W9-CMP-922

CUSCAM
MASCUS
CAMPC
AMASCUS
CASCUS
CAMP

TOR
PUBLISHING
GROUP * * * * * * NEW
YORK

NIGHTFIRE

CAMP ASCUS

CHUCK TINGLE

CAMP DAMASCUS

Copyright © 2023 by Chuck Tingle

A Nightfire Book
Published by Tom Doherty Associates / Tor Publishing Group
120 Broadway
New York, NY 10271

tornightfire.com

Nightfire™ is a trademark of Macmillan Publishing Group, LLC.

Library of Congress Cataloging-in-Publication Data

Names: Tingle, Chuck, author.
Title: Camp Damascus / Chuck Tingle.
Description: First edition. | New York : Tor Publishing Group, [2023] |
    "A Tom Doherty Associates Book."
Identifiers: LCCN 2023007710 (print) | LCCN 2023007711 (ebook) |
    ISBN 9781250874627 (hardcover) | ISBN 9781250906991
    (international, sold outside the U.S., subject to rights availability) |
    ISBN 9781250874641 (ebook)
Subjects: LCGFT: Horror fiction. | Queer fiction. | Novels.
Classification: LCC PS3620.I534 C36 2023 (print) | LCC PS3620.I534
    (ebook) | DDC 813.6—dc23/eng/20270307
LC record available at https://lccn.loc.gov/2023007710
LC ebook record available at https://lccn.loc.gov/2023007711

Our books may be purchased in bulk for promotional, educational, or business use. Please contact your local bookseller or the Macmillan Corporate and Premium Sales Department at 1-800-221-7945, extension 5442, or by email at MacmillanSpecialMarkets@macmillan.com.

First Edition: 2023

Printed in the United States of America

0 9 8 7 6 5 4 3 2

CONTENTS

CAMP DAMASCUS

1

LEAP
OF FAITH

"You've got no shadow," Martina informs me, gazing down at my feet and then shifting her eyes back up to mine.

I check, and sure enough my friend is largely correct. Thanks to the afternoon sun hanging directly overhead, it appears my shadow has *mostly* disappeared. It's a subtle observation, a phenomenon you'd never really notice unless you were looking for it, and yet Martina has pointed it out with an excited grin.

Of course, closer examination would reveal that my shadow, while small, is still there. Hawai'i is the only state where your shadows *do* completely disappear, and this rare event only happens twice a year. It's called Lahaina Noon.

I don't say this, though.

I think to ask why Martina is so excited about her flawed discovery, one that immediately falls apart after the slightest direct inspection, but I quickly realize I don't have to. I too notice the little things Martina does, logging every tiny quirk of the world regardless of whether anyone else finds it worthy of comment. There are so many beautiful pieces in God's grand puzzle, and you can miss them if you're not careful.

"Yeah, I guess you're right," I offer.

"Like Peter Pan," Martina continues, the smile curling wider across her overwhelmingly freckled face.

With anyone else, this unhinged friendliness might signal a touch of sarcasm lurking somewhere behind their large green eyes, but I know better. At least, I hope I do.

I nod along, smiling happily despite suddenly finding myself in the pop culture deep end with little understanding of what she's talking about. I've never read the book, nor seen any films related to this antique story with questionable motives. There's *enchantment* involved, so I know enough to stay far, far away.

For a brief moment I consider telling Martina she shouldn't read that stuff, that the only magic she needs is the love of Christ, but I hesitate.

I've had these conversations before, and even in a town as God-fearing as Neverton, there are only so many who want to hear it. Most Christian folks are friendly enough, but the second you start rubbing their faces in these little indiscretions they bristle.

The last thing I want to do is make Martina bristle.

"Did you have to read that freshman year?" she asks, clearly noting the pained expression on my face I'm so desperately struggling to avoid.

I shake my head. "No," I reply flatly, rejecting explanation.

The truth is, I do remember *Peter Pan* being assigned in English class, and I remember the reports that accompanied this classic secular tale from James Matthew Barrie. I could easily tell you where the author was born (Scotland), how he died (pneumonia), or even let you in on the fact that he killed off an equally profane and godless character, Sherlock Holmes, in a noncanonical short story well before Sir Arthur Conan Doyle ever had the chance.

These facts about the author create a window into his work, not a door. It's a window I've never crawled through.

Intentionally.

"Weren't you in my class?" Martina continues. "I thought everyone read it."

Once again, I'm put to the test, reaching the familiar crossroads of how forthcoming I think I should be.

I love Jesus, I really do, but Jesus would want me to be cool. He'd want *Martina* to think I'm cool.

Kingdom of the Pine was founded on a bedrock of practicality, after all.

Which brings me back to this conversation, and the sudden realization I've been standing in silence for way too long. I need an answer that will appease both a fellow student and the good Lord above, struggling to walk the razor's edge between the truth of my deeply held convictions and the relaxed sheen of a *perfectly normal* girl.

Not all Kingdom Kids are weird.

"I didn't think . . . I mean . . ." I fumble, struggling to craft an excuse and coming up short as my mind tumbles and churns. "My parents didn't want me reading it," I finally reply, submitting the truth and letting the chips fall where they may. "Magic, you know?"

Martina's already enormous green eyes widen in shock. "Wait, really?" she blurts.

Her expression is not what I expected, flooded by sudden excitement and genuine interest. I now realize she might be *impressed* by this moral objection, and my mind begins to race as I wonder if she's proud of me.

Well, not *prideful* but . . . something like that.

I've known Martina for a very long time, although we've only recently started talking in a meaningful way. Could she have similar convictions? Could this be the start of the deep, authentic friendship I've been hoping for?

"That's fucked up," Martina finally continues, immediately prompting me to pump the proverbial brakes on my enthusiasm. "That's *way* fucked up, Rose. I'm sorry your parents are so crazy."

I can't help nodding along, the muscles of my neck taking on a life of their own.

"Yeah," I reply, rolling my eyes. "Way . . . messed up. Parents, right?"

The second these words leave my lips I feel the deep ache of regret, a guilty pang that shoots down my spine as a sinful reminder. God's watchful eye has noticed.

Martina smiles, though, and suddenly this regret is met with something else, a surge of joy that counteracts the holy venom like ANAVIP through the bloodstream of some poor soul who crossed a Pentecostal pit viper.

I've gotta pull back on the snake handling.

"Alright. See you at the bottom," Martina says.

My friend promptly turns and breaks into a run, sprinting with her bare feet across the short, rocky runway. It's as though the frozen universe has started rolling on again, the rustle of the trees and the splash of water far, far below filling my ears.

The other kids who've gathered around these cliffs watch in amazement, their hair wet and stringy as towels drape across them for a fleeting moment of dryness before the next brave leap. Everyone here is used to jumpers taking their time for a big show, standing at the edge of the cliff for a good while and gazing down as though considering their surrender. Of course, once they've gotten to the rocky ledge they rarely back down, and everyone watching knows this. It's all part of the performance, a temporary ringmaster gathering as many eyes as possible before rushing to the edge and hurling themselves over. They tumble down into the cool water below with a mighty splash, followed by excited cheers from their temporary but adoring fans.

Martina doesn't need any of that.

"Fuck!" she cries out as she springs from the rocks, her body rocketing forward while arms and legs continue pumping in the air. I can see the exact point that gravity catches hold of her body, gripping tight and then yanking downward in a sharp change of trajectory that would make Newton proud.

I lose sight of Martina's long strawberry curls as she drops, but I'm too frightened to rush to the edge and witness her plummet. Seconds after disappearing from view there's a loud splash, followed by a joyful eruption from the crowd. Their applause carries out through the forest around us, washing through the trees like audible water.

Carefully, I creep to the edge and stare down into the swimming hole that lies below, the dark water still rippling from Martina's plunge. A few sunbathers lay out on the shore nearby in various states of undress, many of them less covered up than I'm comfortable with, and a handful of swimmers float at the outer rim of this dazzling natural pool.

It's a hot day in Montana, so the falls are packed.

I continue gazing, waiting for Martina to resurface as my heart rate needlessly quickens. She's done this jump hundreds of times, and it appears none of them have resulted in disaster so far. There's no *logical reason* for Martina to have any trouble this time around, but as I stare down at the reflective surface below, I can't help the tiny seed of fear that blossoms at the pit of my stomach.

For some reason I've found myself caring *a lot* about how things turn out for her. It feels, in a word, *weird.*

A wave of relief pulses through my body as Martina breaks the surface, taking in a big gulp of air and instinctively whipping her red hair from side to side. She begins swimming gracefully across the water, making her way to the shore.

From up here I can see her body move in a completely new light, propelling forward with majestic elegance. She looks like a frog as she kicks her legs, but that comparison sounds brash and awkward, while Martina is nothing of the sort.

"You gonna give it a shot?" a voice abruptly questions from behind, breaking my focus and causing a startled breath to catch in my throat.

I turn around to find my friend Isaiah, his shirtless body already deeply tanned in the afternoon sun. His hair is still wet from the last leap, and I have no doubt he'd love to make another running launch off this cliffside. However, Isaiah has taken a moment away from his own madcap antics to nurture my growth as a future daredevil.

"I was thinking about it," I admit.

Isaiah cracks a smile. "It's not as hard as it looks. I mean, we're only thirty feet up. You're not gonna die."

"People died while jumping here in 1977, 1980, and 2016," I inform him. "So . . . it's possible."

"Oh," Isaiah replies, his enthusiasm abruptly deflating. He narrows his eyes as a confused expression crosses his face, suddenly confronted by an unexpected kernel of self-doubt.

The average speed of a dive is fifteen feet per second. Therefore, a swimming hole between ten and fifteen feet deep could paralyze you in *less* than a second.

I don't mention this.

"You're still not going to die," I assure him. "The chances of fatal injury are phenomenally low. If you want to increase your survival odds, just make sure you jump feet first. Never dive."

Isaiah nods along as I pull him back into mental alignment.

"Plus, God's watching over you," I continue.

Isaiah smiles a toothy, all-American grin. My friend reaches out and places a hand on my shoulder in a gesture of reassurance, lingering there a little longer than I might've expected. "Amen."

Finally, I let out an awkward laugh and my friend removes his hand.

"Let's see it, then," Isaiah says, nodding toward the cliff's edge. "What you got, Rose?"

Isaiah backs away and motions for the other kids up here to clear a path. They're waiting and watching now, their eyes trained on me in anticipation of the leap to come.

Nine out of ten accidents occur when people are playing near the water's edge, *not* when they're focused on jumping in.

I pull off my long dress and toss it to the side, revealing the most decidedly modest black one-piece I could find online. Unlike Martina, however, I'm not yet comfortable enough to flip myself into oblivion without a good look below.

I know I'll be fine, that most of the danger here is nothing but an illusion, but my brain *understanding* this is one thing and my body appropriately reacting is another. My heart is slamming hard within my chest, thundering away as a sizzling hot tingle makes its way across my skin.

This is your fight-or-flight response. Your sympathetic nervous system is releasing catecholamines and making you hyperaware of your surroundings.

The solution, of course, is grounding and prayer.

I spend a moment observing the scene around me, taking in faces on every side of the watering hole. Across the way, on the opposite cliff, even more of my peers watch with excitement and anticipation.

The Lord is my light and my salvation; Whom shall I fear? The Lord is the strength of my life; Of whom shall I be afraid?

Some people come here to jump, others just wanna be a part of something. As the school year comes to an end and we all prepare to leap from our own metaphorical cliffs into adulthood, it's easy to get restless. We're all pretending it's midsummer and we're finally free, despite the fact that tomorrow we'll be right back to the Monday grind.

I get the distinct feeling I'm living in what will someday be a fond memory.

With that, I command my foot to take its first step toward the edge.

My body refuses to move.

"The Lord is my light and my salvation," I repeat. I take a deep breath and center myself once more, focused on compelling my body forward.

Still, nothing.

I remain motionless, staring out at a sea of classmates on the opposite cliffside while they gaze back at this curious standoff between mind and body.

"It's not so bad once you start running," Isaiah says from behind. "Once you reach the edge, the hard part is over."

His words are kind, and I appreciate this vote of confidence, but in a practical sense it does absolutely nothing. I'm displaying textbook freezing behavior, and Isaiah has no more control over my basolateral amygdala than I do.

Suddenly, another familiar voice chimes in, hooting like a baseball coach from the dugout. "Let's go, Rose!"

I glance over to find Martina has already climbed back up, soaking wet with a towel wrapped tightly around her body. Our eyes meet and she smiles warmly, immediately melting away the anxiety and fear that had paralyzed me with its icy grip. She winks.

I grin back, basking in this feeling for a moment, then return my focus to the cliff.

Feeling renewed, I prepare a third attempt to compel myself forward, but before I get the chance my gaze falls onto something strange across the ravine. The other side of the cliffs is fairly close, some forty feet across with a small waterfall carving its way down the middle in a never-ending cascade. Fellow classmates in their colorful swimwear line the opposite edge, but tucked back into the forest is another figure that watches with stoic intensity.

I squint a bit, struggling to parse whether my eyes are playing tricks on me through the shady wood.

A frighteningly pale woman is standing in the forest, her hair long and black as it hangs limply over her face and around her bony shoulders. It appears she's staring directly at me, but it's difficult to tell because her eyes lack irises or pupils. They're solid white globes.

The woman is smiling, her expression frozen and her teeth unusually stained with dark brown and black smears. The teeth themselves are crooked and long, as though her gums have receded to provide an unnatural length.

Yet despite all of this, the strangest thing about the woman's appearance is what she's wearing. She sports a deep red polo shirt with a stark white name tag pinned to the chest. It's the kind of top you'd expect to see worn by someone arriving to fix your wireless internet or telling you which aisle to check at a department store. She also wears a thick metal band around her neck, pulled tight like a collar, and khaki pants.

"Uh . . . do you see that?" I question, whispering to Isaiah as my gaze remains fixed on the woman in the woods.

Across the way, nobody seems to notice this peculiar figure, despite the fact that she's standing less than ten feet behind them in the underbrush.

"See what?" Isaiah asks.

I point to the other side of the swimming hole, but just as Isaiah follows my gesture the eerie woman steps back into the lush Montana forest, disappearing just as quickly as she arrived.

I peer into the shadows, struggling to catch sight of her but coming up empty.

"There was a woman over there," I continue. "She looked . . . kinda off."

"Off how?" he asks.

"I don't know," I reply, then shake my head as though this futile gesture might clear out the cobwebs. I certainly don't intend to make a scene out of some poor old woman who happens to appear, well, frightening.

Maybe she's sick.

"Could've been someone's mom checking in on them," I suggest, offering this explanation more to myself than to Isaiah.

"I really don't see anything," he says, genuinely apologetic, then lowers his voice a bit. "Hey, if you don't wanna jump, it's all good."

Someone else steps up next to us, a girl I don't know who's anxious to get things going again. "Are you gonna jump?" she asks, clearly annoyed.

I glance around to find a line has formed behind me, folks waiting their turn while I stare off into space and let my imagination run wild.

"Oh, sorry," I mumble, stepping back.

Martina isn't as receptive. "Chill out, she's getting ready," my friend retorts angrily from the sidelines.

I push away any thoughts of that curious lady in the woods, or the height of this drop, or the fact that school is ending and life is waiting for me with wide open jaws like the whale ready to swallow Jonah whole. Instead, I focus on the simple act of putting one foot before the next.

I take one final look at Martina, just about ready to step forward, when something startling and warm slips between my fingers.

Glancing down, I find that Isaiah is gripping my hand in his, an unexpected gesture of friendship.

"We'll jump together," Isaiah offers.

I was about to go on my own, but a little more support couldn't hurt.

A strange coo falls from the lips of everyone watching, a sound I'm not quite sure what to make of as expressions shift into knowing smiles and glances are exchanged between this cliffside and the next.

I begin to recite a short verse under my breath, repeating it to myself in quiet anticipation. "It is the Lord who goes before you. He will be with you; he will not leave you or forsake you. It is the Lord who goes before you. He will be with you; he will not leave you or forsake you."

"Go on three," Isaiah proclaims. "One. Two. Three!"

We take off down the short runway, our feet thundering against the dirt until there's no ground left to slam against. I push off with my final step and erupt into the air, unable to keep myself from crying out with a long scream of equal parts fear and excitement.

There are a few precious moments of high school left, but this one feels like the pinnacle of summer.

An electric tingle surges across my frame as gravity catches hold, Isaiah and I plummeting toward the deep blue below. It's a strange sensation that my brain immediately struggles to analyze and dissect, but before I get the chance to understand it fully I'm slamming into the cool water.

My senses are swallowed by darkness, the sound of the world around me sucking inward and holding tight as I struggle to get my bearings. I'm still plummeting, just slower now, and for a brief moment my feet touch the welcome clay of the riverbed below. I push back against the bottom and swim up in a cascade of tiny bubbles, finally breaking the surface once again.

The resulting rush is incredible, my body fresh and rejuvenated in a way I didn't quite expect.

That was my first jump ever; a welcome baptism.

I run fingers through my long blond hair, pushing it away from my face as I spit out some of the water that managed to force its way down my throat. As I sputter and cough, Isaiah emerges next to me in the dark pool.

"You alright, Rose?" He chuckles as he watches me awkwardly pull myself together.

"I'm amazing," I reply. "I can't believe I just did that! God is good!"

Isaiah is unable to keep himself from smiling even wider as we tread water next to each other, savoring the unexpected calm following such a gaudy stunt.

Silence falls, bathing the scene in an awkward hush.

I was so relaxed and now this is tense. Why is this tense?

Finally, I can't take it anymore. I splash some water in Isaiah's face and let the pressure deflate with a good-hearted laugh.

"I'm going again," I announce before slipping below the surface and swimming toward the rocky shore nearby.

*　　　　　　　*　　　　　　　*

As we drive home in Isaiah's old Jeep, I can't help noticing the way his eyes dance across the heating panel of his center console, focused on a dial that sits precariously shifted to the blazing hot side. I get the feeling Isaiah is struggling to tell me something—or maybe he wants *me* to ask something of *him*?—but he's too afraid.

Truth be told, this is becoming a theme with Isaiah, and I just can't figure out why. We've been close for a long time, and I've always appreciated the way he's there for me through thick and thin, a reliable shoulder to cry on and a source of great Christian companionship on these long days.

"What is it?" I finally ask.

Isaiah plays dumb, glancing over from the driver's seat as his vehicle rumbles onward. The trees of the forest have finally started giving way, revealing the modest suburban homes of Neverton.

Tucked against the side of a horseshoe-shaped mountain range, these foothills feel distinctly separate from the rest of the world. While a vast landscape of rolling golden farmlands extends to the east, the majority of this county is swathed in mysterious evergreen forest, hiding our hamlet like a secret as looming peaks rise beyond.

I recognize every intricate step of this route, the signs and sidewalks etched into the depths of my soul. It's a humble Montana town of 15,000 locals, so finding your way around isn't much of an accomplishment, but it certainly makes you notice when your driver isn't paying attention.

"That was the turn," I remind him, charting a route we'd traveled a thousand times before. "Just get the next one."

"Sorry," Isaiah apologizes, shaking his head and wiping his brow. He glances at the heater once again. "You sure you want it that warm?"

I notice now that he's getting a little red, sweating as the car continues to fill with hot air.

"Are you feeling okay?" I ask.

"It's . . . really hot in here." Isaiah finally cuts to the chase. "Can I turn the heat down?"

I nod.

Lately, it feels as though I can't warm up for the life of me, trapped in sporadic states of frigid discomfort. It comes without warning, and the curious part of my mind wonders if this might be a symptom of a larger medical issue.

It hasn't been worth bringing up with my parents yet, because by the time I'm irritated enough to do something about this sensation the chill has thawed.

I say nothing as Isaiah adjusts the temperature slightly. A notable pause lingers between us.

"Long day, huh?" my friend eventually states.

I nod again, gazing out the window as a slate of familiar faces pass us by. I recognize most of the folks strolling around this evening: merry, God-fearing families out for brisk walks as they enjoy a flourishing purple sunset above.

"I really like spending time with you," Isaiah declares.

I glance back at my friend, appreciating the sincerity of his words. "Thanks. You too."

"You too?" he repeats, as if my reply needs more explanation.

"I really like spending time with you, too," I clarify. "You're a good friend."

Isaiah appears confused by my response, but I don't know what else he wants from me. I'd love to dive deep and figure out what's going on with him, but right now I'm partially distracted by just how ravenously hungry I've become. Isaiah wasn't kidding when he mentioned the length of the day, and after five or six cliff jumps and subsequent climbs back to the top, I've found myself yearning for the sweet relief of fat and sugar in my bloodstream.

Thankfully, Mom and Dad assured me dinner would be waiting when I got home.

We ride in silence a while longer before Isaiah reaches out and readjusts the heater, pushing forth the warm air once again and bending to my wishes.

"Thanks." I chuckle graciously.

"No problem," he replies, strangely taciturn.

Eventually, Isaiah pulls up to my house, his Jeep turning into the gravel driveway and slowly rolling to a stop with a satisfying crunch.

"Thank you for driving," I offer, anxious to get inside for dinner.

I throw off my seatbelt and double-check that my backpack and towel are in tow. Swiftly, I throw open the vehicle door and give a slight wave goodbye before hopping out and slamming it shut behind me, then hurry up the front walk.

I've only made it a few steps before another loud metallic slam answers my own. Curious, I turn and discover Isaiah has climbed from the driver's seat and is marching after me.

"Rose!" he calls out.

I wait up, and soon enough we are standing face-to-face. There's an intensity to his gaze, a tidal wave of emotion welling up within my friend. I can sense the impending cascade of feelings, but its shape and tone remain abstract.

I have no idea what Isaiah could possibly want.

My friend doesn't say a word, just stares at me blankly as unknown thoughts spiral through his mind. I've seen this expression a lot lately, but today it has grown to a boiling point and, to be perfectly frank, it's starting to frighten me.

"What *is it?*" I demand.

Isaiah leans forward and kisses me on the lips, a swift movement that's met with my immediate repulsion.

I pull my neck away in alarm and confusion as our faces meet and then quickly part. My mind is struggling to keep up, desperately piecing together what just happened.

"I'm sorry," I blurt. "I didn't . . . that was . . ."

"Oh, I—I thought—" Isaiah stammers.

Gradually, the true nature of this moment falls into place with breathtaking clarity.

I shake my head, my lips tightly sealed as I let this gesture do the talking.

"So, you're not . . . ?" Isaiah is still having trouble completing a sentence.

"Definitely not," I reply.

"But I thought," he repeats, a surprisingly meek moment for this typically stalwart guy.

"Nope," I say as my head continues to shake from side to side.

Isaiah takes a moment to straighten up, processing this information in a state of awkward rigidity. I can tell he's fighting some powerful internal battle, struggling to calm down.

Suddenly, he turns and begins the march back to his car. Before making his way around to the driver's side, however, Isaiah erupts in a startling display of violence as he punches the passenger door.

I jump as the Jeep makes a hollow metallic thump, startled at first and then concerned for his hand.

That probably hurt.

Isaiah doesn't react to the pain. Instead, he stomps around the vehicle and climbs inside, slamming the door behind him. He starts his car and hits the gas, peeling onto the road in reverse and scattering gravel everywhere.

I watch in silence, still not sure how to react as Isaiah's Jeep disappears down the road.

Eventually, the front door opens behind me and my father sticks his head out, his chiseled jaw and familiar black-framed glasses shadowed in the dying light of day.

"Was that Isaiah?" he calls. "You should've asked him to stay for dinner."

Seconds later, my father realizes the porch light is off and makes an awkward *humph* sound that it seems only dads are capable of. He quickly flips a switch, illuminating the scene.

"There's my girl," he says.

I solemnly retreat to my father, still completely silent as I wrap my arms around him in a warm embrace. We stand like this for a moment as I allow his protective paternal aura to envelop me, then I finally pull back as my stomach gurgles.

I can already smell the garlic spaghetti sauce as it bubbles and churns on our kitchen stove. I'm thrilled Mom opted for pasta this evening.

My father, Luke Darling, is a kind-eyed man with dark features and thick glasses that make him look like Superman. Of course, just like *Peter Pan*, I've never actually read a Superman comic, but the cultural relevance of this secular hero has somehow permeated my life.

It's concerning. Jesus Christ is the only true superhero.

"I'm so hungry," I announce.

"Hi, So Hungry. I'm Dad," my father retorts, prompting a playful groan to escape my throat.

We head inside and I immediately find myself bathed in spiritual warmth, a cozy sensation that causes the ice in my veins to melt away. That lingering chill has finally taken its leave, disappearing with such little fanfare I hardly remember it was there in the first place.

My mother, Lisa, greets me in the kitchen with a loud and excited wail. "Rose!" she cries out as though I've been gone for years, a sauce-covered wooden spoon gripped tightly in her hand. "My baby is back!"

Mom wraps her arms around me and plants a firm kiss on my cheek. When she pulls away, she immediately motions to the dining room table, coaxing me toward my place setting at the end.

"Hope you're hungry," she continues. "I made spaghetti."

"I can smell that," I reply warmly, "with extra garlic."

My parents exchange excited glances, thrilled by this culinary transgression. We're being bad tonight.

Mom is always well put together, but this evening she's looking especially done up with a lime green dress and a string of pearls around her neck. Her makeup is less subtle than usual, a little extra red in the tone of her lips that she wouldn't dare try if we were leaving the house this evening, and her stark blond hair is held back with a white band across the top of her head. She's a small woman but full of energy, and tonight her natural beauty is on full display.

People say we look alike, and right now I can truly appreciate what a compliment that is.

I take my seat at the end of the table while my mother continues to move back and forth across the kitchen, hard at work as she guides this meal across the finish line with radiant enthusiasm.

Eventually, my father makes his way over and sits down next to me, a peculiar look in his eyes. He's staring like he's got something to say, an amused smirk just barely visible at the corners of his mouth.

"What?" I question.

"I see the light of the Lord in you tonight," my father informs me, a compliment I'd take to heart if not for the fact that this loving message feels tethered to something I don't understand.

Seconds later, Mom is setting down an enormous dish of spaghetti before us, steam rolling off the bright red sauce as it floods our nostrils with a robust aroma.

"Luke!" my mother blurts playfully. "Give her a *moment!*"

My dad smiles and leans back in his chair, still eyeing me mischievously.

"Okay, what's going on here?" I glance back and forth between them as my mother takes her seat.

My query goes ignored as our conversation takes a sudden intermission, Luke and Lisa reaching their hands out to take my palms in theirs as we lower our heads. Nobody has to say a word as the three of us fall into our nightly routine.

We offer our prayer in unison, eyes shut tight as these words bounce from our mouths in a familiar cadence. "Bless us, O Lord, and these Thy gifts, which we are about to receive from Thy bounty, through Christ our Lord. Bless us so that we may know our place in His kingdom as servants. Bless us so that we may give service to the Lord and the righteous lambs will be spared when the scale of ends meets the scale of means. Bless the Kingdom of the Pine for lighting the darkened path that our Shepherd walks. Amen."

I begin to lift my gaze, but before I get the chance my father launches into an additional blessing. He's clearly caught the spirit this evening. "And bless the Prophet Cobel, for the wisdom he has bestowed. Bless the Four Tenets that guide us. But, most of all, bless our beautiful daughter on this important day. Amen."

"Amen," my mother and I respond in turn.

The three of us lift our gazes once more, taking a beat before getting to work and dishing out some pasta.

Lisa can't help chuckling to herself. *"Most of all,"* she repeats, shaking her head. "Don't get cute, Luke."

She's referring to the part where my father placed *my* blessing above that of the Four Tenets and the Prophet Cobel. This is bad form and I'm a little bothered by it, but we're playing it fast and loose tonight.

All I can do is refrain from pride and do better when it's my turn to lead.

Out of respect, I run though all Four Tenets in my head, with a particular focus on number three this evening.

Respect—I will honor when I do not understand,

Integrity—I will believe when I do not witness,

Service—I will strive when my sin is heavy,

Excellence—I will persevere when my body does not.

"So," Mom begins, curiosity overwhelming her tone and elevating it into a playful singsong frequency. "How was your *date?*"

I raise an eyebrow as I stab the mass of noodles before me, utterly confused. I begin to twirl my utensil. "What date?"

"With Isaiah!"

I can't help laughing. "At the falls today?" I question. "It was fun, but that wasn't a date. We're just friends."

The cold chill I'd felt earlier immediately surges through my body, causing my hand to seize up and my body to shift awkwardly in the hard wooden chair.

My parents exchange glances again, as though passing some unspoken relay baton between them. My father clears his throat for a moment, ready to take over.

"He's a handsome guy, don't you think?" Dad suggests.

I shrug. "I mean, sure."

Mom butts in, unable to wait longer than a single question and answer before leaping back into the fray. "You don't like that?" she demands to know. "You don't want a boyfriend?"

I can't help the barely audible scoff that escapes my throat.

We all love Jesus in the Darling household, but my parents are typically the ones who hoist this flag the highest and elevate my faith on a daily basis. I'm thankful to have two spiritual warriors consistently by my side, and through their pious diligence I've come to carry my own innate parental severity.

The idea of them actually *encouraging* me to have a boyfriend is shocking. I suppose my recent twentieth birthday could be the marker that set them off, but the turn they've taken is so alarming I'm left wondering if it's a trap.

"I think I should be focused on school right now," I offer, hoping this is what they want to hear.

My mother reaches out and places her hand over mine, causing me to return a fresh spool of spaghetti to the plate.

"Honey," she begins softly, "the Lord *wants* you to start a family. You're a woman now, and finding a partner is a very important part of His plan. I know we've been a little . . . strict about this before, but you should know it's okay."

I'm not sure how to react, staring down at the table before me.

My father clears his throat, a sign he's about to launch into a brief diatribe of religious theory. "You know, when Tobias Cobel established the Four Tenets he did so in a way that was pretty genius. A lot of people see him as a man of faith *and* entrepreneurship, which he was, but he was also a family man."

"Tenet number four: Excellence," my mother chimes in. "*I will persevere when my body does not.*"

I already know where they're going with this, but I honor the moment and listen respectfully.

"To *live on*," Dad continues. "That could mean your spirit ascends to heaven, or a business you've built keeps turning a profit. It could also mean your family line lives on."

I nod. "Understood" is all I can think to say.

"You like Isaiah, don't you?" my mother pushes, repeating her initial question. "Bill and Anna tell us he's *really* into you."

I now realize any denial regarding this supposed date will promptly be discarded and we'll be taking another spin around the maypole. Clearly, there's an answer my parents want to hear, and if I hope to enjoy this plate of spaghetti I'll have to give it to them.

Still, I refuse to lie. That's a sin.

"Today was good," I reply, stretching my enthusiasm as far as it can possibly go. "Isaiah is really . . . nice."

Immediately, the tension in my mother's hand softens. She releases her grip as both of my parents sit back in their chairs, finally allowing me a moment of rest.

I don't look up as I eat, but from the corner of my eye I see them watching with absolute satisfaction. They're not even touching their food, just allowing the gratitude to wash over them as though I'm a toddler who finally learned to walk.

Eventually, the evening kicks back into gear and my parents plunge into their food. It seems my simple answer was *just* enough to satisfy whatever they were looking for.

Still, a host of questions continue to linger in the back of my mind. Why were they talking to Isaiah's parents about our day at the falls? Everyone in Neverton is pretty closely knit, especially members of the congregation, but as far as I knew Bill and Anna didn't have a strong rapport with my folks.

I try letting it slide and moving on, but the circumstances of this meeting remain firmly planted in my mind, unable to budge no matter how diligent my attempts to slip past.

Finally, I turn back to my mother, my curiosity getting the better of me.

I open my mouth to speak, but instead of any coherent words spilling from my throat, I find myself erupting with an unexpected cough.

Instinctively, I reach for the tall glass of water on the table next to me, swiftly downing the cool liquid and trying again. However, this time I'm met with the same result at an even larger scale.

Something's tickling the back of my throat, flooding me with frustration as I struggle to speak or even breathe. I begin to cough harder as expressions of grave concern wash across my parents' faces.

"Are you alright, hon?" Dad asks.

A sudden, final cough unblocks my throat as air pumps forcefully from within, blasting forth the seed of my discomfort in a singular heave.

I gag slightly, struggling to collect myself as my father pats me on the back with loving grace. "Something go down the wrong pipe?" He chuckles.

I nod, taking another long sip from my water glass. I gaze down at the plate of spaghetti before me, hoping to find the culprit, and gasp abruptly—nearly choking all over again.

A small black insect wriggles atop my pasta, slathered in sauce as it hopelessly flits its wings in a futile attempt to escape.

"Oh my *word*," my mother blurts, leaning forward to get a better look.

My father does the same, adjusting his glasses as he struggles to take in this tiny, unexpected guest.

The whole family is silent for a moment, reeling.

"Must've accidently swallowed the poor thing," Dad suggests.

I open my mouth to reply, but this simple movement causes an abrupt spasm to overwhelm my throat. I let out a loud, animalistic retch as a cascade of black erupts from deep within me, pouring through my esophagus and spilling across the plate.

The upheaval is so sudden that my parents nearly fall backward in their chairs, letting out cries of alarm as they reflexively push away.

When this ejection finally stops, I stare down in utter horror, my body trembling as my mind races to understand the bizarre, squirming mass that's now heaped onto my pasta and scattered across the table.

This black pile is churning and moving, crawling over itself as tiny wings flutter and miniature legs kick the air. I scream as I realize this is not some toxic liquid but a dark porridge of living creatures, little flies born deep within my body before their sudden expulsion.

2

CALL
NOW

Luke's eyes go wide as he bears witness to the crawling, fluttering insects. He glances at my mother, then springs into action.

"It's okay, it's okay!" Dad yells, leaping to his feet and rushing to the sink. He crouches down and throws open the cabinets, rummaging around before pulling forth a handful of large garbage bags.

Immediately, my father yanks open a bag and begins to shovel flies inside with his hands, scooping the whole mess across our dining room table, spaghetti and all. I'm still in shock, frozen in abject horror as time continues rolling on around me.

I can hear my mother praying under her breath, but the second she begins my dad reaches out and places his hand on her forearm. This stops Mom in her tracks.

The interaction lasts no more than a few seconds, and thanks to the other bizarre occurrences erupting simultaneously around the room, I might have missed it. However, my father's action is arguably stranger than the sauce-covered insects scattering in every direction.

Never before have I witnessed Luke Darling silence a prayer.

"Everything's fine," my mother abruptly pipes up, desperately helping my dad clean the table. She gets to work swatting some of the renegade flies that've managed to keep their wings dry and take flight. "Accidents happen."

"How is that an accident?" I blurt, my voice even more shrill and panicked than expected.

My father cinches his bag of sauce and insects and stands abruptly, stomping out our back door and disappearing around the corner. I hear the loud thud of a plastic trash bin echo through the darkness, then nothing.

I stare quietly at the open door for a moment, realizing now that Dad is hesitating before making his return. A few seconds pass before he reenters, only this trip over the threshold has drained any sense of urgency from his expression. Not only is Luke calm and collected, but the vague hint of a smile has crept its way into the corner of his mouth.

He seems amused.

"God's plan can feel pretty crazy sometimes, huh?" Dad says.

I glance over to catch the flicker of doubt on Mom's face suddenly transforming into agreement. She's nodding along.

"What do you mean?" I retort. "I'm *sick*."

"Oh, honey," my father continues, shaking his head as he sits down and takes my hands in his. "You're not sick. You must've just swallowed something at the falls."

"A bug in the water," Lisa chimes in.

My instinctual reaction is to reject this idea, but there's something about it that *kinda* makes sense.

Regardless, I've yet to come up with a better explanation.

My father is right about one thing: God works in mysterious ways.

"You think I swallowed a bug? In the water?" I repeat.

Both of my parents are nodding along, agreeing profusely.

"And it . . ." I start, then cringe as I trail off, disgusted by the thought. "Laid eggs?"

"I guess so." My father nods. "Nature can be pretty weird!"

"I don't know many insects with a life cycle that fast," I say, running through a sudden barrage of potential variables in my head and speaking the thoughts out loud as they come to me.

My dad notices my mind working overtime and interjects. "Hey, don't stress yourself out. Right now you've got more important things to worry about," he offers. "You're about to graduate."

Mom gently pushes my enormous glass of water toward me, encouraging a drink.

I take a long, satisfying gulp as the cool liquid soothes my irritated throat.

I finish and set the empty glass back down. "Don't you think I should go to the doctor?" I ask with lingering unease. "I've been feeling really cold, too."

"Let's just keep an eye on it," my mom suggests, placing her hand gently against my hair and running her fingers along the back of my head in a deeply soothing gesture. "I'm sure everything's fine."

"Well, not *everything's* fine," my dad chimes in. "I don't know about you, but I'm not really in the mood for spaghetti anymore. Who wants to order a pizza?"

*   *   *

My eyes scan the screen with deep intensity as I carefully work my way through an enormous wall of pixelated text. Above the cascading sentences is a photo of an insect, similar to the flies I coughed up earlier but lacking a select few distinguishing features.

Over the course of the last hour I've gone from anxious and worried to deeply fascinated, consumed by a flood of information regarding the common *Hexagenia limbate*. While the average housefly has the lifespan of one month, *Hexagenia limbate* experiences an entire lifetime over the course of a single day.

That being said, their larval stage lasts much, much longer. If I were to swallow enough larvae at precisely the right time, then *maybe* I'd find myself in a situation like the one I just experienced over dinner.

The bedroom doorway to my left is open and vacant, revealing the darkened hallway beyond, and my eyes keep returning to this gaping frame. All the trappings of a loving home are here, wrapping themselves around me in a confident assurance that everything will be just fine.

Everything's *always* just fine.

Yet for some reason my gaze keeps drifting over to the darkness, lingering a while just to make sure nobody's there.

I shake my head, taking a moment to refocus on the task at hand.

I typically love this kind of research, digging deep and unwrapping the skin of a mystery until I understand every moving part, but my usual state of hyperfocus can't quite latch into place this evening.

Something's off, all of today's bizarre sand grains finally coalescing into one troublesome metaphorical pebble in my shoe.

This time I deliberately maintain my focus on the digital words, actively battling any sense of distraction. It lasts all of three seconds.

From the corner of my eye I sense a vague figure adjusting in the shadows, a shape in the darkness that makes my blood run cold. I freeze, struggling to stay present and recognize my imagination must be conjuring up that dark-haired woman from the falls, until the figure suddenly raises its arm—

—Two quick wooden knocks ring out, prompting my body to jump in alarm. I gasp loudly, only to discover my father standing quietly with a thoughtful expression on his face.

"What's going on, hon?" he asks, his voice calm and soothing.

"I'm just reading," I blurt. I glance back at the luminous screen on the desk before me. "I think I might've swallowed some *Hexagenia limbate* at the end of their larval stage."

"*Hexagenia lim*-whata?" Dad teases.

"Mayflies," I clarify.

My father laughs. "Why not just say that?"

"*Latina sit amet*," I state in return. "Because Latin is fun."

My father lets out a long sigh and casually crosses the threshold of my room, sauntering over to my bed and perching on the edge. "You're a *very* smart girl," Dad offers. "You're also very curious."

I already know where this is headed, and I brace myself for the same conversation we've been having for years. Intelligence is a virtue, but curiosity is something else.

"You know, the Lord doesn't ask much of us," Dad continues. "The Bible tells of great sacrifice, but I'm not Abraham, and you're not Ruth. We're on easy street. We don't have to pay money to walk in His shadow. We don't have to abandon our families. All we have to do is have faith. *Real* faith."

"I know, I know," I reply. *"I will believe when I do not witness."*

Tenet number two.

"You know, honey, sometimes I'm not so sure you will," my father continues, a great weight in his tone. "Seems to me you've been up here all night reading about fruit flies instead of trusting in His plan."

"Mayflies," I correct, "and maybe learning this stuff *is* a part of God's plan."

"It's good to be thoughtful, but when the desire for more knowledge takes over your life, what you're really saying is, 'even in the presence of God's light, I am not full.' Do you understand?" Dad continues. "It's a sin, hon. That feeling you call *curiosity* is fine in small doses, but when you turn it into a habit it becomes *gluttony*. A hunger for knowledge is still hunger."

I hate to admit it, but he's right. I've been up here in my bedroom frightened and scared, turning to these digital walls of text instead of trusting in the Lord. I'm obsessing over something that I'll never be able to make complete sense of, while the *real* answer sits right there in front of me.

"God *is* mysterious," I finally concede.

My dad smiles. "He really is, honey."

"How's Mom doing?" I ask, still concerned about her reaction to all the chaos. Lisa was really shaken up.

"She'll be fine," Dad replies. "She's still downstairs watching TV.

God put a lot of resilience into that woman, just like he put a lot of resilience into you."

We sit in silence a moment longer before my father climbs to his feet, then strolls across the room toward me. He leans down to give me a kiss on the forehead, and with another swift movement he reaches out and shuts my laptop. My father scoops up the gray rectangle and tucks it under his arm.

Of course, my first instinct is to protest, but I already know that approach is going nowhere.

"I think you've had enough computer time for a while." Dad turns and heads toward the doorway once again. "Alright, lights out."

He disappears down the hallway.

I stand up and walk to the threshold, ready to shut my door and turn in for the night, but stop in my tracks. I stare at the frame in confusion, stepping back and forth through it a few times as though I might find better understanding from the opposite side.

There's no bedroom door, only a frame.

"Uh . . . Dad?" I call out. "What happened to my door?"

My father appears at the opposite end of our upstairs hallway, peeking out from his bedroom. "You never had a door, honey." He laughs, a curious expression working its way across his face.

I narrow my eyes, glancing between my father and the empty frame.

"Pretty sure I had a door," I counter, a little more aggressively than intended. As the sentence leaves my mouth I immediately back down, remembering my place in the Darling household. "Sorry."

Luke's good-natured demeanor falters. My father removes his glasses and rubs the ridge of his nose for a moment, clearly frustrated. "We both know how you can get sometimes." He sighs. "When you fixate on little things, you stop noticing the world around you."

Dad returns his spectacles to their rightful throne.

I'm racking my brain, desperately searching for answers to help this all fall into place. I have very distinct memories of opening and shutting a door in this very spot, but admittedly none of them are recent.

However, I certainly have no recollection of taking a door *off*.

"You still don't believe me?" my father finally continues.

Luke stares back at me with searing intensity, the face of a hero now dismissed.

The hair on the back of my neck has quietly bristled. This is a warning sign from my sympathetic nervous system, one I don't entirely understand.

Piloerection: small muscles at the base of one's hair follicles involuntarily contracting in response to shock or fright.

My father has asked me a direct question, but his abrupt shift in demeanor makes me uncertain if he really wants an answer.

"Check for a hinge. Check for screw holes," Dad challenges, his words less of a friendly suggestion and more of a command.

I carefully turn my attention back to the frame, searching for any disturbance in the structure. I run my fingers across the place where holes or wet paint should be if construction had occurred at any recent time, and I find myself greeted by smooth, dry paint. A door *could've* been removed from its hinges right here, but certainly not today.

I turn my attention back to my father. "Weird" is all I can think to say, sensing a pang of guilt at the pit of my stomach.

Tenet number one: Respect. I will honor what I do not understand.

My father's burning gaze stays fixed on me a moment longer, then dissolves just as quickly as it arrived. He grins wide and nods, chuckling to let me know the bit is over.

He's just messing around.

"It's been a long day," Dad announces. "I don't blame you for feeling a little out of it. Do you want us to get a door for your room?"

"I . . . guess," I reply.

He nods. "I'll head down to the hardware store when I have some time and see what I can do. Should be an easy fix. Night, hon."

With that, my father turns and heads back into his bedroom, shutting the door behind him.

The house falls quiet once more.

I creep back into my room under the soft yellow glow of my bedside lamp. I undress and pull on a long green T-shirt featuring the logo of a classic condiment. RELISH is written across the top of this familiar design, while the center part continues with two words: SWEET JESUS.

I slip under the covers and turn off my bedside light, but I don't shut my eyes. Instead, I stare at the ceiling above me, my mind flooded with all the curious thoughts I've been explicitly told to avoid.

Whether or not I swallowed a mouthful of mayfly eggs, the creatures are still absolutely fascinating.

You know how you can get, my father said, a phrase I've heard before.

Focused. Tuned out. Obsessive. Single-minded.

Curious.

I glance back at the empty doorframe, searching for any movement in the dark hallway beyond and then finally sliding over to the edge of my bed. I reach out and grab my phone, which rests on the side table, then quickly turn down its brightness as the device springs to life.

Having technologically illiterate parents can be frustrating, but it also has its advantages. Case in point: the fact I can access all the same information on my phone that I can on my laptop seems completely lost on my father.

I open up a new tab and do a quick search for *Ephemeroptera*, which means the whole mayfly order instead of any specific species.

I slowly peruse this endless trove of information, the dim light of my phone a pale glow in the darkness. Several pages that I've already read appear, but I scroll onward in search of fresh information.

Strangely, the more I read about these insects, the less I think about my traumatic expulsion over dinner. I'm filling my brain with just enough logical stimulation that the rest of my consciousness can take a break.

While mayfly larvae eat plant matter, the adult mayfly is a rare example of an animal that has no diet. They don't live long enough to eat.

"Whoa," I gush aloud, my eyes dancing across the tiny screen as I scroll onward.

The next search result is a local story about a man who claims he discovered a new species of leech in the deep Neverton County woods. A photo is included, showing a clearly fabricated invertebrate that is nothing more than a pale sagging balloon wrapped around someone's deflated football. Stringy hair has been pasted along the ridge of the mysterious creature's "back."

I remember when this story came out and a wave of sadness washes over me. The hoaxer was a deeply disturbed man, a lost soul who would eventually take his own life.

He was a nonbeliever.

My phone buzzes, a notification appearing at the top of the flat rectangular screen.

"Martina Coachman has tagged you in five photos," I recite under my breath, reading the words out loud against my own volition.

I click the notification, my hush-hush and wholly top-secret social media app filling the screen as it displays an assortment of pictures from today. I don't remember posing for any photos, and as I scroll through these uploads I find my recollection to be correct.

However, I *did* end up in the background of several shots, and Martina was kind enough to tag me.

I take a moment to swipe through today's images, glowing with appreciation at my inclusion in this gallery that feels both familiar and deeply foreign. Many of these people are my friends, but a few nonbelievers have wormed their way into the mix.

I see kids making hand signs that I don't understand or recognize. There are swimsuits covering way too little, and T-shirts with logos that seem nothing short of occult.

Fortunately, there's just as many shirts featuring Bible verses to balance things out. I smile when I see one that reads, I GET HIGH ON THE MOST HIGH, which is about as lurid as I'm willing to get. Even then, I feel guilty about my reaction.

In one photo Isaiah flexes for the camera, a display that makes me wrinkle my nose and unconsciously frown. In another, one of the guys has pulled the bottom of his shirt into his own collar to create the approximation of a bra. I'm in the background of that one, standing by myself and struggling to act natural.

The next photo features Martina flanked by two girls I only vaguely know, the three of them doing some kind of secret-agent finger-gun pose I've seen before but can't seem to place.

I can't help making note of how pretty Martina is, a strange feeling bubbling up inside me as I observe these digital representations of her smiling face. The emotion coursing through my veins is uncomfortable, an ache that burns and sizzles awkwardly.

It feels a little like jealousy, but not entirely.

I dive even deeper into my friend's archive, my fingers gaining a mind of their own as I swipe from one image to the next. I'm no longer just perusing snapshots from today, but bounding back in time to various activities, outfits, and hairstyles.

I stop at a photo of a strangely innocuous moment, a portrait Martina appears barely ready for. She's standing on her couch midlaugh, casually clad in a blazer and a white button-up shirt that's way too big for her.

I've never noticed just how many freckles Martina has dancing across her skin, even today at the swimming hole.

So jealous.

Martina's strawberry hair is up in a messy bun, renegade strands falling around her shoulders in a way that somehow appears both completely random and perfectly planned. One eyebrow is cocked high above the other in a silly face—a face that would probably be deeply unflattering on anyone else—but for some reason her expression slips right between my ribs like a perfectly placed spear to the heart.

My body flushes with heat as I shift my weight in bed, turning from side to side. My skin is tingling.

Suddenly, however, the rising temperature comes to an abrupt halt. A wave of cold washes over me, chilling me to the bone.

My breath catches in my throat, and I'm unsure of how I should respond to this bizarre thermal shift. I look to the bedroom window, wondering if I'd accidently left it open and allowed the cool of the evening to slip inside.

I didn't.

What I *do* notice, however, is the slightest bit of movement from the corner of my eye.

It's so fast I barely have time to react, and even when I turn my head fully there's nothing there. It *feels* as though I'm witnessing some residual presence, the ethereal ghost of someone who stood in my doorway just moments earlier.

I gaze into the darkened hallway, struggling to perceive anything as my eyes adjust from their warm visions of Martina's freckly grin on the brilliant phone screen.

"Dad?" I call out with quiet apprehension, my voice soft as it floats through the darkness.

No response.

I lock the phone screen and place it flat against my chest, waiting for my pupils to dilate and listening intently for any sign from the shadows. It takes a beat for me to realize just how tightly clenched my muscles have become, and I consciously relax. I focus on my breathing, appreciating the steady in and out as my chest moves up and down against the blankets.

On one hand I begin to drum out my finger patterns, counting down in specific arrangements. I've done this since I was a child, sometimes when I'm bored, but mostly as a way to soothe my body in times of high tension.

Suddenly, a spasm in my throat. I cough and sputter as the steady flow of air is broken, this brief moment of chaos escalating to a final heave that ejects a tiny, fluttering insect from my mouth.

I can't see the single fly, but I hear this creature buzzing around my room. It zooms from one corner of darkness to the next, rattling against the glass of my bedroom window before finally coming to rest.

Mayflies don't buzz like this, I realize, unable to stop my analysis.

The wings of my mystery insect are much more powerful than any mayfly, humming along with the relentless vigor of a common housefly in search of ripe decay.

Overwhelmed with disgust, I sit up and turn on my bedside lamp once again, hunting for the tiny intruder but unable to locate this now silent insect. I'm not sure if the horrible taste in my mouth is really there or just a product of my own subconscious mind after the lone straggler made their esophageal exit.

Either way, I need a glass of water.

Climbing out of bed, I search my windowsill one last time for the renegade insect. My parents hauled away the trash pretty quickly, leaving me to research from memory, and it'd be nice to procure a live sample. I consider waiting around for the fly to buzz again, but after a patient moment the atrocious tang in my throat is just too much to bear.

Quietly, I creep into the hallway and make my way downstairs, guided by nothing more than the light of the moon as it streams through nearby windows. With every step, the soft chatter of the distant living room television grows in volume, and from the house's main foyer I can see its flickering glow dance across an opposing kitchen wall.

Shivering, I press onward, the dull chill still lingering within me.

Rounding the kitchen corner, I now have a full view of the dining room and the living room beyond. It's here my mother sits, the back of her head silhouetted by a flashing TV screen before her. Her neck has a slight cant to it, revealing that she's fallen asleep while watching her favorite show.

In the Darling household our television options are limited.

Temptation comes in many forms, including an overwhelming number of secular channels. They've been blocked with parental controls, leaving us with four appropriate networks to choose from.

By now, I know all the commercials by heart, including this local offering from my very own Kingdom of the Pine church.

The familiar advertisement flashes into view, Pastor Pete Bend strolling calmly across a field of brilliant green grass. Behind him, several rows of stark white cabins stretch along the edge of the forest, and beyond these is a metal flagpole hoisting a massive American flag.

The site is immaculate and clean, fresh paint and tightly cut lawn immediately letting the viewer know this is more than just another cozy summer camp.

A I-800 number appears at the bottom of the screen, and it remains there for the entire duration of the commercial. It's a bit excessive, but it's also good marketing, and I'd be remiss to say Kingdom of the Pine doesn't know how to market themselves.

It's what this church was founded on.

"For all have sinned, and come short of the glory of God," Pastor Bend offers in a casual, direct-to-camera speech. "In other words, nobody's perfect. We've been blessed by the Lord to walk in the sun on this beautiful day and smell the fresh Montana air, but what we *do* with this blessing is up to us."

Pastor Bend skirts the line between a young man with older features and an older man who happens to be surprisingly youthful. He's always dressed in the current trends, yet gray hair overtook his temples long ago. The man's face always seems to fall in a natural smile, and his eyes are brilliant and excited. He's wearing an earth-tone jacket, decidedly fashion-forward and trendy.

Around the man's left wrist is a familiar band of red fabric, a recognition of Tobias Cobel's sacrifice.

The pastor stops his casual stroll and his expression changes slightly, becoming more serious as the camera begins an achingly slow zoom toward his face. "Does the temptation of unnatural lust have a hold on you or someone you love? Has someone in your life found themselves in the unholy grip of same-sex attraction? Don't be ashamed. Don't be embarrassed. Be proactive."

The camera cuts away from Pastor Bend to show a montage of footage from around the camp. Young people are playing baseball together, hustling around the bases and sliding into home. A group of joyful teenage girls rows a boat on the surface of a mirror-calm lake. Two young men with massive crucifixes on their T-shirts playfully razz each other over dinner at the camp dining hall. A Christian rock band plays enthusiastically on a beautiful outdoor stage, the guitarist a youthful dark-skinned guy with an arm full of religious iconography in the form of brilliant ink.

This place is *cool*.

"A life free from sin *is* possible, and it's waiting for you at Camp Damascus," Pete Bend continues in voiceover as the inspiring footage continues. "Kingdom of the Pine has developed a one-of-a-kind reparative therapy program for homosexual youth. We believe that a sympathetic yet firm approach is what makes Camp Damascus so special, but it's also what makes it so effective."

The screen jumps to a new shot of a young man with tousled blond hair. He's sitting in one of the cabins and a wide smile is stretched across his face. Below him, a title bar appears reading JORDAN, 16, EX-GAY.

"How would I describe my time at Camp Damascus?" he replies to someone just off camera. "Life-changing. I'm so thankful for all the counselors here, and for Pastor Bend. They saved me."

Moments later, another talking head appears, his smiling face perfectly framed as a quiet lake stretches out behind him. It's the handsome guitarist from earlier. SAUL, 22, COUNSELOR.

Saul gazes straight down the lens, his showmanship immediately palpable. "Purpose. Community. Connection," the man offers with stalwart confidence. "You're gonna grow here, but you're also gonna have a lot of fun."

The screen cuts back to Pastor Bend, who's standing in a modest outdoor amphitheater surrounded by lush forest. There are bleachers positioned on either side of him, and they've been divided down the middle with men on the left and women on the right. Pastor Bend stands tall at the center of it all, addressing the camera directly once more.

"Behind me are more than three hundred Camp Damascus graduates, but over the last thirteen years we've helped *thousands* of young people go on to lead healthy, normal, heterosexual lives in the presence of God," he passionately explains. "The facts speak for themselves: we are the most effective ex-gay ministry on the planet, boasting a 100 percent success rate. In the long history of Camp Damascus, there has not been a single reversion to same-sex attraction."

The screen fades to a long, slow pan across the bleachers, prompting me to recognize a few notable faces from my own high school mixed in with others from across the globe.

This is the only issue I have with this commercial. With a 100 percent success rate, there's no need to hire actors, yet the handful of acquaintances who ended up in this crowd shot claim they never went to Camp Damascus. A few of them *did* actually go, but when I prod about what it was like to shoot this commercial they always have trouble finding the words.

Must've been amazing.

"So call the number below and begin the process of embracing a better life for you or someone you love," Pastor Bend announces confidently. "With a little help, every one of us can . . ."

He pauses for a moment as the whole camp joins in for a raucous cheer.

"Love right!" they cry out in unison.

The commercial fades to black and my mother's late-night program returns to the screen, an hour of preaching from an ultraliberal California pastor she probably shouldn't be watching but tunes in for after Dad's gone to bed.

I hesitate a moment and bask in the gratitude that suddenly washes over me. Today may have been strange, but at least I'm not dealing with the torment those poor souls at Camp Damascus are constantly battling. At least I'm not gay.

The second I register this thought, I catch an unexpected vision slinking along with it: a stowaway. The fantasy comes in a flash, a startling image of another girl and me at a diner. It feels warm and cozy as we sit across from one another, sipping coffee and giggling over some inside joke. I reach out and touch her left hand across the table, and she hoists her drink with the right. The silhouette of a cartoon crocodile is on her mug, but the thing that really draws my attention is just how beautiful and deep her dark brown eyes are, framed by a bob of jet-black hair.

As soon as the thought arrives, however, it disappears. I'm left feeling strange and uncomfortable, my mind and my body at odds with each other in their reaction to this imaginary scene of some hypothetical other life.

I remind myself that 94 percent of people report having intrusive thoughts.

Moving on, I quietly turn to the cupboard, opening it up and pulling out a tall glass. I fill the cup with tap water, listening to the pitch of the faucet's soft hiss for timing, then turn back around and creep toward the stairs.

I only get a few steps before halting in my tracks, a potent surge of adrenaline coursing through my body. A humanoid figure now stands next to the television set, tucked away in the darkness and perfectly still.

I blink a few times, staring at this mass in the shadows as I attempt to make sense of it. I've gone from a bright screen to pitch black so many times in the last few minutes that my vision is struggling to keep up, fighting to sort through the things that are actual threats and the things that are nothing more than a coat rack or a standing lamp.

Or is that a hanging arm and a leg? I think to myself.

My mother remains motionless on the couch, completely unaware of the tension that fills the room around her.

My body is trembling, the glass of water in my hand vibrating as I wait and observe.

"Mom" is all I can think to say, attempting to wake her up in a hushed tone.

The figure remains still, utterly motionless in the dim, flickering light of the living room.

"Mom, do you see that?" I continue, a little louder this time.

My mother stirs a bit, but she doesn't wake.

"Mom!" I finally blurt, enough force behind my voice to pull her from her slumber.

The figure erupts toward me in a horrifyingly confident march, abruptly revealing themself and prompting a frightened shriek to escape my throat. I stumble back, dropping my glass against the kitchen tile with a resounding crash.

I immediately recognize the intruder, this glimpse in the darkness all I need to recall the woman at the falls. Her stark white eyeballs and strange, mangled grin come surging back to me, flooding my mind with abject terror. She's wearing the same deep red polo as before, and her stringy black hair flows behind her as she rushes forward.

I stumble against the dining room table, knocking it back with a hollow *skert* as I fail to catch myself. I hit the ground hard, feeling the cold chill of spilled water soaking through my shirt.

Suddenly, however, my intruder alters course. The woman turns at a crisp 90-degree angle, heading toward a nearby closet and disappearing into the darkness.

The next thing I know, my mother is blasting on the living room light and rushing toward me with a look of belligerent alarm. "Rose! Oh, son of a *gun!*" she cries out.

A moment later, she steps on a shard of glass and erupts with an unbridled howl. "Shoot!"

"There's someone in the house!" I scream, tears streaming down my face. "She's in the closet!"

A look of grave concern crosses my mother's face as I say this, glancing between me and the nearby door as she hobbles over and crouches down.

"What are you saying?" Lisa questions. "*Who* is in the closet?"

"The lady from the falls!" I clamor wildly, losing myself in the mighty flood of emotion that courses through my body. "She had these *blank eyes* and *weird teeth!* She's wearing a uniform!"

My mother's eyebrows furrow as I say this.

Dad arrives in the kitchen doorway, panicked and out of sorts.

"What's going on?" he asks, hurrying over until my mother raises her hand to stop him in his tracks.

"Glass" is all she says, prompting Dad to glance down before taking a cautious step back.

"What's going on?" my father repeats, calmer this time.

I struggle to follow his lead, pulling it together as much as I can before pushing onward. "There's a woman in the house," I inform him. "She was standing in the dark and she just ran at me. I saw her earlier today at the falls and she must've followed me home."

"She had blank eyes," my mother adds, strangely calm now, "and a *uniform*."

With this new information my father's expression flickers slightly, changing in a way that's so subtle I'd barely notice if not for the fact that I'm looking right at him with my senses on high alert.

My father points to the closet door. "In here?" he questions.

I nod.

Dad creeps toward the door as my eyes widen in fear. He's got nothing to defend himself with in the frightening event that this intruder has a weapon, but he doesn't seem to care.

"Wait!" I blurt, terrified by the thought of what lurks within.

Before I have a chance to stop him, however, Luke yanks open the closet door.

My father halts abruptly, staring into the darkness for a beat and then reaching out to turn on the light.

There's nothing in the closet.

A startled gasp escapes my lips—I'm both confused and relieved.

Dad turns around, a solemn look on his face as he returns to me. He takes his time to avoid the shattered glass that covers our kitchen floor, then eventually kneels down so we're eye to eye.

"It's been a long night," my father announces, reaching out and placing his hand on my shoulder. "Everything okay, honey?"

My first instinct is to protest, to tell him I'm perfectly fine and the strange woman must've slipped past him somehow, but the words won't form. Instead, I start crying again, even harder than before, as I allow the feelings to sweep me away like Noah's ark.

My parents soothe me from either side, hushing gently as I collapse into their arms.

3

TRUTH

I wait patiently in a small wooden chair, trying my best not to eavesdrop but latching on to fragments of the muffled conversation anyway.

"Yes, I know . . . well, it's not an exact science . . ." the familiar voice explains, anxious but assured. "There's variation in every breed . . . yes, I know. Understood."

The talking abruptly halts as a landline phone slams back down onto its wooden desk. There's a brief moment of silence, then footsteps marching toward the office door that flies open moments later.

"Hi, Rose, come on in," Dr. Smith offers, smiling warmly to greet me.

My therapist is a bespectacled, bearded man with soft features and kind eyes that always seem to bear a look of deep concern, whether I'm telling him something important or not. He's relatively short and his hair is stark white, still sitting thick atop the man's head despite his age.

Our sessions typically occur on a set monthly schedule, but today he's fitting me in.

"I used to love days off from school," Dr. Smith reveals as we step into his office, motioning toward my usual leather chair as he takes a seat in his own. "Dentist appointments. Doctor visits. I know it can be scary but I always looked forward to missing some class."

Dr. Smith chuckles to himself as he says this, thrilled by the rebellious nature of his childhood. He settles into his chair even more, allowing this blue-and-white piece of furniture to envelop him. The striped colors pop against the leathery tones of this otherwise academic basement office.

"My parents thought I should come in first thing," I reply.

"And what do *you* think?" Dr. Smith continues.

I mull this question over. "I think they're right," I finally offer. "I've been under a lot of stress."

Dr. Smith nods, but doesn't say anything. He stares quietly, waiting for me to continue.

"Who were you talking to just now?" I ask.

"Dog breeder," he replies, "but we're not here to talk about my Newfoundland puppy."

More silence, the pressure of this reticent moment hanging over us like a sword above John the Baptist's neck.

"I saw something strange yesterday," I finally inform him. "*Really* strange. I was at the falls with some friends, and I could've sworn I saw a lady in the woods. She was odd-looking, but you know, I didn't think much of it. She disappeared pretty quickly."

"Odd-looking? What was so odd-looking?" Dr. Smith asks, jotting down a few notes.

I close my eyes a moment, picturing the woman's bizarre face. I breathe in and out slowly, settling into the darkness and then allowing this aberrant figure to emerge from the wings of my subconscious brain. In my mind's eye, this stranger is even paler than I'd thought, her skin wrinkled and saggy but not with age. It's as though she's waterlogged, bones and membrane with nothing but putrid liquid hanging between them.

"She's . . . frightening," I offer. "Her hair is long and black, and it's patchy. Looks like it's falling out. She's got crooked, dirty teeth and her eyes are white."

My brain is taking brief, fragmented glimpses and sewing them together, completing a picture that felt quite abstract up until this point. In this dark room I've manifested, my gaze drifts down to her hands, coming to rest on something I hadn't considered much until now.

"I think her fingers are *very* long," I continue. "They stretch out like sharp white sticks."

"Sounds like you got a pretty good look at her," my therapist offers, prompting me to open my eyes again.

"Not really," I reply, shaking my head.

"Sure seems like it, though," Dr. Smith continues, gently adjusting his perfectly round glasses. "Unless your imagination is doing some heavy lifting."

A defensive surge pulses through me.

"What are you saying?" I counter.

"Just observing," Dr. Smith replies, deftly maintaining his open and warm demeanor.

We sit in silence for another long moment, allowing our conversation to settle. I can't help letting my eyes wander to the assortment of plaques mounted on his wall, the metallic rectangles hanging around him in an authoritative halo.

"Do you think she's real?" my therapist finally asks, cutting to the chase.

My immediate instinct is to defend myself, but in the name of objectivity I somehow manage to pull back on the reins.

"I don't know," I finally reply.

"When your parents called, they mentioned something about you seeing this woman walk into the closet? Your father followed her in, correct?"

I nod.

"And what happened?"

"She wasn't there," I admit.

Dr. Smith takes a deep breath and lets it out, shifting his weight a bit. "I'm disappointed in you," he finally announces. "I speak with plenty of young children who see monsters in their closets, but you're not a child anymore, Rose."

"I know," I reply, shaking my head, "but what about the flies? Something *strange* is going on."

"Swallowing that much insect larva is a *medical emergency*. It could cause someone a lot of stress, and stress is no good," Dr. Smith continues. "Stress can make even perfectly rational people see things that aren't really there."

I lower my head a bit, shaking it from side to side as I struggle to sort through everything. Something feels very wrong, as if the whole wide world is in on some joke that I'm completely oblivious to. Things aren't *quite* adding up, but I can't for the life of me figure out how the pieces actually fit.

Everyone is telling me to chill out and destress, that this feeling of being pulled apart like a baby before King Solomon is perfectly normal as I take the leap into adulthood.

Right now, however, it certainly doesn't feel normal. I want to trust my elders and my community, *yearn* for that familiar blanket of security, but the proposed retelling of these events is simply refusing to fall in line.

"What if it's a demon?" I question.

Dr. Smith hesitates. I can tell he's forcing himself to shift gears, to approach this particular topic from a calculated angle.

"Demons *are* real," he bluntly replies, his eyes now burning into mine, "you and I both know that. But they're also not little guys running around with pitchforks and horns, and they're certainly not scary ladies in red polo-shirt uniforms. Demons manifest *abstractly*, through addiction and sin and moral decay. They manifest through *temptation*. So I guess my question back to you is . . . have you felt any temptation lately?"

I shake my head confidently. "No."

"Sometimes when we're feeling something we *know* is wrong, it's hard for us to accept responsibility," Dr. Smith explains. "We create someone or something, like a monster in the closet or an imaginary friend, and we place the blame on them. When that happens, there's only one way to stop it: we must *turn away* from the feelings that create the monster. We must reject the temptation."

I'm listening, but I remain quiet. I drum out a few patterns on my fingers, the movement soft enough that Dr. Smith won't notice.

He laughs to himself a bit. "Truth be told, most of the time it doesn't get this far. People tend to turn away from their demons once things get truly frightening. Have you ever heard of Petrov's dogs?"

"Pavlov's dogs," I correct him.

Dr. Smith just brushes past my amendment, barreling onward. "Petrov rang a bell every time he presented his dogs with food. He did this for a long time, training them, until one day he rang the bell and delivered no food. Even though there was no food, the canine bodies *reacted* to his bell, salivating profusely. Now, what do you think would happen if he *scared* the dogs every time he rang his bell?"

"They'd be afraid of the bell," I reply flatly.

He nods. "God is ringing a bell for you, Rose. He's telling you to steer clear of temptation, but you're much more thoughtful than the other pups. You're curious, and that can be a virtue, but it can also be a curse. Do you know what happened to the dogs that were too unruly for Petrov's research?"

"They didn't have to worry about someone experimenting on their salivary glands," I say.

Dr. Smith smiles. "They were taken out back and shot in the head."

"That's . . . not how the scientific method should work," I counter.

"God doesn't use the scientific method. So I'll ask you again, Rose. Do you have any temptation in your life?"

I hesitate, then confidently shake my head no.

Dr. Smith lets my reply marinate for an uncomfortably long time. Finally, he relaxes. "Well, that's good. Maybe what's going on here *seems* to be some massive, cataclysmic event, but what we're really looking at is a stressed-out young woman at the end of her senior year. When you consider your Tenet Intensives, plus kindergarten, that's a fifteen-year journey."

Every child raised in Kingdom of the Pine takes two years away from traditional schooling to study the tenets, focusing on *respect* and *integrity* after fifth grade, then *service* and *excellence* after tenth.

Dr. Smith knocks twice on the arm of his chair as the tension dissipates from the room.

"What I'd recommend is a hearty dose of *fun*," my therapist enthusiastically suggests. "Your parents let me know you're going to Isaiah's birthday party tonight after school."

"They did?" I ask.

Dr. Smith leans in a bit, lowering his voice as though he's letting me in on a little secret. All this, despite the fact there's nobody else in the room to overhear us. "What I think you should do is just . . . have a good time, you know? Let loose a bit. The congregation understands kids are gonna be kids, that's what these youth excursions are all about."

"Okay," I reply with a nod.

"Good," Dr. Smith offers in return, slapping his knees and standing up. He strolls over to the office door and opens it, waiting for me to follow his lead. "We don't need a long session today. This was just a little checkup."

I stand and head for the door.

"Have fun with Isaiah," my therapist imparts with a wink.

"Sure," I reply, trying my best to sound enthusiastic.

Dr. Smith closes the door, plunging me into the stuffy silence of a church basement once again.

I stand uncomfortably for a moment, still struggling to process our conversation. I came here for answers, but the dichotomy blooming at the depths of my soul still sits awkward and jagged.

Eventually, I make my way up to the main floor of the church.

At least this KOPTOC, or Kingdom of the Pine Therapeutic Outreach Center, is located conveniently, positioned just a few blocks from school and easily walkable.

I wave to some familiar volunteers and head out into the sun on my quest for second-period calculus. It's a beautiful day, and as I amble along I can feel *some* of my haunting anxiety beginning to slip away. I'm relieved, but there's one thing that lingers in the back of my mind.

I hadn't mentioned the red work polo my intruder was wearing before Dr. Smith brought it up in our session; not to him, not to my parents.

Or maybe I did, and it just slipped my mind.

I shake my head, rattling loose any doubt that still desperately clings tight. I need to take the advice I've already received and just relax— have a good time!—especially given the fact that my parents are *actually* letting me attend a mixed party this evening with both Kingdom of the Pine and secular kids in attendance.

Hopefully things with Isaiah won't be too weird, I think to myself. *At least Martina's gonna be there.*

There's a faint tickle at the back of my throat, but I ignore it.

*   *   *

I gaze across this suburban basement packed with friends and class-mates, the whole gang spreading out before me in a perfectly imperfect balance. It's as though they were placed here by some artful Renaissance painter; Veronese, maybe. Music is blasting from the nearby stereo and fellow students struggle to shout over it as they lean casually against walls or laugh together in small pods. Any observer might see this as a quintessential teenage party scene, but a careful eye reveals assorted cru-cifix jewelry and T-shirts sporting various God-centric catch phrases.

I'm feeling reasonably confident thanks to my social preparation routine—a large notecard of potential discussion topics, interesting facts, and small-talk questions. This card is folded and tucked away in my pocket for quick reference, though I don't think that'll be necessary. I spent enough time on this one to recite it from memory.

The word "muscle" is derived from a Latin term, meaning "little mouse."

The shortest sentence in the Bible is two words. Do you know what they are?

What are your biggest fears?

Most of the partiers are holding red cups, but these plastic goblets are full of root beer, not *beer* beer, and the safe yet faintly abrasive music is upbeat Christian pop-punk with a positive message.

I love it.

Suffice to say, this whole experience is a lot less intimidating than I expected.

Of course, half these kids are members of the congregation anyway, people I've known since I was a child. The other half are Neverton citizens who may not be Kingdom of the Pine members, but they're God-fearing enough for our parents to approve.

Neverton is quaint in size, but strong in Christian presence thanks to Camp Damascus. While Kingdom of the Pine remains a modest sect internationally, this town is chock-full of believers, a stronghold of faith.

Despite the chaos yesterday, I actually find myself feeling pretty normal again, happy to begrudgingly accept these strange events as nothing more than a natural buildup of stress in a young, exhausted mind.

"Hey" comes a familiar voice.

I glance over to find Isaiah, the man of the hour, sliding up beside me. He hoists his plastic cup and the two of us give a hearty cheers, taking large sips of the carbonated beverage.

Root beer was created in 1866 and first commercially available in 1875. It was sold in syrup form and made from sassafras root, which has since been banned for causing cancer. The plan was to call it "root tea," but the name was changed last minute in an attempt to capture the Pennsylvania coal miner market.

That one's not from the card. I just know my root beer.

"Thanks for coming," Isaiah continues, yanking me back from my journey into beverage history. "I wasn't sure if you'd make it after the way I acted."

"It's fine," I offer, still gazing across the party.

"No, it's not," Isaiah continues.

I turn to face the birthday boy, giving him my full attention and making sure he believes I've genuinely accepted his apology. Truth be told, this little moment of forgiveness is the last thing on my conscious mind. "Thank you for saying something," I reply, struggling to give my voice enough emotional weight so we can finally move on.

The regret in my friend's expression melts away, gradually transforming into a smile.

We stand a moment, sipping our drinks and gazing out across the party. The music does a great job filling in space between the break in our conversation, but I'm still not all that comfortable just standing here.

"The word 'muscle' is derived from a Latin term that means 'little mouse,'" I blurt.

"What?" Isaiah asks, although I'm not sure if he couldn't hear me, or if he *could* hear me and doesn't know how to respond.

I stare at him blankly, my mind seizing up.

"Hey, come with me," Isaiah finally offers, shifting gears.

The next thing I know he's taking me by the hand and leading me through the open floorplan of this crowded basement. Peers immediately turn and watch us go, whispering to one another with looks of tittering excitement.

Soon enough, we're making our way down a dark hallway, the music growing quieter and the raucous atmosphere evolving into relative calm. We reach a door, and Isaiah pushes through to reveal a small circle of friends sitting cross-legged on the floor. A television is on behind them, playing Christian music videos and casting the proceedings in an eerie dancing light. It's muted.

"Wanna play truth or dare?" Isaiah asks.

My first instinct is to decline and retreat, disappearing back into the wash of the party, but before I get the chance I catch sight of Martina chatting away within the circle. Immediately, my demeanor changes, and I struggle to act natural as I heartily accept.

"Yeah!" I chirp, climbing down to join the others. "Sounds fun!"

I've never played truth or dare, and to be honest, the prospect sounds terrifying. Still, I find myself compelled to sit. Martina is one of the coolest people I know, and maybe spending a little more time around her will help some of that innate coolness rub off on me.

It appears the game has already started when Isaiah and I join, the group loosened up after several rounds of wild dares and raunchy questions. Morgan, a guy I know from school, has just completed his dare and is now tasked with selecting another target.

His eyes slowly move around the circle, drifting from person to person. He's careful not to rush this important decision, finally arriving on the last option I'd ever want: me.

"Rose. Truth or dare?" Morgan asks, a mischievous flicker in his eye.

A hush falls over the crowd as I take on their undivided attention.

It's a simple enough decision, only two possible outcomes presented and each one just as mysterious as the other, yet I find myself utterly tongue-tied.

When the awkward silence becomes truly unbearable, I somehow manage to spit out a single word. "Truth."

Morgan nods, a pleased king who has formally accepted my response. "Alright, alright," he offers, chewing his lip as he considers the query. Morgan has suddenly been thrust into a position of incredible power, and he wants to make the most of it.

Along with the expected tension of this moment, I get the feeling something else is going on behind the scenes, some inside joke I'm clearly not a part of. While most eyes remain trained on me, other kids are quietly shooting glances at Isaiah.

"Okay," Morgan finally begins, "how many times have you done it?"

The circle immediately reacts, quietly chattering with excited guesses over the answer to come. I pick up tiny fragments of these whispered conversations, nuggets of brutal honesty that bubble faintly across my ears.

There's a clear consensus to the guesses: zero.

"She's two years older, though," someone murmurs. "All Kingdom Kids are."

"Doesn't matter. Virgin," comes a confident reply.

I feel a flush of anxiety wash over me, and I'm well aware my face is turning red despite my efforts to remain calm. I laugh awkwardly, shaking my head and immediately pushing the question out of my mind.

"I—I don't know," I stammer, my fingers dancing a mile a minute.

I force them to stop moving.

Morgan raises an eyebrow. "You *don't know?*"

This reply was instinctual, a sympathetic response straight from the medulla with no rhyme or reason other than a quick-release social eject button, but in this moment of panic a flash of vivid imagery slips through my mind. I see the same arresting dark-haired girl I pictured last night, imagine her kissing me deeply and feel the weight of her body against mine. I sense flashes of a mischievous smile, of her voice, and of the comfort I feel when she's close.

Meanwhile, the attention of the circle remains fully transfixed, waiting for a coherent response.

"I . . . uh. Let me think about it," I falter, struggling to right the ship.

"*That many?*" someone loudly jokes, causing a wave of laugher to erupt across the group.

More flashes of the beautiful black-haired girl rip through me; memories of an aching, burning sensation at the pit of my stomach. Impressions of warm, bare skin. Her face is right there at the forefront of my mind: olive complexion and startlingly dark, wide-set eyes that make it seem like her pupils are filling the whole iris.

From where I'm sitting there's a direct view of the muted television set. The screen is dancing with light and movement, showing off familiar clips of a bleach-blond, spiky-haired punk band with crucifix tattoos. Slowly, however, the images begin to roll and mutate, hues shifting as these visual representations become more and more difficult to understand. Random bursts of intermittent analog snow pierce the transmission.

I'm the only one who notices, my eyes glued to the screen with fascination and confusion.

"Rose?" Morgan continues, a hint of genuine concern now coloring his tone.

By now, the music videos have disappeared completely as another set of images struggles to push through the static. I can faintly make out the blurry shape of a bald, humanoid figure in a chair, their body held tight by a series of straps. The body is slumped over, and as this scene grows clearer I notice additional captive figures in the dim light, the shapes restrained in a variety of awkward, painful poses. Some of the forms are bent backward over outlandish metal contraptions while others are fastened upside down against a stone wall. The transmission hue has been skewed a deep red, giving these characters a bizarre, other-worldly look.

A nauseated sickness floods my stomach as I watch, but nothing could make me tear my eyes away. Curiosity has gotten the best of me.

Back in the realm of reality, a circle of friends is vying for my attention, waving and shouting my name as they struggle to break the trance. I know they're here, but my attention is fixated elsewhere.

Onscreen, the point-of-view camera creeps onward, making its way through this chamber of crimson figures. It passes the chair-bound form and arrives at another body, this one twisted haphazardly over a metal bar and locked into place by multiple straps. Closer and closer this visual perspective draws, details sharpening until a horrific realization surges through me and my breath catches in my throat.

The television hue is just fine. These figures are deep red because they're missing their skin.

The camera is so close now I can make out every detail of these mutilated corpses, the ripples of muscle and sinew glistening under dim light. The face of this particular body is hauntingly still, eyes glazed over in a reminder of just how delicate our mortal shells really are.

It's utterly repulsive, yet I can't bring myself to look away.

Suddenly, a breath of freezing cold air visibly pulses from the lips of the luminous face onscreen, still gasping despite their fully peeled state. They're alive.

I let out a startled scream, the imagery finally too much to handle as I scramble away from the television.

The room of friends immediately flies into a state of chaos, class-mates glancing between the screen and me.

One of the partiers jumps to their feet and hurries over to the tele-vision set, turning it off in frustration. "This is why we don't watch secular media!" he announces. "Who thought it was funny to put on a *terror film*?"

Someone else rolls their eyes. "Holy cow! We're not all Kingdom Kids here. God has better things to worry about than scary movies."

"Hey!" Isaiah snaps, pointing to them then motioning toward the door. "Not cool! Go!"

The pandemonium is a lot to keep up with as my body reels from the shock of this grotesque imagery. Isaiah puts his hand on my shoulder in an effort to calm me down, and this human connection actually helps pull me back to reality.

"Hey, it was just a movie," Isaiah offers. "It's just makeup and effects."

I nod along, half listening.

"Liberal Hollywood will do anything to make money," Isaiah con-tinues. "That kind of violence is disgusting, but it's not real. It's fake."

I keep nodding, gradually starting to believe him.

Of course it's fake.

I take a deep breath, hold, then let it out, now mostly terrified by what a fool I've made of myself.

Hoping to craft a social antidote, I abruptly sit up straight and pull it together.

"Sorry," I blurt. "Let's keep playing."

The crowd begins to settle as I say this, reforming the circle once again. There's a clear shift in mood, but it's not as bad as it could've been.

Eventually, Morgan loudly clears his throat. "Let's just move on to someone else," he suggests, glancing around the circle. He stops on Martina. "Martina. Truth or dare."

This question has power, immediately tugging the room back into a state of quiet intimacy and simmering tension.

Let no one deceive you by any means; for that day will not come unless the falling away comes first.

I find myself repeating this phrase over and over, the mantra cascading through my mind and rushing across my brain like soapy water. I'm okay. Everything is fine.

It was just a stupid movie.

Martina considers the query, taking her time. Her facial expressions begin to playfully shift, each one revealing something new and exciting.

The next thing I know, a ridiculous terror film is the last thing on my mind.

"Dare," Martina finally replies.

My skin tingles faintly as she says this.

Morgan smiles, unmistakably craving this answer. It appears he has a great dare locked and loaded. "I dare you to get in the closet for *seven minutes* with the person you like."

My blood runs cold, a surge of chilly discomfort drifting through me. My eyes are trained on Martina like a hawk's, deeply invested in her decision as she surveys the group.

I'm flooded by a bizarre state of self-awareness, yearning for Martina to choose me but struggling to accept the context of this desire. The emotions are so powerful that I'm actually trembling, shivering with nervous anticipation.

What is it about my friend that I find so utterly fascinating?

I want to be near her, but not in a *weird* way. Obviously.

It's not like I'm gay or something.

As Martina's sparkling green eyes pass over me I feel my body clench tight with anticipation, aching for her to stop and prompt the whole group to erupt in a giant laugh. We'd go with it, heading into the closet where we could giggle together over this little comedy bit.

Martina's gaze suddenly halts in my direction.

Thank you, Jesus.

"Parker," Martina announces, pointing at the guy sitting next to me.

A wave of aching disappointment pulses through my frame. While the rest of the circle lets out a fit of excited chatter, I just stare at Martina and watch as she rises to her feet. Parker stands as well, and soon enough the two of them are heading toward the bedroom closet for a stomach-churning bout of alone time.

Parker's not even religious, I suddenly realize. He's not a congregation member, not even a CAPE Catholic or some other kind of lukewarm backslider. What the *heck* does Martina see in him?

What doesn't she see in me?

Martina and Parker slip inside the closet and shut the door, disappearing from view.

The nauseating, heartbreaking sickness within me has done nothing but grow, and soon enough I've found myself too overwhelmed to remain still any longer. My breathing heavy, I climb to my feet and make a break for the exit.

"Rose!" Isaiah calls out, startled by my sudden departure.

I leave the bedroom and slam the door behind me, so overwhelmed with raw emotion that tears are welling up in my eyes. I'm as analytical as they come, yet in this moment I find myself unable to parse what's happening within my body. These sensations don't make any sense, but my understanding of that fact doesn't taper their ferocity.

It just upsets me even more.

I stand in the dark hallway, struggling to catch my breath as I drift between worlds. Behind me is the closed door of a childish truth or dare game, a place that's suddenly brought me immense sorrow and confusion for reasons I still can't comprehend.

Before me is the rest of the party, a raucous scene where secular kids I've never met mingle freely with congregation members in a hedonistic free-for-all. It's a spiritual battlefield, and while it doesn't offer as much pain as the room behind, there's still plenty of chaos.

"Hey" comes an unfamiliar voice, a tall, messy-haired partier stumbling down the hallway. He stops before me, bracing himself against the wall as he sways in and out of my personal bubble. "You're hot."

I say nothing in return.

"Trash party, huh?" the sloppy visitor continues, his words tumbling over one another. "Isaiah's pretty cool, but these kids are fucking cringe. You want a drink? Like, a real drink?"

He holds up a water bottle, but the scent causes me to wrinkle my nose in disgust.

"Uh, hello?" the guy pushes onward.

I should probably be more annoyed, but all I can think about right now is Martina. My heart was viciously ripped from my chest, and now nothing else seems to register.

I close my eyes and count the rhythmic tapping of my fingers, struggling to calm down.

5, 4, 3, 2, 1.

4, 3, 2, 1.

3, 2, 1.

2, 1.

1.

Then repeat.

"Be strong and of good courage, do not fear nor be afraid of them;" I recite softly under my breath, "for the Lord your God, He is the one who goes with you. He will not leave you nor forsake you."

I can hear my suitor mumbling to himself, his frustrated tone growing steadily quieter as he returns to the fray.

When I open my eyes the partier is gone, but my solitude is short-lived.

There are two rooms here at the end of the hallway: the one we were playing in, and a second bedroom mirroring the first. They are similar in size, and if I had to guess I'd say this other one belongs to Isaiah's older brother.

He's not around tonight, but it appears someone else is enjoying the space.

Standing at the center of this dimly lit room is the pale woman, smiling that same crooked grin and silently gazing at me with her vacant white eyes. This is the best look at her I've gotten, and as we stand motionless I carefully take her in.

Cadaverous. Eldritch. Puzzling.

"You're not real," I find myself announcing. "You're just . . . stress."

To be honest, she doesn't feel like stress. Now that I'm seeing this woman up close, the idea that she's just some figment of my imagination is getting much harder to swallow. Previously, her appearances were fraught with movement and shadow, a vague glimpse of something otherworldly.

This moment, however, is as quiet and grounded as it gets. The pale woman has weight in my world, a substance to her form. For the first time, I can fully make out the bizarre length of her fingers, approximately three times as long as any typical human digits. They're thin and spidery, twitching ever so slightly in the shadows.

The collar around her neck is so tight that it makes *me* feel like I'm choking, a sturdy iron band that clasps in the middle.

From here I can make out the name tag on her peculiar red work polo. It reads: PACHID.

I know that name, though just barely, the unique title ringing a faint bell in the darkest recesses of my mind. It takes a moment for all of the pieces to add up as I sort through hazy memories of various religious tomes until, suddenly, a spark of recognition becomes a roaring blaze.

Pachid is a demon.

I'm shaking so hard that my teeth are chattering, not just out of fear, but from the gelid sensation that overwhelms my body.

"What do you want?" I ask, the words barely rattling their way from between my lips.

The woman says nothing. She slowly tilts her head to the side, as though this is also *her* first time really taking me in.

It feels like this moment lasts forever, the two of us just watching each other with genuine curiosity until finally, and without a shred of warning, the pale woman turns and walks directly toward the wall.

Pachid doesn't slow down as she approaches the barrier, causing a startled gasp to escape my throat when she walks right through it and disappears completely. A faint blue sizzle lies in her wake, flickering with uncanny illumination then disappearing just as soon as it arrived.

Seconds later, the shrieking begins.

I burst back into the truth or dare room to find everyone staring at the closet door in wide-eyed horror. A few loud thumps rumble from within, but the more apparent sounds are a gut-churning cacophony of Parker and Martina screaming in hysterical fear.

It's only now that I realize this closet is directly behind the wall Pachid just walked through.

The frantically spinning gears of my mind catch and I spring into action, marching in a direct route to the closet door.

"Get them out of there!" I scream.

I reach out to grab the handle, but before I get the chance the door flies open so hard it punches a hole through the wall beside it. I cry out in alarm, jumping back as Martina topples out with a tremendous thump and lands on the floor, her eyes huge and glassy as she stares up at me in a frozen expression of grotesque panic.

There's something confusing about her pose, and it takes me a moment to realize Martina's head has been violently twisted in a perfect half rotation. The bones of her neck have shattered, pressing awkwardly against the inside of her skin and threatening to punch through.

Meanwhile, the pale woman is nowhere to be found, but Parker's complexion is just as pallid as he stands in shock, mumbling to himself while tears stream down his face.

The room erupts in a choir of screams.

4

DARKNESS
ON THE EDGE
OF TOWN

When you shuffle off this mortal coil, your senses will likely take their leave one by one. Depending on the way your body meets its end, the exact order of these fading perceptions can vary, but everyone seems to agree on one thing: your hearing goes last.

The final spark in Martina's awareness was her friends screaming in panic and horror, blubbering over a body that couldn't feel and eyes that couldn't see.

I'm supposed to be fine with this because she's in a better place now. She wasn't a member of the congregation, but she loved Jesus above all others.

That counts. At least, that's my take.

Other things I've learned:

Around 150,000 people die every day across the globe, Martina being one of them.

Cotard's syndrome is a rare mental disorder that makes people believe they're dead.

The Turritopsis dohrnii jellyfish lives forever. As far as science can tell, it's the only immortal species on record.

I've buried myself in death facts, devouring everything I can find on the subject. My behavior is obsessive, and I know it, but it's better than staring at the wall for hours on end, watching shadows gradually creep across my bedroom as a thousand intrusive questions dance through my mind.

What kind of god would let this happen?

Is Martina really happy now?

Because she certainly didn't look happy with her head cracked around backward, her spinal column shredded, and her shattered bones rending her flesh like hundreds of tiny knives.

A shudder rolls across my frame as I revisit this terrible image, tears forming at the corners of my eyes that I swiftly wipe away. I dive back into the massive blocks of text on my phone, returning to an article about the burial customs of ancient Greece.

"You okay?" my mother's voice sounds from the doorway behind me.

I scramble to tuck away my device, which they've made clear is for emergencies only. In any other circumstance I'd be receiving a hearty taste of parental discipline, but it appears Lisa has momentarily holstered the whip.

Mom steps onto the wooden porch and stands behind me, gazing across the backyard. There's not much of a view here, just a huge patch of grass and an abrupt line of trees at the far end, but it's quiet.

"Wanna go on a walk?" my mother asks.

I don't, but after sitting inside for two weeks this idea might be the lesser evil.

I glance back at her, struggling to plaster on the most natural expression I can manage. Typically, I'm great at masking, but right now the cracks are simply too profound to maintain.

"Sure," I offer, my voice wavering slightly.

Right-handed people live an average of three years longer than left-handed people.

I stand up and move past her, making my way into the house as I gather my things. I grab a jacket and pull on my shoes, ready for a temperature drop as the evening settles in around us.

Soon, we're heading down the front steps and taking our usual right turn up the quiet suburban street.

This walk is a ritual for Mom and me, a little moment for us to connect in ways directly spoken and otherwise. The modest neighborhood loop has gotten me through a lot, but nothing quite like this.

We remain silent at first, the soft pulse of our middle-class hamlet filling in the spaces between words. Sprinklers shuffle and churn as dogs bark in the distance. I pick up on children laughing behind the fence next door, and the faintest chime of a bicycle bell rings out just a few blocks onward. It's not as crowded as other neighborhoods, with plenty of distance and swaths of forest between the houses, but this time of the evening it seems like everyone's up to something.

After we pass by a handful of familiar abodes, my mother points over at a home on the corner.

"Adultery," she offers. "Husband is cheating on his wife with . . ."

Mom drifts off for a moment, considering her options.

"The maid," she finally concludes.

I remain silent, unable to play along. I refuse to turn and assess the target.

"Come on, Rose," my mother continues.

All I can do is shake my head, then abruptly stop in my tracks as tears begin to well.

Mom sees it coming, but she doesn't demand I pull myself together. That's what my dad would do.

To be fair, though, he's absolutely right.

Tobias Herrod Cobel wouldn't have accomplished a damn thing without perseverance and sacrifice, and that spirt runs deep through the congregation. The Industrial Revolution wasn't a great time for a workplace accident, especially one that took his hand and stole two months of his life in a coma, but without that horrible moment the Prophet would never have received his vision, and without his vision we wouldn't have Kingdom of the Pine.

Prophet Cobel managed to pull himself up by his bootstraps, and he had it much worse than this.

My mother doesn't recite any of the tenets, however. She doesn't remind me of Tobias's story or tell me to have faith. Instead, she opens her arms wide and wraps me in a tight hug.

We stay like this for a long while, until I finally pull back and instinctively reach up to brush the tears from my eyes. There's nothing to wipe away, however. I'm all cried out.

My mother starts walking again and I follow her lead.

"Husband cheating with the maid," she reminds me.

I glance over at the light blue structure, warm light emanating from the kitchen where a family loudly clinks their dishes and laughs with their whole bellies. It's hard to picture the story Mom's created, especially given that the Kimberlys live here and we know them very well, but I go with it.

"Send the couple to church counseling," I offer. "Fire the maid. Remind them of John 3:18, Ephesians 5:33 . . . Exodus 20:14, obviously."

Mom nods along, my skills of biblical recollection so precise that it actually prompts her to chuckle in amazement. "That's great," she offers. "Consider them saved."

We continue onward, strolling up the next lane as it curves and sweeps around a large hill. This section of the route is a little more forested than the rest, trees stretching out over the road and a modest creek trickling parallel to cracked pavement.

A car passes, slowing to a crawl as the driver offers a friendly wave. I have no doubt our neighbors would take this care either way, but by now the news of Martina's death has permeated our community and soaked into everything like spilled ink. Everyone knows I was there when it happened.

Deep in the forest, another home can be seen perched atop its own modest hill.

"I love this place," my mother announces. "So quiet."

She says this every time we pass, and although this little comment has been deeply ingrained in my mind, I never understand it.

Lisa is a warm, beaming member of the community, a blond-haired, blue-eyed beacon of light at every church function and a consistent host of book clubs and women's prayer groups. Almost everything I've learned about navigating social cues I picked up from her, a brilliant teacher whether she knows it or not.

This house on the left, however, is the last place I'd ever picture Lisa Darling yearning for. It's the smallest home in the neighborhood, much older than the rest and featuring a single chimney that's likely the only source of heat. It's a one- or two-room cabin, barely visible through the woods: a place of solitude.

"Secular influence," my mother begins, nodding toward the cabin as we pass. "The daughter brought home *terror fiction* from her school library; public school, of course. She's starting to act out."

This one is easy.

"Remove the secular influence. Schedule a youth pastor one-on-one," I suggest. "Assign a meditation on I Corinthians 10:31 and a reading of Romans I, top to bottom."

"The whole thing, huh?" Mom questions.

"Sure," I reply.

My mother is impressed.

As our walk enters its second half, I find a strange, creeping dread beginning to simmer deep within. The overwhelming sadness I've been feeling has been momentarily sidelined, and for that I'm thankful, but this method of ignoring the problem can only hold for so long.

We can't keep walking forever, and as vast as the subject of death remains, I'll eventually run out of facts to fill my skull like dry bandages.

The spiritual bleeding hasn't stopped. In fact, it's gushing more than ever.

Once I've finished tackling death and trauma, there's only one topic left to shift over to. It's a question that hangs like a specter in the back of my mind, haunting me.

What does it mean to see things that aren't really there?

Even more frightening: What if they really are?

Kingdom of the Pine is strict in its teachings about demonic forces, taking a firm but realistic approach over the last decade. We live in the modern age now, and we're fortunate enough to understand these creatures as a metaphor for the dark cravings within ourselves.

But when's the last time you saw an abstract metaphor shatter anyone's spine?

"Rose!" my mother snaps angrily, her sharp tone breaking through my haze of concentration. "Fingers!"

I glance down to realize I've been doing my counts, a massive transgression in the Darling household. My hands immediately stiffen, then relax.

Lisa's face remains stern over the remaining block, finally relaxing by the time we've reached our next sharp turn. This area transitions back into newer suburban houses, a cozy lane featuring some of my favorites. Other Kingdom of the Pine families are clustered here.

Mom gestures to another house as we pass, the porchlight on and a lazy orange cat sitting confidently on the front stoop. Inside, the television chatters, a prayer service drifting out through the cool evening air.

"Suicide," my mother suggests. "The father took his own life."

I'm always trying to impress her with my responses, answering these hypothetical queries of spiritual warfare with a quick and firm solution. This time, however, I falter.

I know exactly what she wants me to say, but as I open my mouth the words refuse to emerge. Something doesn't quite fit.

"For the family?" I finally manage to question.

"For the sinner," my mother clarifies.

Martina didn't take her own life, but the weight of her death is undeniably tethered to this topic all the same. I can't help wondering if my mother is doing this on purpose, but the innocent look on her face says otherwise.

A far more heartbreaking realization washes over me, one that doesn't require any ulterior motives or discreet social manipulation from my mother.

The truth is, even *I* wouldn't have found this question sickening until recently. On any other day I would've jumped right in with a pitch-perfect prescription, a way for that poor soul to repent even after they've left this earth.

Maybe I'd even reply it was impossible; what's done is done.

Now, however, the simmering dread has reached a boil. Everything feels wrong. It's not just this particular question that has grown distasteful, it's the whole exercise. Judgment as sport, whether fictional or not, has taken an undeniable toll on me, a weight that's likely even more caustic than any encounter with some hallucinated demon.

Or a real demon.

"What do you think?" Mom prods, waiting for my response. "Can he be saved?"

I feel nauseated, the world swaying awkwardly below me as I struggle to maintain my composure. There's a tear in my soul, a rip that started with Martina's death and continues unraveling with every passing day.

The Four Tenets were built for moments like this, reminders of my higher purpose in the face of doubt and despair, but the stitches this mantra provides can't hold back what's coming.

Respect—I will honor when I do not understand,

Integrity—I will believe when I do not witness,

Service—I will strive when my sin is heavy,

Excellence—I will persevere when my body does not.

I've followed this path since I was a little girl, and with a community of cheerful faces at my back and a loving family by my side, it always felt righteous and good.

It doesn't *feel* righteous anymore, and with that feeling gone, something even more potent has continued to blossom within me: curiosity.

I suddenly realize how long I've been silent, scrambling for an answer that doesn't exist. "Hey, you wanna grab ice cream after dinner?" I finally blurt.

My mother raises her eyebrow ever so slightly, hesitating. She's considering whether or not to let me move on.

Eventually, Lisa erupts in a sharp cackle of laughter. "Sure, honey," she replies, clearly thrilled by our breakthrough.

Her horrible question drifts away into the ether, unanswered.

✳   ✳   ✳

I've been a patient of Dr. Smith's for years now, the therapist carrying me diligently through good times and bad, and while the circumstances of my life have changed plenty, the feeling of his office has not. This has always been a place of safety and warmth, a port in the storm of young adult angst that swirls around any girl my age.

In the past, I've actually felt *guilty* over the security I find here. *The only one I should feel this welcome around is Jesus,* I'd worry.

Back then, I'd been so solid in my convictions, my faith the steady foundation from which everything else was constructed. Sure, I was much keener to explore science and nature than my parents would've liked, but that was only because I appreciated these subjects as an extension of God's love.

And I still do. At least, I *think* I still do.

But the fact remains, something in this bedrock is cracked and wobbling, a key bracer that was mentioned in the blueprints but was never really there. The more I look around, the more these bracers come up missing.

It's a little frightening, but after that night at Isaiah's birthday party, what *isn't* a little frightening?

"Where are those plaques from?" I blurt.

Dr. Smith follows my gaze, turning in his striped chair and gazing up at the sweeping assortment of metallic rectangles marking the wall behind him. "All over the place," he says. "Would you like to take a look?"

I stand up and cross the office, passing Dr. Smith and arriving next to his desk where these awards and accolades hang proudly. I begin to look them over, moving slowly from piece to piece as I silently take them in.

2018 Montana Christian Fellowship Mark of Excellence

2009 Church of the Crossroads Honorable Service Award

2021 Ignite Ministries Youth Outreach Medal of Appreciation

As I move from one side of this display to the other, I discover a whole section of the wall is dedicated to certificates from Camp Damascus, ranging from 2014 to now.

"Almost a decade at Damascus," I observe.

Dr. Smith watches me closely. He nods as I say this, but doesn't speak in return.

Eventually, I reach the end of the plaques and turn around. "Why are these all from Christian organizations?" I ask flatly.

My therapist laughs. "What else would they be? Buddhist?"

"But you're a doctor," I continue. "Why don't you have your doctorate hanging up?"

"I learned much more from the Bible than I did in any schoolbook," Dr. Smith retorts. "I choose to display the things that matter to me."

I stand in awkward silence, two distinct halves of my brain tugging in opposite directions. While I usually have a simple enough time finding a middle ground between my faith and my curiosity, it's a dichotomy growing more and more difficult to synthesize. Dr. Smith's reasoning is both perfectly understandable and overwhelmingly frustrating.

He motions back toward my chair and I follow his lead, returning to this familiar seat.

"You don't seem like yourself," he observes.

"Well, yeah," I reply. "I saw my friend die two weeks ago."

"You seem angry," Dr. Smith clarifies.

"I *am* fricking angry!" I snap, then gasp at my own rage. "Forgive me."

The two of us sit awkwardly for a moment, my unexpected outburst hanging in the air as I struggle to understand what just happened. I'm ashamed, but the shame feels confusing and unjustified and ultimately just makes me even more frustrated.

"Who are you angry with?" Dr. Smith asks.

I let out a long sigh. "I don't know."

"Me?" he asks, taking a direct approach. "Your parents?"

I ignore the second part of this question, a bridge I'm not quite ready to cross, but the first half is intriguing.

"You lied to me," I declare.

Dr. Smith raises his white eyebrows, nodding along from behind circular glasses. "Care to elaborate?"

"You told me demons weren't real," I continue, barreling onward in a way that admittedly feels cathartic.

Dr. Smith and I have been meeting every other evening since Martina's death, but most of that time has been spent in quiet introspection.

These feelings—these questions—have been bubbling up inside me for a very long time, and finally purging them from my body feels incredible. It doesn't matter how Dr. Smith responds, only that I'm allowing myself to speak freely.

"I never said that," my therapist immediately clarifies. "In fact, I told you point blank that demons *are* real, just not in the way you think."

"You said they were abstractions," I push. "What I saw wasn't an abstraction."

It's taken a while for this conviction in my demonic visions to form, but now that it's here the results are powerful. It feels amazing to say these things without qualification or doubt.

My therapist sighs, shifting his weight for a moment.

"People who witness the things you've described rarely know they're illusory," Dr. Smith counters. "Subjects *think* they're real, because that's what their senses tell them. They trust their eyes and ears and heart, but these are all easily corruptible things. You are trusting your *flesh* over God. And for what? For a murderer?"

"Parker Torrance didn't murder anyone," I retort.

"Kingdom of the Pine is paying the legal fees for Martina's family," Dr. Smith informs me. "I've seen the case against him and . . . it's not great."

"But *why* are they paying to go after him?" I press, growing more and more heated by the second. "Martina's not a member of the congregation. Why is Kingdom of the Pine even involved?"

"Are you against charitable work now?" my therapist questions.

"It's just . . ." I start, even more overwhelmed than before. I want to loudly exclaim that none of this makes any sense, that the two sides of my personality are threatening to tear me in half. I don't say this, however, instead focusing on my next question, the one that's been hacking through the stitches of my aching heart like butter.

"Have you ever heard the name Pachid before?" I ask.

Dr. Smith hesitates, the moment so slight that it barely registers. He's been working a long time because he's darn good at his job, but I'm beginning to wonder what Dr. Smith's *job* actually is.

"I think I might've heard that name before," he finally admits, sifting through the depths of his memory bank. "One of the minor demons, right?"

My heart skips a beat.

"So you've read *Abramelin the Mage*?" I continue. "Because Pachid isn't anywhere in the Bible, only an obscure text from fifteenth-century France."

"I read all kinds of spiritual texts," Dr. Smith admits. "It's part of my job, Rose. What's your point?"

"I mean, I understand being familiar with some random nonfiction bestseller by a pastor who gave a TED Talk, but *Abramelin the Mage*? Kingdom of the Pine considers his work to be, and I quote, 'an occult abomination of lies and sin,'" I say. "Why are you reading that book if nobody else is allowed to? More importantly, why are you suddenly telling me it's *canon*?"

"Why are *you* reading it?" he asks. "You're filling your mind with these satanic diatribes, then you wonder why your guilt has manifested as imaginary demons?"

"My guilt?" I shout. "Over what?"

"Over sin!" Dr. Smith bellows, finally losing his cool as his face turns red and he lunges forward in his chair, unleashing the words like a holy tidal wave. "Over *temptation!* I read these books because it is my duty to *God*, Rose. Do you understand? These texts are not meant for the impressionable minds of curious little girls who think they understand the world but know absolutely nothing!"

His intensity is so suffocating that I finally pull back, unable to withstand the torrential rage of the man before me.

When Dr. Smith finishes seething he takes a moment to pull himself together, removing his glasses and wiping them off before returning them to the bridge of his nose. The man straightens his tie a bit, then clears his throat.

"I'm sorry about that," he says, returning to his usual soft-spoken demeanor. "This is just . . . difficult for me to see. Listen, Rose, I understand it's your nature to question these things, but I think it's time you started looking at the actual facts and accepting the reality of this situation."

"That's what I'm finally doing," I inform him.

"*Are you*, though?" Dr. Smith counters. "Because, here's the thing: it's been two weeks since the murder, and during that time these demonic visions of yours have fully disappeared, isn't that right?"

I nod.

"Maybe that's because you've realized temptation just isn't worth it," my therapist offers.

I narrow my eyes, not quite sure I understand the meaning behind this.

Dr. Smith smiles. "Think about it," he continues with a nod. "Consider what *you* can do to walk in the footsteps of Jesus, because blaming all this on Pachid isn't going to fly. Your sin is real, but she is not."

My body abruptly freezes.

"What?" is all I can think to reply, barely able to keep my voice from quaking as it tumbles from between my lips.

"Your sin is real, but she is not," Dr. Smith firmly repeats.

"Who?"

"Pachid," he confirms.

It feels as though the air has been sucked from this room, all of reality upended by a single statement.

After learning that name, I dove headfirst into my research, secretly pouring over volumes of biblical lore and far-reaching occult theories that would likely give my parents a heart attack if they had any idea what I was doing. Thankfully, these days I'm expected to mourn in deep thought and prayer, providing the perfect cover to let the most obsessive parts of my curiosity run wild.

I've moved on from fun facts about death.

At this point, it's my sincere belief I've read every scholarly work on Pachid in existence.

And Pachid, like most demons, is always described as a man.

Your sin is real, but she *is not.*

Dr. Smith's words repeat in my mind, washing through me as a vision of the pale woman emerges from the darkest recesses of my subconscious.

Regardless of how much research I do on these occult forces, I'll never understand them completely. They are powers well beyond my mortal understanding, which I'll gladly admit. For all I know, demons present themselves in various ways to different people, or change their physical manifestation over time.

But why, for the love of all that is holy, would Dr. Smith say *she*?

Unless he knows.

"Rose?" He breaks through my mental haze.

"Yeah?" I reply, refocusing my eyes on his.

"I'm gonna do something I don't normally do," he continues.

Dr. Smith stands up and walks over to a large iron cabinet at the corner of his office, the safe built into his wall like a bank vault. He bends over and enters a three-number combination, struggling to cover it up with his left hand and doing an absolutely *terrible* job.

11, 14, 15.

There's a hollow metallic clang as the lock pops open and Dr. Smith reaches within. He pulls forth a small bottle of pills, bringing them over and placing them in my hand.

"While I don't condone your flirtation with science over faith, I'm more worried about treating you than winning any sort of ideological battle," my therapist explains. "This is an antianxiety medication. If you feel like you need to calm down, take one of these."

I nod, gazing at the small white bottle.

The label indicates it's a drug called Cebocap, a powerful substance that's been used to treat all kinds of ailments in one form or another since the beginning of time. This particular version is made from lactose, something most folks coming in here would never realize because they don't constantly devour seemingly random information like I do.

These are sugar pills, from the Latin word meaning "to please."

It's a placebo.

"I think that's all the time we have for today," Dr. Smith announces, ambling back toward the door of his office and opening it for me. "That was a difficult session, but I think we made a lot of progress."

"I think so, too." I climb to my feet. "I'm gonna focus on stamping out temptation instead of making excuses."

"That's great to hear," my therapist replies, placing his hand on my shoulder, making my skin crawl. "I'll see you in two days, Rose."

I leave, Dr. Smith closing the door behind me, then make my way down the hallway before heading up into an empty church outreach center. It's late, the shadows stretching like long fingers as the sky blooms above them in glorious purple and orange. Objectively speaking, it's a breathtaking display, but my mind is humming along too fast to pay much attention.

Head spinning, I make my way out into the parking lot. There's so much to unpack that it feels as though I might fall over, my legs threatening to buckle under me at any moment.

One thing's for sure, I'm in no condition to drive.

Still, I climb into my car and sit for a moment, allowing this anxiety to pump through me in the hope that it might run its course and fade away. I start running through my finger patterns, counting them down over and over again, but the solace this typically provides me comes on muted and slow.

It's not working because another pattern keeps getting in the way.

11, 14, 15.

This is likely a cheeky reference to Numbers. *I cannot carry all these people by myself; the burden is too heavy for me. If this is how you are going to treat me, please go ahead and kill me—if I have found favor in your eyes—and do not let me face my own ruin.*

Therapist humor?

It could theoretically connect to any volume in the Bible. I consider Second Corinthians.

And no wonder, for Satan himself masquerades as an angel of light. It is not surprising, then, if his servants also masquerade as servants of righteousness. Their end will be what their actions deserve.

Who knows if there's any *real* connection to be made here. After all, this combination of digits could easily be nothing more than Dr. Smith's three favorite football players, but lately I've been enjoying this feeling of trusting my instincts.

Not some abstract cosmic faith, but *my own* instincts.

This recognition sends another shockwave through my body.

It's getting dark, and I should be heading home, but right now going home to my parents feels like a bridge too far. Instead, I pull out into the unknown.

I turn on the radio and start driving, allowing the road to lead me wherever it desires.

Righteous, thundering drums flood the vehicle as a slippery vocal line begins to croon across the top, rhythmic and precisely tuned.

I used to love this song, a rousing pop-rock anthem that could just as easily be about letting Jesus into your heart as letting someone into your bed. I try focusing on the former interpretation, but by the time they start belting out "fill me with your love, spill your grace into me," I have to turn it off.

It feels like I'm seeing through everything.

The car plunges into silence once more, my only soundtrack now the soft hum of asphalt under tires.

I've always been wise for my age, and part of that wisdom came from having a profound sense of who I was and what I liked. I understood my place in the world: I was a daughter, an American, a member of the congregation. I played soccer and loved brownies. I was curious and full of joy. I was excited to try new things and I had a past, present, and very specific future laid out for me. I was committed to the Lord.

Some of those things are still true, of course, but as more and more of my characteristics fall into question, I find myself testing the relevance of them all. What happens when every identity marker slips away?

Do you disappear?

I glance down at my hands as they grip the steering wheel, double-checking that the appendages haven't faded into mist.

Still here.

On the passenger seat, my phone buzzes. It's my father calling, likely wondering how my session with Dr. Smith went and worried about where I am. A brief moment of panic vibrates through me as I recognize that I've already been gone for way too long, but the anxiety is swiftly quelled as I reconnect with my own needs.

Not the needs of my parents.

Not the needs of the church.

Not even the needs of God.

I reach out and dismiss the call.

*   *   *

My body is on autopilot as I drive into the blossoming sunset. I'm off the main highway now, twisting and turning through a generously forested region on the county line. This place is familiar, but not in any specific way, just a strange aching memory that seems to hang over everything.

Soon enough, I arrive at a small hillside park, this modest view offering a nice enough glimpse of some trees and a winding creek that slices through its lush green field. There's a playground to the left, and half a basketball court to the right, both of which are being used while the citizens of Neverton fight valiantly against the looming nightfall.

I pull into the parking lot and stop, a bizarre surge of déjà vu pulsing through my body.

Climbing out, I take a deep breath of the cool evening air, smelling the sweet pine of the forest around me. I've lived in Neverton all my life, and I still can't get over this glorious landscape I've been blessed with.

Who blessed you? comes a deep and powerful voice from the back of my mind.

I don't know.

I walk to the front of my car and perch on the hood, pulling my legs up as I sit and watch the happy people below me going about their business. Out on the open field some Kingdom of the Pine members throw a Frisbee back and forth, hoping to get a few more tosses in before heading home in the dark.

Gradually, my gaze drifts from one side of this park to the other, taking in the whole scene as indigo hues gradually leak into the purple above, swelling and overtaking the last ounces of light in this vast Montana sky.

The scent of pine inhabits my nostrils, carried on the gentle breeze that tickles my skin.

Eventually, my eyes come to rest on a young woman in the grass nearby, her eyes transfixed by the same glorious sunset as she leans back on her elbows and gazes skyward. There's a blanket laid out below her and a bottle of beer held loose in her hand, a bold move in Neverton even on the distant edge of town. Jet black hair tops her head in a short, chin-length cut, this stark color matching her equally dark sweater and torn charcoal jeans. She looks to be around my age, but I don't recognize her from the congregation, or from school.

She must be a nonbeliever.

An old film camera sits to this stranger's left, suggesting she's come here on a photographic expedition.

Somehow feeling my gaze against the side of her head, the figure turns and glances over at me. The two of us freeze clumsily, our brains struggling to keep up with the visceral reaction of our bodies.

I've seen her before, not in any concrete sense, but in the abstract depths of my mind. This girl has haunted my imagination, and there's no mistaking that stunning face with huge features and deep, soulful eyes. She was lurking in the back of my mind at the party, and before that I saw her in the living room when Pachid made her frightening house call.

While I've been seeing visions of this stranger for quite some time, I never knew what to make of them. I could never be sure they'd manifested from any connection to reality.

Now, I know the truth.

This mysterious young woman turns her gaze back toward the sunset, avoiding eye contact and attempting to act natural. She's pretty good at it, but the subtle tension of her body language quickly gives her away.

I gaze out at the dying light of the day, then back at the stranger, struggling with how to approach this situation. Maybe she really *is* a random girl who wanted to catch the sunset and would rather not be pestered.

Still, I've gotta find out for myself. Of all the qualities that may or may not survive my currently transforming identity, nosiness is still one of them.

I hop off the hood of my car and start walking over, hoping to find a balance between casual stroll and confident stride that only makes me breathtakingly awkward. I'm sure the girl senses me at this point, but she refuses to offer a glance of acknowledgment.

I stop next to her, not quite sure where to begin.

"Hey. Do I know you from somewhere?" I finally ask.

She doesn't even look up. "I don't think so."

"Really?" I press onward. "You look super familiar. You're not a member of the congregation, are you?"

She scoffs at this suggestion. "No."

My heart hammers away as my mind struggles to connect the dots, this mystery a little more difficult to parse than I'd expected. I briefly consider turning around and leaving it be, but with one final surge of desperation I take my shot.

"Mind if I sit down?" I ask, affixing the mask of a cool, confident young woman. "I was watching the sunset from my car, but it's a little uncomfortable."

"Yes, I fucking mind!" the stranger snaps, whipping toward me in a flare of anger and frustration.

The second I see her face up close, however, everything changes. I recognize this girl immediately and *deeply*; she is absolutely the one who has been haunting my dreams and clouding my mind with strange, passionate visions. Up until now this connection has been strong but abstract, a tug in my subconscious that I couldn't fully comprehend.

Now, however, there's nothing abstract about it.

Suddenly, entirely new visions are erupting through the depths of my mind, glimpses of some other life that's been lurking in the shadows far too long. I witness an endless ocean of the past, memories cascading over one another like crashing waves. I see a birthday cupcake with a single shimmering candle. I see a movie night. I see a chance meeting in a bookstore. I gaze deep into her eyes, knowing that I've seen them thousands of times even if I don't understand how.

She's crying, tears spilling down her cheeks as she stares back at me with fury, defeat, and aching sorrow.

"Leave me alone," the mysterious girl growls. "I don't fucking know you!"

"I'm sorry," I flounder, backing away. "I just . . . You seem *so* familiar."

"I don't *fucking know you!*" she repeats, even louder this time.

The gang playing Frisbee nearby halts abruptly, glancing over at us with concern.

Not knowing what else to do, I turn and make my escape back toward the car. My whole body is shaking from the adrenaline of this conflict, an avalanche of brand-new emotions filling me to the brim with no release in sight.

When I reach the vehicle I open the door and throw myself inside, slamming it behind me and erupting in a fit of tears. My body is quaking, not just from the emotions throttling my senses but thanks to the chill that has suddenly enveloped my form. I'm freezing cold, as though I've found myself trapped in some invisible icebox.

My hands trembling, I reach out and start the car, blasting the heat and still finding myself without a shred of relief.

Maybe leaving the old me behind wasn't such a good idea, I suddenly realize. *Maybe this is just a taste of what happens when you turn your back on God.*

I glance over to discover the girl has gathered her blanket, camera, and beer before disappearing into the gloaming. The whole park has plunged into relative darkness, stars flickering to life above me in a river of spilt glitter.

My phone rings through the car stereo, prompting me to jump in alarm. I answer quickly, pressing a button on the dash.

"Hello?" I start, terrified of the tone that will soon announce itself on the other end of the line.

"Honey?" comes my father's voice, not nearly as fuming as I expected. "Are you okay?"

"Yeah," I blurt, sweet relief overwhelming me. "I just had a . . . weird session with Dr. Smith today."

Dad lets out a long sigh. "It's alright, hon. I understand."

My father keeps talking, but as he does the signal begins to crackle and cut out. I can tell he's trying to be supportive, but the words are too choppy for me to understand.

"I think I'm losing you," I explain. "Service is bad out here."

There's no response, just waves of static washing across my ear. I listen intently, struggling to make out my father's voice through the fuzz, and gradually a faint vocal tone begins to rise above the din. It's a peculiar and distant sound, tough to place with all this noise swirling around it, but gradually I begin to comprehend the unexpected wail.

It sounds like someone's screaming, not in anger but blinding pain.

The more I listen, the louder this tortured choir grows, and soon a whole cascade of shrieking and groaning has overtaken the static hum coming from my car speakers. Suddenly, the dashboard lights of my car begin to flicker on and off wildly, and my headlights follow suit.

I hang up the phone and toss it onto my passenger seat, prompting an abrupt end to the chaos.

The car falls into silence once more, headlights holding steady as warm air billows across me.

Thump! Thump!

I jolt in shock as someone knocks hard against my driver's side window.

The girl with dark hair stands stoically in this unlit parking lot, her eyes dry but puffy. She makes a cranking motion with her hand, a sign for me to roll down my window.

I follow her instructions, retracting the glass that separates us.

"I-I'm so sorry," the young woman stammers, a desperate thing swimming in her large black sweater. "I'm so, so sorry."

"What are you talking about?" I reply, confused.

"I shouldn't even be doing this," she mumbles, the words tumbling under her breath before she barrels onward in a state of panic. "Fuck!"

The girl shakes her head from side to side, abruptly shifting emotions.

"What's wrong?" I beg. "Can I help you?"

"No!" she cries, suddenly finding her direction. "You can't help me, Rose. That's the point!"

My breath catches. She knows my name.

Gradually, her expression softens as a potent realization washes through her.

"They really did a number on you, didn't they?" She finally sighs. "All to avoid this exact moment."

"Whatever it is, looks like it didn't work," I retort. "We're here."

For the first time, the girl cracks a smile. Truth be told, I'm not exactly sure what I meant, but I'm glad she found the slightest kernel of joy in it. I find myself compelled to ask a question that seems ridiculous at this point, especially given the intimacy that we may have once shared.

"What's your name?" I finally question.

The girl winces and places her hand over her mouth, acting as though this gesture might keep the pain at bay.

"I'm sorry," she blurts. "I don't know what I'm doing here."

"What's your name?" I repeat, desperately yearning for this connection that's swiftly pulling away.

The stranger shakes her head. "I'm not gonna tell you my name," she says, stepping back from the car. "That's the point. Forget about me. Forget about *all this* and go back home."

"I don't understand!" I cry. "Why can't you just tell me what's going on?"

"Because the longer we stand here, the more I start to miss you, and the more I start to miss you, the more danger we're both in," she states with a cogent intensity. "Stop looking for answers. They've won. It's over."

"If you really knew me then you'd understand I can't do that," I reply.

"Understand this," the girl continues. "If you approach me again, you might as well bring a gun and shoot me in the fucking head. There's a mark on both of—"

Before she can finish, the girl erupts with a sudden cough. She staggers a bit, holding her throat, then coughs again with even more force. This time, whatever's caught in her windpipe dislodges and spills from her lips, a handful of flies that immediately take off buzzing in every direction.

"Oh fuck," the stranger gasps. "I'm so sorry. I love you."

She turns and sprints back toward the park, disappearing into the darkness and leaving me to sit in a state of complete shock.

"I love you?" I repeat back to myself, these final three words the most unexpected part of our encounter.

I'm not sure how, but the longer I sit with it, the more it makes sense.

Eventually, I pull out onto the road, beginning the winding trek back through several pockets of tree-covered neighborhoods and the deep, dark woods. I'm a long way from home, all the way across town, and after the emotional roller coaster of this evening I'm exhausted.

Neverton transforms in these twilight hours, becoming a strangely lonely place. There are no other cars on this desolate stretch, just a single set of headlights slicing through the great, evergreen-covered abyss of Montana wilderness.

I gradually return to the radio, hoping to find a semblance of company and distract myself from the chaotic ruminations running wild in my head.

I'm trying not to think of those flies, the ones that blossomed deep within my body as a once-in-a-lifetime fluke that no longer seems so once-in-a-lifetime. I try not to consider what else I encountered that evening, especially since I've been recently convinced that my demon days are behind me.

As the radio clicks on static fills my car, a station that had been perfectly clear during my trip to the park now drowned in chattering fuzz. It sounds a lot like what happened during the phone call with my dad—chaotic screaming hidden somewhere deep within the mysterious tangle of sound waves.

I shut the radio off, disappointed by my timing on this particularly desolate stretch of signal-free road.

According to the National Safety Council, the likelihood you'll die in a car crash is 1 in 101.

Approaching a stop sign, I slow and pop on the blinker, making a gradual turn as my headlights sweep across the heavily forested scene.

The second my turn completes, however, I gasp and slam on the brakes.

Someone is standing in the middle of the road, a bizarre figure brilliantly lit by my headlights' yellow glow. The shape is frozen in place, clad in familiar attire that makes my neck hair bristle.

They're wearing the same red polo shirt that Pachid sports, and their hair is equally dark and stringy. They offer me the same crooked smile full of dirty broken teeth, and the same stark white eyes gaze at me from within their sunken sockets. They have long, spidery fingers that hang by their side, twitching restlessly.

This figure, however, is not Pachid. This is a man, just as thin-limbed but sporting a rotund belly that pushes out from the center of his lanky form. His hair is just as long, but it only sprouts from the rim of his head, leaving the top completely bald and sickly pale.

I've been struggling to understand what I saw that night, struggling to make sense of the evidence as it piled up before me. Everything seemed to point in such an obvious direction, yet I was *still* desperately hoping to avoid this crushing cosmic truth.

Sitting in the driver's seat, shivering terribly as I stare at this bizarre and unholy sight, there's no longer a doubt in my mind.

I'm looking at a demon.

5

MEMORY LANE

From this distance, I can barely make out what's etched into the demon's oval name tag. Squinting through the brilliant illumination of my headlights, however, the word becomes apparent.

It reads: RAMIEL.

As the pale man and I stare at each other, I find myself faced with an unexpected test. Beside me is the car's automatic shifter, currently sitting in the drive position but tempting me with retreat in the form of a little glowing *R*.

When it comes to sin, Kingdom of the Pine teaches *avoidance*, to win the battle against temptation before it even begins. In the congregation, so much focus is placed on averting your eyes and shielding your heart that we rarely get around to discussing what happens once these forces have taken hold.

You conquer your metaphorical demons by restricting them from your life in the first place.

But what happens when a demon is standing right in front of you, watching over you with twitching fingers and sagging skin, his meandering teeth locked in the knowing smile of a hunter who has cornered their prey?

The church leaders would likely tell me to run, to cut off the infection and remove this demonic force from my life. Excommunication is a powerful tool within Kingdom of the Pine, and it works.

The thing is, I'm beginning to doubt these philosophies apply to me anymore.

In a sudden jerk of movement, the pale man goes from frozen to agitated. He marches directly toward my vehicle, prompting a surge of adrenaline to erupt through my veins.

"Oh *shoot!*" I blurt.

Instinct takes over, but I don't reach for the shifter in retreat. Instead, I slam on the gas.

My vehicle rockets forward, roaring to life with a loud squeal that pierces the dark forest around us. The force pulls my head back against my seat, and as the demon looms larger and larger in my windshield I brace for impact.

When the pale man and my car meet I expect a loud crunch as he's thrown over the hood, maybe the crack of a windshield or some shattering glass.

This doesn't happen.

Instead, Ramiel's body phases through my sedan, these two pieces of solid matter slipping through one another with ease. It happens so fast that I barely catch a glimpse of this bizarre, shimmering moment, the pale man's torso whipping past me in sizzling blue.

I snap my head back to find he's stopped in the road behind me, unharmed and standing as still as the night around him. My eyes go wide; I'm spellbound by the tangible magic I've just witnessed.

Abruptly, a violent rumble forces my attention back to the forward path. I instinctively slam on the brakes, but it's already too late. The next thing I know I'm careening off the pavement and bouncing down a sharp incline, struggling to maintain control as a massive tree looms before me.

Then, darkness.

A vast endless nothing.

My senses numb, I have no choice but to drift in this immeasurable void. If I had lungs, I'd focus on my breathing, but right now there are no organs to pump and no air to inhale.

Maybe this is it, I consider, speculating on the bizarre state I've suddenly found myself in. *Maybe this is all there is when you die, endless black nothing. Forever.*

When heaven and hell are so deeply ingrained in your psyche, alternate versions of the afterlife don't often worm their way in. Even *considering* other ideas in a simple thought experiment would be strictly prohibited by the church, but fortunately we live in a world without mind reading.

The possibility of something this vacant and lonesome has slipped into my quiet brain from time to time, a horrifying manifestation of death as a perpetual vacuum that we remain eternally aware of. It's tough to wrap my mind around what endless eons would feel like as they float past, trapped forever while time stretches on and on in a haze.

There's no logical *reason* for things to end like this, but I suppose there's also no logical reason they wouldn't.

At least eternal torment in hell gives you something to do.

The second I think this, I feel the first hint of a growing warmth below me. Orange light dances across the black abyss, accompanied by the pop and crackle of licking flames.

I'm growing hotter, quickly regretting just how flippant I was with my existential observations.

But death hasn't come knocking just yet.

My eyes flutter open, pain surging through my body as I witness the dancing blaze that has made its way across my passenger seat. Smoke is filling the vehicle, but before I can open the door and crawl out I notice something even more dangerous watching from the dark forest nearby.

Ramiel is standing there with his bulbous belly and bald, wrinkly head. He's wearing that familiar, unsettling smile, the light of swiftly growing flames dancing across his awkward visage. His pure white eyes gaze straight ahead, watching me through the glass of the passenger-side window as he waits some forty feet away.

I can't just sit here and burn.

Drawing on centuries of demonic lore, I reach out and snatch the little metal crucifix hanging from my rearview mirror, gripping the beaded rope tight in my hand. I push open the driver's side door.

Battling through the aches and pains that overwhelm my broken form, I make a first attempt to escape the burning vehicle. I clench my teeth as a mighty sting erupts through my left leg, the appendage badly twisted after the front of my car crumpled inward.

The strain is too much. I fall back into my seat, tears welling up in my eyes.

"Son of a *gun!*" I cry out, the rarely used words sizzling against my lips.

I glance over to see the pale man still standing, still watching. Making a run for it was likely never an option.

Still, I can't just succumb to the fire.

One in 101, I remind myself.

I take a deep breath, bracing for the pain and trying again. This time I'm ready for the discomfort, and by some miracle I manage to pull myself up. I balance against the side of the car and thrust my cross toward the demon, crying out with a fitting prayer.

"Saint Michael the Archangel, defend us in battle!" I shriek through the billowing smoke. "Be our protection against the wickedness and snares of the devil. May God rebuke him we humbly pray; and do thou, O Prince of the Heavenly Host, by the power of God, thrust into hell Satan and all evil spirits who prowl about the world seeking the ruin of souls! Amen!"

The second I finish my diatribe the demon rushes toward me, propelled swiftly through the forest in the exact opposite direction I was hoping for. It didn't work.

"Oh no, oh no, oh no," I gush, fear erupting through me as I instinctively duck back into the blazing car.

It's a strange move, but with no other safer haven this is the only option I've got. If I limp into the woods I'm a goner, and as far as I know any fate delivered by a demon is much, much worse than burning alive.

I'll be burning even longer if I go with him.

Sweat pours from my body as I stall in the driver's seat, accepting my fate and praying with all my might.

"Even though I walk through the darkest valley, I will fear no evil, for you are with me; your rod and your staff, they comfort me," I repeat over and over again.

From the corner of my eye, I expect to see Ramiel gazing into my vehicle, his face pressed against the cracking glass as he watches the life gradually melt from my body.

But the demon is nowhere to be found.

Confused, I look out and discover the pale, pudgy creature has retreated slightly, returning to his former position some forty feet away from my burning car.

"Wait, what?" I allow my analytical mind a welcome return to the captain's chair.

The demon's behavior is odd, but an idea is emerging. This creature certainly didn't mind the crucifix in my hand, nor the holy words spilling from my throat, but when I got back into the car he retreated.

Thinking fast, I move to climb from my car again, watching the pale man closely from the corner of my eye. I can barely see him through the smoke now, but I *can* make out his silhouette stepping closer with every inch I slip from my vehicle.

When I drop back into the driver's seat, the demon retreats.

I've managed to formulate one or two theories, but I'm not thrilled about any particular hypothesis. Nothing about this makes *complete* sense.

Why would a demon from the pits of hell avoid, of all things, fire?

I've only got one shot at this, I realize, coughing loudly as smoke completely fills the vehicle. On one hand, I've had years of coaching through my faith, Christian lore offering a time-honored process of facing down demons with a cross in your palm and the holy spirit in your heart. On the other hand, a crazy—but seemingly evidence-based—idea is brewing.

I spring into action, holding my breath as I reach into the car's backseat and gather as much junk as I can. There are a few jackets strewn about, as well as an assortment of books and various clutter that any high school senior has. I push through the painful ache that surges through my body, then drop my trash next to the open driver's side door with a thud.

At the same time, I slip from my vehicle, tumbling to the ground and setting my gaze across the forest. I focus on the demon's bare feet.

The pale man instantly marches toward my car, and as he approaches I slowly crawl even further under the broiling machine. It's only now I realize just how burned my skin has gotten; the whole right side of my body is throbbing like I've caught the worst sunburn of my life.

Fortunately, the more adrenaline surges through my veins, the more this searing pain becomes a dull ache, unpleasant but manageable. My leg is still mangled and my joints are stiff, but this is no time to nurse my wounds.

It's time to act.

Ramiel continues his approach, gradually slowing as he makes his way around the blaze. My eyes are glued to every movement, and I react accordingly to avoid detection.

Soon enough, I'm creeping out from under my flaming vehicle and slinking into the woods, hobbling slightly but refraining from the painful yelps that beg to escape from within me.

The demon rounds my car and stands before the mysterious heap that rests outside my door. It's difficult to see, the fire providing a shield of visual disorientation and prompting the pale man to keep a slight distance.

It all comes down to this, I realize, hesitating before making my approach. I'm fully aware of just how foolish this plan is, but right now it's the best one I've got.

This is how I take matters into my own hands.

The demon leans down, investigating the heap of jackets and books in search of my crumpled, unconscious body. For creatures who typically move with such intention, it's the first time I've seen one of them tepid in their interactions, frightened even.

Now that I've crept into position behind the pale man, the time for action has finally arrived. I rush forward and kick him as hard as I can in the small of his back, the pain that surges through me nothing more than an afterthought as adrenaline fortifies my frame. The demon launches forward, tumbling into the billowing car as a horrifying screech erupts from his throat. Flames engulf him.

I slam the door shut, holding it closed with my foot while struggling to put some distance between this roaring fire and the rest of my body.

The monster immediately flies into a squealing panic, slamming against the driver's side door as its body pulses with flickering blue energy.

My eyes go wide as sparks of recognition erupt in my mind. I've seen this bizarre shimmer before, first when the pale woman walked through Isaiah's bedroom wall, and even more recently when this demon phased through my vehicle.

While I'm in no position to understand the *how* or *why*, it appears these creatures can move through solid matter at will. However, a new variable has entered the equation: fire.

The demon quickly gives up and scrambles to the other side of my car, pushing against the passenger door but finding its mechanics compromised. Big thanks to the massive tree that crushed my door shut like an aluminum can. The pale man desperately attempts to phase through this door, as well, but his abilities are once again thwarted by the blaze.

Frantic, he even tries climbing into the backseat, but by now the demon's screams are nothing more than a hissing gurgle that melts away into nothing. The creature collapses in a charred heap, his body fully engulfed by the roiling blaze.

I stumble back, thankful to put some space between myself and this astonishing heat.

"Whoa. Okay," I sigh, the words falling awkwardly from my mouth in a series of reflexive huffs. "Alright."

The human body contains enough fuel to burn for seven hours.

Running on metaphorical fumes, I use the last of my energy to scale the roadside embankment, then collapse at the asphalt's edge.

After cremation, a magnet is used to separate metal objects from the remains.

I slowly breathe in and out, the stillness of my body finally revealing just how broken and bruised I really am.

Gazing out into the darkness of the forest, I spot a distinct, pulsing flash of red-and-blue lights as they slice through the trees, rocketing toward me down the long, winding road. I watch as they grow larger and larger, my vision blurring as a haze of exhaustion overwhelms my senses.

Firetrucks get to work subduing the flame and EMTs tend to my body.

At some point, I'm loaded into an ambulance.

A man and woman stand over me now, treating my injuries with expressions of deep focus while I inform them of a demon in the wreckage. They ignore this earth-shaking revelation. The man tells me everything's gonna be fine, but he's a terrible liar.

There's panic in his eyes.

"They're real," I advise.

The man nods along, but I know he's not listening, not actually registering what I'm saying. The implications of something like this are, after all, a little much to reckon with over the course of an ambulance ride.

The walls rattle and hum as our emergency vehicle hurtles through the night, shelves of various medical equipment creating a distinct tone that wraps around me like a warm blanket. The light hanging above is extra bright, glowing like some holy tunnel to the afterlife, and I close my eyes to escape its overpowering presence.

I feel as though I'm reclining on the world's softest cloud, a pillow woven by angels from a golden loom.

Painkillers, I suddenly realize, noticing the intravenous drip in my hand for the first time. *Probably morphine.*

"We're losing her!" the man above me cries out, prompting an unexpectedly affable smile to spread across my face.

I'm not allowed to watch medical dramas, but even *I* can pick up on how notorious this line is.

"Epinephrine! Now!" the man instructs, prompting his partner to rummage around in the cabinets to my left.

Epinephrine, also known as adrenaline, concentrates blood around the vital organs and is one of the first pharmaceutical lines of defense against a heart attack.

Am I having a heart attack?

Suddenly, the chaos falls away and disperses like a low-lying fog.

It's the second time I've disconnected from reality this evening, but the sensation of this round is much different than my first. There is no endless abyss, no blank void of empty space stretching forever and ever around me, because this time I'm not unconscious.

I'm just really, *really* high.

When I open my eyes I find the ambulance has fallen away, replaced instead by a chamber of dark, wet stone. Torchlight flickers and dances across the walls around me, illuminating a circular gathering of mysterious figures in jet-black robes.

As otherworldly as this setting is, I get the distinct feeling I've been here before.

Large doses of epinephrine can be helpful with long term-memory loss, I inform myself.

With this in mind, I'm able to observe the scene without fear or anxiety, calmly watching as the story unfolds. I'm not really here, and the implication of this is incredibly palliative.

Or maybe it's just the morphine.

One of the robed figures who stands behind me is reading from a book, his words authoritative and well rehearsed. I'm much better at understanding Latin than anyone my age should rightly be, and even *I'm* having trouble keeping up with the flowing ancient language that cascades across his lips in a powerful rhythm.

That's the thing about Latin: no matter how good you get at reading or writing it, you'll still have a little trouble understanding the spoken word.

My mysterious host stops abruptly, prompting the rest of the robed figures to repeat his last phrase back in unison.

Something about an "unholy union."

The lead voice begins again as torches flicker and dance, illuminating the ring of figures. Their faces are covered, but I see their chins bouncing as they continue trading lines with their moderator.

The whole chamber is belting out a mantra now, shouting at the top of their lungs while I watch in awe. I know this is just a dream, or a memory, or a combination of both, but at this point my heart is starting to pick up speed. The choir of thundering vocalizations is simply too much to ignore.

A sharp prick on my arm causes me to flinch, and I struggle to glance over but am unable to turn my head. I can barely make out the gloved hands of someone working diligently next to me, their attire much different than the others.

They're dressed in light blue nurse's scrubs.

"Uh . . . is this a memory, or are you from the ambulance?" I find myself asking.

I'm completely ignored as the nurse continues their business, drawing a full syringe of blood from the crook of my arm as the chanting reaches a crescendo. The second my nurse finishes and extracts their needle, the sound dissipates and the torches plunge into darkness.

Moments later, a dingy fluorescent light flickers to life above me, illuminating the stone room with a pale glow.

"And that's enough of the boring stuff," the voice behind me announces. "Is our little friend back in his tank?"

"Safe and sound," one of the robed figures replies.

"Let's get to work."

Now that he's speaking English, I immediately pick up on something familiar in the man's tone. I've heard his voice before, and not just in some mysterious recovered memory.

I *know* him.

Two of the robed figures get to work pulling a large rolling cabinet into position, the metal structure filled with an assortment of crackling computer servers and hardware boxes buzzing along. This is sophisticated equipment, while the previous ritual felt like the polar opposite.

A computer monitor rests on the middle shelf of this cabinet, along with an empty vessel about the size of a shoebox. Heaps of cabling spill from the backs of the machines, snaking out of view along the cold cement floor.

The fully scrubbed nurse approaches this apparatus, sliding a vial of my blood into the chamber and closing the door. This prompts a powerful sucking sound, followed by a loud metallic click as some interior latch falls into place.

"Sanguis link is locked in," the nurse announces.

One of the robed figures approaches with a glowing tablet in their hands, reading aloud from the digital screen.

"Coordinate X: seven, zero, zero, point, one, nine, four, two, two, nine. Coordinate Y: five, two, one, nine, point, six, eight, two. Coordinate Z: six, point, zero, two, six, seven. Moving on to timeline. Coordinate A: seven, four . . ."

As this figure with the handheld device drones on and on my nurse diligently types away before their monitor, inputting enormous strings of code.

Remembering this is nothing more than a memory, I am fascinated by the sheer amount of detail, detail that can't possibly be accurate. While I have faith in the broad strokes my brain is painting, there's no way I could remember these long coordinates. My mind is just filling in the blanks to conjure a coherent picture.

The question is: How much of this *really* happened and how much is some fantastical leap?

"Last one of the night! Places!" the man behind me calls out, prompting more of the robed figures to spring into action. They start making preparations in various parts of the stone chamber, one of them carefully testing the hinge of a large metal ring while two more roll the cabinet holding my blood into a very specific position. They're glancing down, turning the cabinet so it aligns with some particular arrangement of unseen floor markings.

"Ready for tether," announces the nurse.

Machinery springs to life, whirring louder and louder as the fluorescent lights above me flicker and sway. Several of the figures step back and make room, clearly on edge.

Gazing down from my position on the table, I notice sparks of pale blue light swirling through the air. They dance and ignite just past my feet, surging with arcane power as the hum of computers escalates. Soon enough, the crackling flashes stir a surge of energy, tearing through the space before me like a knife across taut canvas.

Frigid air erupts through this bizarre opening as distant, caustic screams flood my ears.

Above me, the robed figure steps forward and leans over so I can finally bear witness to his familiar, smiling face. Gazing back at me is Dr. Smith, who places his hand on my shoulder in an attempted gesture of care.

I flinch.

"Sometimes to walk in the light you need to spend a little time in the shadows," he submits.

The tear that hovers before me grows larger and larger, the edges glittering like embers of a turquoise fire. A figure approaches through this supernatural hole, reaching out with long, pale fingers as they climb through the slit.

My eyes fly open.

I find myself laid out in a similar position, tucked into a hospital bed with various plastic tubes pumping me full of fluids and painkillers.

The chaos of roaring computers and flickering lights has bluntly ceased, leaving me to enjoy the quiet peace of a single, softly beeping monitor on my right.

"Dr. Smith," I whisper aloud, the words barely slipping from between my cracked lips.

I'm smart enough to know these drug-induced walks down memory lane can be skewed and distorted, that an epinephrine-fueled trip into the depths of my psyche should be the *last* thing I count on while considering the surgical removal of faith from my life. After all, how can I turn away from the congregation's wild leaps and unfounded teachings if I'm making wild leaps of my own?

I refuse to walk that path any longer, and hazy memories are not enough.

I need evidence.

Still, there's nothing wrong with a little psychedelic imagery to point me in the right direction.

I settle into my hospital bed and gaze at the ceiling, anxious to heal. My body can barely move, but my mind is working overtime, plotting away.

Beware a curious person whose attention has been piqued.

11, 14, 15.

I remind myself of Dr. Smith's private safe code, mentally repeating the digits over and over again.

The door flies open and my parents rush inside, overflowing with raw emotion.

"My baby!" Mom cries out, making her way to one side of the bed while my father moves to the other.

A nurse follows them in, making sure my folks don't get too riled up and accidently yank out some important medical tube from its socket.

"How are you feeling, Rose?" the nurse asks.

"Tired." I struggle to push the word out.

"Any pain?" she continues.

I slowly nod my head, prompting the nurse to offer an expression of sympathy. "We'll bump up the morphine for you."

The woman strolls over and makes some adjustments. My pain instantly dissolves.

"I'll give you all a moment," the nurse explains sweetly, "then I'll come back to go over some technicalities. The important thing is that you're here, and you're stable."

I consider replying with heartfelt thanks, but this would require far too much energy. Instead, I offer a long, slow blink, which the nurse seems to have no problem translating.

"She's a fighter," the nurse informs my parents, prompting them to exchange glances.

The nurse takes her leave and soon enough it's just the three of us basking in the glow of my gentle heart monitor. I hadn't realized it, but they've already started praying.

I don't join them, thankful to have a decent excuse at the moment.

As soon as they finish, Luke and Lisa stand up and kiss me on the forehead, gazing into my weary eyes with profound love.

"I know you're feeling really tired," Mom whispers, "but there's a few questions your dad needs to ask you. It's very important for you to think hard about your answers before you give them, okay?"

"Okay," I croak.

"I know you weren't a part of that scene," Lisa coos before stepping back.

As my mother says this I sense my heart quicken, and it takes every ounce of discipline I can muster to calm myself. The monitor next to me registers this petite spike, but my parents are too wrapped up in their questionnaire to notice.

"What happened out there, honey?" Dad asks.

A little broad for someone who can barely speak.

I rack my brain, struggling to connect the dots.

I know you weren't a part of that scene, my mother said, but for the life of me I can't imagine what scene she's talking about.

The crash? Of course I was there. It was my car.

There's a hidden layer of anxiety in my father's voice, a hint at his intention with this particular line of questioning. After all, going through an interview checklist isn't usually the first thing parents do when their daughter is in a horrible car wreck. Even the nurse had a better bedside manner.

I get the distinct feeling there's something he wants me to say—*needs* me to say—and my job now is to parse exactly what that is. I tread carefully.

"I hit a tree," I offer.

My father nods.

"Must've fallen asleep," I continue. "Driving back."

"That's it?" Dad pushes. "Didn't see anything else out there?"

"Bad dreams," I reply, my heart rate leveling out again. I take a moment to focus up. "Gotta make some changes. Gotta get right with the Lord."

My father's gaze intensifies. "Some people say there's a trick to ending your nightmares when you're in them, did you hear? Folks would pay a lot of money for something like that. That's a million-dollar secret, right there."

Despite my best efforts, my heart monitor is speeding up.

"Imagine that," Luke continues. "Nightmares have been around for a *long time,* and suddenly there's a cure! You'd probably get some real trouble from the folks selling chamomile tea!"

My father forces a laugh, glancing back at my mother as if she might also find this hilarious, but Mom doesn't react.

The key to making a good joke is subverting expectations, and the easiest way to do this is through the element of surprise. To spark that involuntary laugh, you've gotta tickle a part of someone's nervous system that's expecting one thing and is presented with another.

Personally, I don't even *try* doing this.

My dad makes a lot of jokes, however, and while I love to hear them, I can attest that these little nuggets of humor are not exactly *funny*. I always know what's coming next, because I spot the setups—the little white lies.

I stare at my father for a long time, mustering up all the fake sincerity I can manage with what little energy's left in my battered body.

"Dad," I groan. "I have no idea what you're talking about."

Unfortunately, I do have *some* idea, and the implication of this causes a wave of nausea to bubble up at the pit of my stomach.

The sparkle I catch in my father's eye is undeniable, however, a sign I've hit the correct response. His body language immediately changes, relaxing as he settles in.

Moments later, Dad takes off his glasses to reveal that he's crying. He wipes his eyes. "I'm so glad to hear that, honey," he gushes.

I tightly squeeze the man's giant hand.

"After they're done at the crash site, some folks from the church are gonna come and ask you similar questions," my father continues, his speech staggered and broken as he navigates this welling spring of emotion. "Just tell them exactly what you told me. Everything's gonna be fine."

Why is anyone from the congregation at my crash site?

My father takes a moment to fully calm himself, and during this time a deep emotional ache starts blossoming within me. Lying, withholding the truth, bending the facts; whatever you wanna call it, I'm not used to this kind of relationship with my parents. As far as I've come, and as devastated as I am by their possible involvement in something nefarious, it still hurts like hell.

I consider what might happen if I told my father I *knew* there was another body in the wreckage, and I knew that body belonged to a demon. What if I informed him Dr. Smith and Kingdom of the Pine were likely a part of all this?

"Rose," Lisa suddenly chimes in, breaking through the haze of my chaotic thoughts. "You okay?"

"Yeah," I confirm.

My mother smiles. "You were under for hours. We're just so glad to have you back."

But I'm not back. They don't realize it yet, but I'm a completely different person.

6

LATE-NIGHT SECULAR PROGRAMMING

You think you know yourself, but you don't really *know yourself* until you're laid up in bed for three weeks with absolutely nothing to do, rebuilding your strength and slowly healing minute by minute.

Plenty of time to read and learn, you might think, and you'd be absolutely correct had my parents not confiscated my phone.

"You need to focus on getting better," Dad told me.

I've requested books, but all I've received is my Bible and a handful of celebrity gossip magazines that a particularly kind nurse snuck from the waiting room. At least there's a TV.

The first few days were the worst, my body so stiff that just tilting my head up to eat or drink caused surges of immense pain, but gradually my limbs loosened up and the doctors weaned me off my painkillers.

A breakthrough came once I could walk around my floor of the hospital, hanging IV bag in tow as I traversed the giant loop I've dubbed "going out to lunch." There's a vending machine at the other end of this wing, and while I typically wouldn't be allowed to munch on sweet treats at home, here at the hospital there's rarely anyone to stop me.

My parents swing by once each evening to see how I'm doing, and congregation members make pop-ins to ask me about the crash from time to time. Fortunately, as distance grows between that fateful night and the present day, they come around less often.

It appears they can live with my answers, and over time I grow better and better at reciting what they want to hear.

Yes, I've been having nightmares about demons, but they're not real.

No, I wouldn't know how to kill one if they *were* real, but prayer is where I'd start.

Yes, I'm ready to reaffirm my commitment to the church and live without temptation.

As I continue to bob and weave through these bizarre verbal tests, it becomes very clear the word *temptation* holds extra weight. Every interviewer will reach this part of the process and hesitate for a moment, their eyes struggling to convey something the rest of their body is clearly not entirely comfortable with.

I answer exactly how they want me to, while maintaining a casual vagueness regarding exactly *what* these temptations are. Still, the thought lingers in the back of my mind: What is it they need me to turn away from?

It's late in the evening and any visitors have long since returned home, leaving the hospital eerily quiet. The only sound is the gentle pulse of heart monitors and the faint drone of one or two televisions left on in this wing while their corresponding patients slumber.

After alternating between aching for sleep and staring at the ceiling, I finally climb out of bed, careful not to tangle my permanent companion: the rolling metal hanger and plastic IV bag that connects to my hand.

"Late night snack?" I ask the hanger, to which the piece of medical equipment says absolutely nothing in return.

I nod for a moment, pretending to listen, then slowly climb to my feet. I shuffle my frail, gown-clad body into the hallway.

At this point, I fully recognize how loopy this long-term stay has made me. My sense of humor has devolved into little more than deeply sincere conversations with inanimate objects.

"Come on, Ivy," I coax, pulling the hanger along as I hobble down this empty hallway.

I'm still shocked by how oddly sickening the atmosphere of hospitals tends to be, the aesthetic of this space making me feel wholly unwelcome even after all this time. Long tubes of fluorescent lightbulbs line the hall above, washing the scene with a strange bluish tint, and the lack of furniture or hanging wall art only adds to the cold design.

Soon enough, I arrive at the vending machine, standing before the rectangular device and gazing blankly at its assortment of sugary selections. There are some healthy alternatives, like carrots and dip in a small plastic pack, but I'm here for the good stuff.

I gradually narrow my choice to a dueling pair of chocolate-covered snacks, but before I can finish, something in a nearby room catches my eye.

I glance over to find the door wide open and a patient lying tucked in their bed, fast asleep. As I assumed, their television's been left on and a movie I've never seen plays across a tiny, hanging screen in the corner.

The first thing I notice is the woman onscreen is absolutely gorgeous, yet casually dressed, with large round glasses covering her eyes. She looks disheveled and sports very little makeup, especially for what appears to be a large-scale, secular Hollywood film. Her eyes are giant, and the second I see them I feel a cold gust wash across my skin.

My gaze transfixed on the screen, I watch as another woman appears next to the first. She crawls across a bed in similarly casual attire.

The two figures stare at each other for a moment, their faces creeping closer and closer as their lips part and then, finally, once the tension has reached a breaking point, they kiss.

It's so cold now that I'm literally shivering, my body unable to handle the sensations flowing through it.

The stimulation is too much.

I avert my eyes, pulling my attention back to the vending machine before yelping in terror.

Pachid, pasty and waterlogged, is somehow knotted up within this rectangular box, her face pressed against the glass no more than a foot from my own. Her bleached eyes are huge and glaring, staring daggers into me as she smiles with her filthy, broken-toothed maw.

I stagger back, hoping to cry for help but instead erupting in a sudden, hacking cough. A handful of flies spills from the depths of my throat, buzzing away.

Somehow, I manage to keep my IV from tearing out, the metal hanger scooting across the floor with me and remaining upright as I back away.

The demon watches me go, her fingers trembling against the glass for a moment before she slips back into the darkness of the vending machine. Pachid dissolves so smoothly it feels like the whole thing was nothing more than a brief waking nightmare, some powerful optical illusion that fades just as mysteriously as it arrived.

The frigid air seems to disappear with her.

My time in the hospital has been dedicated to unraveling a metaphorical ball of yarn, yet my focus has been on the church itself. I haven't yet opened the mental Pandora's box of these otherworldly encounters. I certainly can't tackle these problems out of order.

However, fresh off of a visit from Pachid, my mind is racing.

I'm connecting the dots, considering all the times this demonic force appeared in my life and the circumstances surrounding them. There's more to Pachid's arrival than just her physical presence; there's an emotional weight, a change in the air.

My heart pounding, I creep back to my hospital room with the vaguest spark of an idea swirling in my mind. I feel bonkers for even considering it, but at the same time I can't deny a pattern that's starting to emerge.

Memories from encounters with Pachid and her peers begin to cascade through my hippocampus, a complex equation of cause and effect. I begin to categorize them, and the more I analyze these events, the more my fear begins to drift away. There's something comforting about the brilliant, illuminating light of rational thought.

I enter my room and sit at the edge of the bed, finding my remote and pointing it at the hanging television. I turn it on, immediately greeted by a flickering animation of Peter Pan. He's wrestling his shadow, struggling to catch the mischievous silhouette as it prances and dives about the cartoon room.

Slowly, I begin to flip through channels, going from one program to the next in search of a particular storyline.

I witness all that secular television has to offer. On one channel there's a troop of muscular men in the jungle, huddled around their wounded companion as some frightening parasite crawls beneath his skin. The next channel features two special agents kicking open a door to reveal an inhumanly tall woman with two pupils in each eye. She stands over dozens of crumpled bodies.

"Ugh," I blurt, flipping through the channels a little faster. Secular media is frightening.

The moment two familiar, beautiful women appear onscreen, however, I halt. It's a new scene with the same gorgeous ladies, but the sexual tension between them is just as palpable.

I watch intently, the chill gradually returning to my body as I allow this strange feeling to overtake me. I'm terrified of what it might mean if my theory is correct, but fear is not the only emotion lurking within.

I'm hoping to remain objective, to experience these sensations and categorize them in a way that fits, yet the real tension comes from an obvious truth looming large, staring me in the face and waiting for me to accept it.

My eyes are transfixed on the televised couple, and while their physical presence is just fine, the *story* they're telling makes me ache in a pulpy, scintillating way.

There's no question about it: this is the temptation I was warned about.

I glance over to see Pachid standing in the hallway, putrid grin wide and scraggly hair hanging from her scalp in awkward patches. Those empty white eyes are trained directly on me.

Immediately, I point my remote and turn off the television, forcing any thoughts of illicit sexual tension from my mind. Instead, I think of puppies in a field, the playful creatures bounding through brilliant green grass as they pounce on one another in a haphazard quarrel of furry canine mayhem.

My body is still yearning for those images onscreen, but I gradually manage to relax and let it all go. The ache within me slowly releases and disappears, and along with it goes the demon.

Pachid gently turns and walks around the nearby corner.

Once the demon is gone and my body has warmed back up, I take another pass at summoning her. This time, instead of turning on the television and watching the erotic scenes unfold, I simply dive deep within my own imagination.

I'm so embarrassed by the very notion of all this that I tiptoe around the carnal thoughts within my own mind, treating the ideas like caged animals that could attack at any moment. I'm anxious, not about *what* might happen when Pachid returns, but about the consequences for my identity once the whole truth is revealed.

You already know the truth, I remind myself.

I picture a perfect guy, the most handsome man imaginable standing before me as he delivers a grand romantic gesture with flowers in hand. He's shirtless, and we're on vacation in a tropical location far, far away. He surfs. We're standing on a luxurious deck while the sunset blooms in glorious Technicolor behind us.

Objectively speaking, this imaginary man is very sexy, I guess. He looks like a hunky amalgamation of secular superstar Harry Styles and a specific painting of Jesus I like, but to be perfectly honest with myself . . . I don't really care.

I curiously glance down the hospital hallway, waiting for a return from Pachid that never comes. No matter what romantic or sexual flights of fancy I imagine with my handsome suitor, there's no reaction from the demon.

Not so much as a cold chill or a coughed-up mayfly.

Eventually, I move on, extracting myself from the imaginary bubble and continuing through the labyrinth of my mind. I know exactly where I'm headed now.

It's not long before I arrive at a very specific thought, hesitating a moment before finally diving in.

The moment of truth.

I remember the dark-haired girl at the park, picture the way her frantic words felt hitting my ears. I remember the tone of her voice when she cried "I love you," and how even in that moment of chaos I somehow knew she meant it.

Closing my eyes, I dive deeper.

I flash through other memories with this mysterious stranger, unsure if they are manifestations of repressed reality or some fully manufactured fantasy. Either way, I'm cautiously drawn to these romantic scenes, both attracted to the flame and terrified of getting burned.

A particular memory comes into focus.

I see the girl and me in a cozy, bohemian apartment. We're dancing together, jumping around with large headphones strapped over our ears and two long cables snaking their way across the wood floors to an old, glowing stereo.

Her neighbors threw a fit over the loud music, so this was my solution.

It's the middle of the night, late enough that even the nearby diner has said goodbye to its last-call regulars. We're the only ones left to keep this party going, making each other laugh with just how silly our moves can get.

"I don't wanna leave," I say.

The girl just shakes her head. "What?" she calls out with an exaggerated shrug.

I pull off my headphones, prompting my host to follow suit as her apartment fills with the quiet, tinny rhythm of secular hip-hop.

She's wearing all black still, but the harsh monochromatic style is softened by her lighthearted smile and the playful cut of her dress.

"I don't wanna leave," I repeat, "but I'm gonna have to. This isn't real."

Her expression falters, but this heart-wrenching shift doesn't hold my attention. Instead, I find my focus drifting to the open window behind her, the glass pane slid up as frigid air spills into her place. It's cold, really cold.

I tremble as a mighty chill permeates my bones.

"I'll find you," I assure her.

When I open my eyes again, Pachid is standing directly in front of me, her pallid face hovering just inches from mine.

I expected her arrival, but I didn't know it would be this close. Startled, I take a quick breath as the demon reaches out and snatches my hand.

The second her long fingers wrap around my wrist I'm in shock, the icy temperature urging me to pull away but my body unable to do so. Pachid is incredibly strong, and my instinctual jerk barely registers as she gazes through me with those massive white eyes.

"I'm sorry" is all I can think to say, the words meekly babbling from my mouth.

In a sudden, precise movement, the pale woman reaches up and grips my pinky finger in her other hand. She wrenches it sideways with a loud, sickening crack, tearing tendon and snapping bone.

I let out a blood-curdling howl, any previous thoughts of a dark-haired lover exorcised from my body.

Pachid releases my wrist, prompting me to collapse on the hospital bed as she turns and marches toward the wall. She passes through this barrier with a faint blue shimmer and, just like that, she's gone.

Gradually, the warmth returns to my body, but the pain throbbing across my hand does not subside. I gaze down to find my little finger jutting perpendicular to the rest of my digits; a warning sign.

Echoing footsteps ring out from afar, a night nurse roused by my screams. The sound grows louder as I lay back and stare at the ceiling above.

It hurts, that's for sure, but there's a calm in my soul that no physical pain could ever dampen. I've followed the evidence and finally reached my conclusion, a deduction impossible to believe just a few days ago that now makes perfect sense.

It all fits.

The more I sit with this truth, the more several lifelong points of interest begin to connect like a beautiful web. This is the final piece of a jigsaw puzzle that's been sitting right in front of me.

I may be physically battered and broken, but my soul feels complete in a way that brings tears of joy to my eyes.

Pachid is clearly following a system of rules I don't understand, and her attachment to me is nothing short of a mystery. I still have no idea who the girl with the short dark hair is or why I can't remember her, but there's one thing I *do* know.

I'm gay, and there's a demon out there who *really* doesn't want me acknowledging it.

✳   ✳   ✳

For someone who's happily spent their life under the thumb of strict rules and regulations, I have an uncanny knack for crime.

"Trespassing," I mumble under my breath as I climb over the locked entry gate, quietly dropping to the other side and hustling onward over well-manicured grass.

Of course, fresh from my extended hospital stay with my pinkie and ring finger taped together and a slight limp that might never go away, *hustling* isn't exactly what it used to be, but I make it work.

And forgive us our trespasses, as we forgive those who trespass against us.

It's around one in the morning and without a soul in sight, this large Kingdom of the Pine outreach center takes on a strange, solemn air in juxtaposition to its typically welcoming atmosphere.

I sneak along the building and find a dark corridor between the

CAMP DAMASCUS * 109

church wall and a row of hedges. It's here I'll remain hidden from anyone passing by, but this lane is not without its own challenges. Security
cameras hang from either corner of the structure, and having been inside I know full well they're recording my every move.

Fortunately, I've planned ahead, sporting thin black gloves and a
plastic angel mask.

It's from a church play several years prior, *Paul the Apostle: The Musical.*
Hundreds of these plastic cherubic faces were passed out during a
fourth-wall-breaking conversion scene, and have since made their way
out into every Kingdom Kid's closet. I'm also clad in nondescript sweat-
pants and a hoodie, the latter pulled over my hair to completely obscure
my true identity.

Ordering a different but equally nondescript ski mask was considered when I planned this from my hospital bed, but I decided not to
risk a package showing up for my parents to find.

They're already suspicious enough these days.

I continue along the building, crouching low as I arrive at a very
specific basement window. This is the frame I left unlocked after this
morning's session with Dr. Smith, and I can only hope some good Sa-
maritan didn't come along and rectify my very intentional mistake. I
reach down and test the frame, praying I won't be forced to add breaking and entering to my new criminal record.

Only 5 percent of break-ins require no use of force to get inside.

Fortunately, my planning has paid off in the form of an unlocked
window that can be gently wiggled up. Once the frame is high enough,
I slip my good fingers below and lift with confidence, allowing myself
passage within. I climb through the tiny opening and over the ledge,
hanging a moment before dropping softly to the floor.

Illuminated by faint light streaming through the modest rectangle, I
carefully make my way across the small chamber, eventually finding my
exit and pushing into the hallway. This part of my journey is familiar,
although it feels quite different in the dead of night.

Not only has the still of the evening given this structure a distinctly eerie feel, but my perception of the organization itself has tainted the typically cozy location. Even in the brightest light, this place will never feel as wholesome and welcoming as it once did.

I reach the door of Dr. Smith's office, quietly turning the knob and slipping inside. I don't waste any time, scurrying to the corner cabinet and inputting his code: *11, 14, 15.*

There's a metallic clang as the vessel unlocks.

For a brief moment I freeze, grappling with the wealth of information that lies just below my fingertips.

I've been pushing forward on autopilot this whole time, allowing the fuming, determined part of my brain to take over while the rest of me sits back and enjoys the show. I feel strangely comfortable in this mode, no longer performing the balancing act of two Roses within a single body.

It also keeps me from digging too deep through the untended emotions that float through my soul like restless ghosts.

Slowly disconnecting from your community—from your *family*—is difficult, and while it seems like unearthing their sinister motives and dark secrets might make the process easier, it will never entirely quell the pain.

I've been avoiding this dark ache by keeping my mind busy while my body couldn't be, but it hasn't gone away. The sadness is still there, lurking in the corner like a pale demon in a red polo, just waiting to finally be acknowledged.

That acknowledgment could arrive after several decades, or it could happen tonight, but the time *will* come. Eventually, I'll have to fully contend with this simple fact: the love I was promised is conditional.

That's why I'm so fearful to open this drawer and see what's inside.

Just because Dr. Smith offered a placebo from this particular cabinet doesn't mean a trove of unholy secrets lies hidden within. I had a drug-induced vision on the verge of death (something I never thought I'd get to say about myself, but here we are) and for all I know those images were nothing more than a surreal expression of the blood and oxygen draining from my brain.

It's called a hypoxic-anoxic injury, and yes, it causes hallucinations.

If this is the case—and Dr. Smith has nothing to hide but his questionable credentials—I might be forced to slow down and accept the feeling of loss that lurks above me like a patient vulture.

Vultures are bald to reduce the risk of bacterial infection while plunging their heads inside rotting carcasses.

I need a way to fight back against whatever's going on: a clue, a sign, a fork in the road. I need a way to keep moving forward.

I take a deep breath and pull the top drawer open, gazing down at rows and rows of plastic pill bottles and tiny tinctures. I recognize the little white containers immediately, a massive supply of the Cebocap Dr. Smith is currently prescribing me and I'm happily ignoring. It appears the placebo strategy calms a wide range of patients.

Another swath of containers remain a mystery, however.

I reach inside and extract one of these tiny glass flasks, holding it up to the faint moonlight that streams through a nearby window.

"Holy water," I read aloud from the vessel's tiny engraving.

Looks like this is what the other half of Dr. Smith's patients get.

I continue to the lower drawer, opening it up and discovering a neatly organized rack of manila folders. Each folder sports a patient's name, listed in alphabetical order and running the length of the bin. I immediately scan for my own folder and pull it out, opening it wide and running my eyes over pages and pages of notes.

Dr. Smith's writing is fairly stream of consciousness, documenting a scribbled impression of each session and marking a date at the top to keep things orderly. That's all well and good for a therapist, but within seconds of reading through the freehand pages it becomes clear something unusual is going on.

These notes seem deeply preoccupied with my connection to the church, rather than any internal connection to myself. Dr. Smith also appears completely unaware of my place on the autism spectrum.

My conscious mind was ignorant to the fact that I'm gay, but even *I* knew I was autistic.

Stranger still is Dr. Smith's constant mention of "the assignment."

One passage reads: *Rose Darling has consistently shown resistance to the assignment, which gives reason to keep an eye on other assignments tethered using Ligeian breeds Delta-4 and Delta-5. It should be noted these breeds are also displaying an unusually resilient lifecycle.*

Another entry: *The assignment of Rose Darling is particularly aggressive. It's difficult to determine whether this is a product of Rose or the assignment itself. L and L have been advised.*

I read the last sentence four times before moving on. At first I assumed he was referencing some school project of mine, or a task for the congregation, but it dawns on me "the assignment" is something much more pressing.

Reaching the end of the folder, I discover several invoices between my parents and the church, each one in the form of a charitable donation. These gifts are three hundred dollars a month, transferred directly from my family to Kingdom of the Pine. I was told my therapy is a free service for all congregation members, but it appears that's a lie.

I follow the dates backward until finally reaching an initial payment, then gasp aloud at the enormous number staring back at me in faded black printer ink.

"Half a million dollars?" I blurt. "*What?*"

I snap a few photos with my phone, then slip the paperwork back into its cabinet. I'm just about ready to shut the drawer, satisfied with my discoveries, when another folder catches my eye.

This is the first manila envelope of the bunch, gazing back at me with one simple word printed across its label: ASSIGNMENTS.

I'm just about to reach out and grab it when, suddenly, I freeze.

The faintest shuffling tone crosses my ears and forces me to glance at the door. I hold my breath in the darkness, watching intently for any sign of life and praying my ears were just playing tricks on me.

5, 4, 3, 2, 1.

4, 3, 2, 1.

3, 2, 1.

2, 1.

1.

This little pattern of tension in my fingers is the only movement allowed.

I'm seconds from relaxing when the hallway light pops on, faintly glowing under the doorframe. Panic surges through my body as I'm flooded with thoughts of a silent alarm that must've been triggered at some point along my journey.

The security room is down here in the basement, and as soon as the guards realize this alarm trigger was legitimate, the police will be on their way.

I grab the ASSIGNMENTS folder and scurry over to Dr. Smith's desk, climbing onto it and stretching out to reach the window. These are the same small, high-perched openings that wrap around the whole basement, and fortunately I already know I can fit through them.

It's a lot more difficult on the way out than the way in, that's for sure, but with a boost from Dr. Smith's desk I manage to hoist myself up and slide onto the gravel landing above.

Folder gripped tight, I take off hobbling as fast as I can.

At first, I'm deeply concerned about the missing file my therapist is certain to notice, but my fears are gradually quelled when I acknowledge *anyone* could've taken it. Unlike the other folders with specific names, this selection likely has information on several patients, if not all of them.

But I'm already on their radar.

I shake my head, dismissing the thought. There's nothing I can do about it now, and if things get serious I'll just deny it up and down. Based on what I've already learned, it's unlikely Kingdom of the Pine is free from enemies.

I continue on through the deep woods that surround the outreach center, eventually stopping in a small clearing to catch my breath and rest my throbbing leg as it burns with deep, internal pain. I pull off my mask and flop down on a fallen tree, rubbing the sore flesh of my thigh and clenching my teeth in a grimace of both satisfaction and discomfort.

Once the ache has been subdued I pull out the stolen folder and open it up, gazing down at a single sheet of paper under the light of the moon.

I'm looking at a grid of fifty or so names that run down the left side of a table, followed by a column of complex numbers and another column of mysterious words.

I recognize some of them as Latin names.

On the far right side of this page are two small pillars of checkmarks with the titles RETETHER SUGGESTED and DECEASED.

Across the top of the sheet a headline is emblazoned in bold lettering: CAMP DAMASCUS ASSIGNMENTS.

Here in Neverton, it's hard to ignore the way the camp's presence weaves through daily life. It is, after all, the central cog of our local economy. Without much else to export, having the world's most effective gay conversion therapy program in our backyard has been a boon to the community. Folks fly in from across the globe to change the lives of their lost children.

I'm well aware that Dr. Smith works at Camp Damascus, but I'm struggling to understand how the rest of this data applies to an ex-gay ministry.

"What the *heck*," I murmur, struggling to make sense of the informational cascade.

Relax, I remind myself, *slow down*.

I drum my fingers across the page in a deeply soothing pattern, allowing this peaceful exercise to work its magic.

Meanwhile, the forest around me respires to its own natural rhythm, a faint breeze rustling the leaves as insects chirp and hum.

Starting again, I carefully scroll down the list of names to see if I recognize anyone. While most people who attend Camp Damascus are out-of-towners, it's not uncommon for Neverton residents to make their way through the program.

They certainly don't like to talk about it afterward, but it happens.

When I reach my own name, I stop.

I back up, then read it again, and again.

My hands are shaking, and I do my best to keep from succumbing to the wave of nauseated anxiety that washes though me.

"I've never been to Camp Damascus," I say aloud, my head spinning. "Why would I go to Camp Damascus?"

Because you're gay, an inner voice quips.

My visions from in the ambulance come swirling back like a vicious tornado, tearing through my thoughts. I remember the way that hard cement slab felt against my back, the drone of the chanting figures as it vibrated through my inner ears and crept into my skull.

I still have no recollection of how I got to that place, nor how I left, but I now have a pretty good idea where it's hidden.

As I've allowed myself to blossom and change, breaking the chains of this community that tightly wrapped around my heart for so long, my perspective has also shifted. My outlook creeps along with me, lurking in the background until it's time to gaze out some familiar mental window, at which point I find myself shocked by the view. What once seemed so cut-and-dried has warped into an absolute nightmare.

Growing up in Neverton, I rarely gave Camp Damascus a second thought. As a devout follower of the Lord, it felt good to know this organization was giving people their lives back.

Now that it appears something even more sinister is going on, I'm forced to reassess these feelings and confront the horrific truth that will likely haunt me for a very, very long time: there was *always* something sinister going on at Camp Damascus.

Another wave of aching repulsion sweeps through me and I'm forced to lower the paper, bracing against the log below as I let out a slow breath. After growing up a member of the congregation, guilt is an emotional reaction I know all too well.

Pushing forward and following the clues has been a wonderful distraction. It's kept me from confronting my grief, but it's also kept me from confronting my *regret*. The more I separate myself from the villains in this web of lies, the easier it gets, but the raw truth is that I'm a huge part of this system already. In my own small way, I helped build this town.

I recall participating in car wash fundraisers for families who couldn't afford the program. One year we raised almost *ten grand* to help with renovations on the north cabins.

The roiling emotions within me are finally too much to contain, and the next thing I know I'm erupting in a long, tormented groan. I drop my head to my hands and let it all spill out, losing myself in the moment.

It feels good to expel my feelings in such a visceral way, but I can't express them for long. I'm still too close to the outreach center.

As usual, however, my curiosity gets the best of me.

I open the folder again, blurry-eyed yet determined to understand the full weight of this information. I return to my own row, then slowly read across. The numbers appear to be a system of complex coordinates with twelve points: X, Y, Z (labeled SPACE) and A, B, C (labeled TIME) are each stated twice, a unique numerical string for every variable.

Next to this information is an ancient name that doesn't surprise me in the least.

"Pachid," I read aloud.

Glancing up and down this column I recognize several other names from my studies, minor demons spanning the biblical and occult canon.

Empusa, Leyak, Megalesius, Gressil.

The sudden crunch of a footstep over dry leaves prompts me to glance up in alarm. Someone is headed this way, finding the security footage and following a vague direction of my escape through the woods.

I close the folder and keep moving, forcing my aching body to pick up the pace.

It's not long before I emerge onto the road where my car is parked, climb in, and tear out of there without a moment's hesitation. The guilt is still gnawing away at me, but there's plenty of forward momentum to keep it at bay.

Now that I have this page, something much better than a means of distraction simmers within.

I was taught the importance of perseverance by Kingdom of the Pine, so I suppose they brought this upon themselves.

I was also educated on vengeance.

If I sharpen My flashing sword, and My hand takes hold on justice, I will render vengeance on My adversaries, and I will repay those who hate Me. I will make My arrows drunk with blood, And My sword will devour flesh, With the blood of the slain and the captives, From the long-haired leaders of the enemy.

Luckily, I'm a little less fire and brimstone than the Word of God. I'm hoping for justice rather than retribution, but the heart of the matter remains. I was a cog in a terrible machine for years, and now I'm honored to be the monkey wrench dismantling it.

I marinate on this as I speed through the darkness toward home, focused on my new identity as a ferocious warrior.

In the back of my mind, however, I still know the *real* motivation here, the spark of light that stays tucked away in the depths of my subconscious thought where it won't hurt anyone. I can't dwell on her too much, but I know she's there, the girl who once loved me and who I loved back.

Deep down, I know I'm doing all of this for her. I just can't admit it yet.

7

COMMUNICATORS

As anxious as I am sitting out here in my car, gazing across the street at Zeitgeist Coffeeworks and scanning for familiar faces, it's nothing compared to the tension I've been feeling back home.

Returning from the hospital and sleeping in my own bed was a blessing, but the health of my physical body came at a heavy price.

Suffice to say, Dad never got around to putting a new door up in my bedroom.

It was much easier being under my parents' thumbs before I realized what else was out there, before I noticed all the weeds that climb their way up through the cracks in this little community of ours. Now that the blinders are off, however, there's no going back, and the rotten creep of deception can't help permeating every little thing.

I've been trying my best to act natural, something I wasn't exactly good at even *before* all this happened, and I'm doubtful these efforts have been worth it. My parents know something's up, sense an unspoken change in me.

Now it feels like the only thing keeping me safe is their own denial.

I glance up at myself in the rearview mirror, cringing slightly when I see how disheveled I've gotten. The stress hasn't been kind, bags forming under my eyes and my stark blond hair now greasy and tangled.

Fortunately, I don't have long to dwell. From the corner of my eye

I notice my target, the girl sporting a bright red polka-dot shirt and black jeans. She goes to the only other high school in Neverton, and I've seen her once or twice at various social events. I vaguely recall the two of us holding a brief conversation at a snack bar when our football teams played each other and I was actually allowed to go, but my memory is hazy and I can't be certain.

She's also a Kingdom of the Pine member, but she worships across town.

I reach into my center console and pull out a pen, then unfold my list and place it against the flat surface of my steering wheel. I draw a long line horizontally across one of the rows, blacking out two names.

One is Ally Robertson. Her "assignment" is Lepaca.

This is the sixth person I've checked in with, each one of them under a different cover story and none leading anywhere productive. Nobody remembers a thing.

The mysterious girl with dark hair from the park and my memories isn't on this list, either, since the name of her demon is nowhere to be found. There are several other therapists doing exactly the same work as Dr. Smith, and Ramiel must've been assigned to one of them before his transformation into charred Satanic sirloin.

Still, I keep pushing onward. What other choice do I have?

Ally enters the cafe first and I follow, climbing from my vehicle and limping across the street as the late afternoon sun peeks through stark white clouds overhead. On any other weekend I might be on a neighborhood stroll with Mom, followed by a family dinner and an evening dive into the Scriptures, but things have changed.

The sharp pain in my leg is gone, but a strange ache still rattles through my bones with every step. The closer I get to the coffee shop, the more I consciously balance my stride, forcing myself to push through discomfort. I've worn a long-sleeved shirt to cover up the burns and scarring down my arms.

As I slip into the café, my nostrils are swiftly violated by a pungent, bitter scent.

The Darlings rarely drink coffee, and we certainly don't keep any in the house. While caffeine is one of the rare drugs my parents actually make an exception for, they've strictly forbidden me from trying the stuff while I'm under their roof.

"It's a matter of addiction," Dad once told me. "The Lord didn't design our bodies to run on caffeine, and once it becomes a requirement to find joy, well, you've got yourself a problem."

Truth be told, I'd probably never touch the stuff regardless. The one sip I ever took was enough to let me know the flavor isn't a part of my natural palate.

There are plenty of tables open in various nooks and crannies, and a short line of patrons waits at a front counter. Two baristas are hard at work, jumping between fixing drinks and taking orders with expert proficiency.

My eyes lock on to Ally, but she is completely unaware of my presence as she stands at the back of the line. Her attention is on a large chalkboard that hangs behind the counter, dozens of drink names scribbled in a language that is wholly foreign to me.

I focus, reminding myself exactly why I'm here before making my approach. I mentally refresh my cue card list of questions.

Do you remember Camp Damascus?

Have you seen the demons?

Most important, *Do you know who the girl with dark hair is?*

Truth be told, this little investigation will go smoother if Ally has no idea who I am, and deep down I'm hoping that is the case. If I can get away with a fake name, I'll feel much safer if things go sideways. I'd signed my email with nothing more than an *R.*

"Rose?" Ally blurts, glancing over her shoulder and catching my gaze. She smiles and opens her arms, greeting me with a warm hug.

So much for that plan.

"Hey!" I reply with all the gusto I can manage. "Thanks for meeting up with me!"

"No, thank *you*! What a blessing this is. Seriously," Ally cries, her words randomly curling into high pitched squeaks in a way than I can already tell is a long-term habit. "Let me get you something."

Ally motions to the board of selections.

"It's fine," I insist. "I'm okay."

My coffee date furrows her brow in a playful but scolding way. "*He must be hospitable, one who loves what is good, who is self-controlled, upright, holy and disciplined,*" she recites.

I need to be easy, I remind myself. *Casual. Fun.*

"Fine, fine," I relent, stepping up as the line moves closer. "Do they have chocolate milk?"

Ally pauses, her mind reeling briefly and then finally arriving at an eruption of laughter.

"I forgot how funny you are," she gushes, touching my arm in a way that seems slightly unnatural for how little I actually know her. It's not completely out of line, but it serves as a quick reminder that we *both* have ulterior motives.

I'm calculating too much, I realize, taking a moment to yank my attention back to where it belongs.

A barista suddenly calls out a greeting as the group before us finishes their order, stepping away. Ally approaches the counter, her brilliant smile shining with so much saleswoman pizzazz that it may as well be illuminated. "Venti cappuccino," she instructs, prompting an odd, tight-lipped smile from the barista. Ally then signals for me to order. "I insist."

My gaze returns to the board and I immediately struggle to pick from the confusing array.

"Uh, yeah, sure," I stammer, finally choosing a drink at random. "Americano."

The barista nods. "What size?"

I shoot down the middle. "Medium."

"Room for milk?"

I recall the last time I mentioned milk and take evasive action. "No thanks."

Ally pays, then leads us over to an empty table while our drinks are prepared.

"I always knew you were a self-starter," Ally begins, this observation immediately ringing hollow. She doesn't know me well enough for that kind of reflection, and it's another hint that most of this conversation has been well rehearsed. "What is it about the Kingdom's Young Communicators course that appeals to you?"

Absolutely nothing, but I fully understand I'll need to give a little if I want some trust in return. Ally's strong connection to the church makes her a dangerous interview, but it also means her knowledge could run deep.

I've gotta take my time with this.

"I'd like to be my own boss," I reply.

Ally's grin somehow gets even wider when I say this. "Yes!" she replies with genuine enthusiasm. "Have you read Pastor Bend's new book?"

I'd love to keep smiling and agreeing with every little thing she says, but out of worry I'll be quizzed later on, I'm forced to shake my head *no*. Fortunately, I've read everything else by Pete Bend, but the new-release copy from my parents remained unopened on my hospital bed stand.

Ally doesn't seem to mind that I haven't been keeping up.

"*Craftsman Soul* is incredible," she fawns. "Like, how is he so smart? I know it's just stuff the Prophet said back in the day, but he's got a way of making it really . . . modern."

Now we're getting somewhere. For as little as I know about how to order coffee, I'm extremely well versed in discussions of Prophet Cobel and Pastor Pete Bend. I've been training my whole life for this.

"You're so right," I reply with a nod, "and that's exactly what Tobias Cobel wanted, for his words to live beyond the time and place they were first spoken. He knew the church had to evolve and change with the times, and that's a revolutionary stance to take with something as ancient as the Word of God."

"Yes!" Ally agrees, her eyes lighting up.

"It's *okay* to run a church like a business, because if we don't treat the message of Jesus like a Fortune 500 company, then nonbelievers will certainly do that with messages of their own," I continue. "Religion is more than just faith—it's faith with a brand."

"Did you just make that up?"

"*The Original Leader,*" I reply. "Pastor Bend's first book."

"Holy *moly.*" Ally's expression melts as her rehearsed demeanor slips away. I can tell she's relieved that I know my stuff, thankful our discussion is set to be more of a business meeting than a sales pitch.

I almost feel bad that our conversation will never reach the conclusion she seems so thrilled about. I'm not really here to sign up for the Young Communicators course, although if our paths had crossed in any meaningful way two years ago, who knows what might've happened.

It's our duty as Kingdom of the Pine to spread the message of Prophet Cobel far and wide, to keep his lessons—and the teachings of Jesus— firm in their deeper meaning, but palatable to an ever-changing world. Getting members of the congregation into positions of executive power is an important step in this process, and while some people might find this mixture of business and faith off-putting, for us it's the whole point. For too long, religion has taken a back seat to other organizations that are willing to embrace capitalism—organizations willing to admit that sometimes the ends *do* justify the means.

We are in the business of saving souls, Pastor Bend cried out during one of my favorite sermons. *Let's act like it.*

"Ally!" the barista calls, prompting her to lose focus.

My companion excuses herself, standing up and heading over to the counter to fetch our beverages. I take this moment to collect my thoughts and shift into a new gear, homing in on the reason I'm here. I've built a connection, and now it's time to dig deep.

Ally returns, placing my drink before me and then sitting in her chair. She takes a quick sip of her own beverage and leans down to pull a folder from her bag.

It reads: KINGDOM OF THE PINE YOUNG COMMUNICATORS BUSINESS PATHWAYS—INTERMEDIATE.

"You seem to know what you're talking about, so I have an offer I'd like you to consider," Ally starts. "Through my own current program, I'm eligible to sign up ten other recruiters under what's called a multi-level model."

"Hey," I suddenly blurt, cutting Ally off. "Can I ask you something?"

She seems confused but curious.

"You went to Northcrest High School, right?" I continue, trying my best to feign intrigue as I take in her features. "For some reason, I feel like we spent *a lot* of time together. Do you get that, too?"

"Sure," she replies warmly.

"Do you remember a school trip, though? Or maybe something with the church?" I ask, then try guiding her with a vague recollection of my own. "I have a hazy memory of like . . . a camping trip."

Ally considers this a moment, then shakes her head. "I don't think so," she offers in a way that seems genuinely unaware of where I'm leading this conversation. She notices my untouched drink. "How is it?"

"Oh," I falter, glancing down at the cup of hot, brown liquid. I'm appalled by the smell, but in the interest of playing along I lift my drink and take a quick sip.

The bitter taste immediately overwhelms my mouth. It takes everything I've got to keep my lips in place as my body instinctively struggles to pull them down in an exaggerated frown.

That is *terrible.*

"Wow," I blurt, not sure what else to say as I squint my eyes in an expression of deep thought. "Really good."

The second these words leave my lips I erupt in a sputtering, gasping cough, unable to hold back the reflexive spasm in my throat. I somehow manage to swallow most of the beverage without spitting it out, but that doesn't stop the commotion.

Startled patrons immediately turn in their chairs to look at us, pausing their conversations as they take in the scene of the uncontrollably coughing girl who's now loudly hacking into her hand.

"I'm sorry," I choke, finally managing to pull myself together.

"It's fine, it's fine," Ally assures me, more than gracious.

As my throat settles I turn back to face my companion, but I'm swiftly distracted by a slight tickle within my hand. I glance down, opening my palm ever so slightly and then clenching it tight when I notice the mayfly.

I'd hoped these little critters were out of my system—no outbursts since returning home from the hospital—but it appears we have a straggler.

"You okay?" Ally asks.

I couldn't be less attracted to Ally, but I might've laid it on a little too thick with my holy business acumen. The sparkle in my coffee date's eye might've expressed a little more than just excitement for the sale.

Lepaca is close.

This confirms Ally's attendance at Camp Damascus, but it also means time is a bigger factor than I initially thought.

"I'm good," I insist, quietly crushing the fly within my grip. "Listen, I need to ask you something. Is there a month or two in your life that you just can't remember? Last summer, maybe?"

Ally stares at me, but her expression is no longer confused. It's blank.

"No," she replies.

I lower my voice a bit, leaning in. "Do you ever see things? See . . . *people* watching you?"

Ally says nothing, frozen in place. I notice her body is trembling now, stress hormones flooding her system. She swallows gently.

I wasn't planning on being this direct, but after speaking with five others who gave up no reaction at all, I can't turn back now. Ally is the first person who seems to actually know *something*, who's grappling with these forces instead of just assuming they're a bad dream or blaming an anxious mind.

I hesitate, then jump into the deep end. "Have you ever been to Camp Damascus?"

Ally finally reacts.

"Why would I go to Camp Damascus?" she asks, suddenly just as rehearsed as her initial greeting. "I'm not gay."

The slightest tremble in her voice is the only giveaway that something's off, but the intensity in her gaze speaks to something more. Her look is one of either dread or furious rage.

"You know our dads volunteer at the church together," Ally says. "You know they've been watching you."

"I'm—I'm just trying to figure out what happened," I stammer.

Ally's lips slowly curl up in a pleasant smile, but the fake nature of her expression is promptly revealed as tears begin to well up in her eyes. One of them finally crests, rolling down her cheek, but the grin remains unwavering.

I realize now that Ally's no longer staring at me, but *through* me.

I turn my head to follow her gaze, gradually revealing a dim corner that stretches out behind. While the rest of the coffee shop is bustling and vibrant, the little restroom hallway is quiet and tucked away, obscured from view of the other patrons. Cardboard boxes are piled in a high stack against one wall, and a bookshelf stuffed with old board games rests against the other.

A figure stands confidently in the shadows, eyes staring back at me as solid white orbs. This visitor is the smallest one I've seen, no more than four feet tall. Her skin is just as pale and waterlogged as the others, but her long black hair is slightly less patchy as it hangs from her head in tangled strands.

She's wearing the usual uniform: a red polo with khaki pants below, and the name tag affixed to her chest reads LEPACA.

The demon is grinning an inhumanly wide, crooked-toothed smile, her teeth stained and sooty with some unknown grime as she watches me from the darkness. Her long fingers twitch slightly.

I slowly turn back to Ally, whose face is now streaked with tears.

"We'll get rid of that thing together," I insist. "I just need information."

"*What* thing?" Ally hisses, her jaw clenched tight as she snarls through her teeth. "There's nothing there."

Her words hit me like a punch to the gut.

"I don't think the Young Communicators course is for you," she continues. "Now get the *fuck* out of my face."

I heed her advice and spring to my feet, turning abruptly and hurrying from the shop.

My heart is slamming hard within my chest as panic overwhelms my senses, but it's not the demon that has me worried.

You know our dads volunteer at the church together.

This time I pushed too far, got a little too excited by the prospect of new clues, and got burned in the process.

There's a version of this where Ally would rather ignore *everything*, pretending our little meeting never happened and the curious girl who's out to unravel these mysteries is just as fake as the demon watching Ally sip her cappuccino.

The other version, however, feels much more likely. In that one, Ally calls her father, who then calls mine, and soon enough a deeply unfortunate conversation happens at Kingdom of the Pine about the girl who simply refuses to leave things well enough alone.

"Five, four, three, two, one. Four, three, two, one. Three, two, one. Two, one. One," I repeat under my breath as I limp across the street to my car, drumming my fingers against the side of my aching leg with the hand that still works.

I glance back one last time to see Ally in exactly the same place I left her, staring off into the darkness as tears stream down her face.

At least she doesn't have her phone out.

I knew this would happen sooner or later, I scold myself. *This is the path I took when I decided to turn my back on faith. I chose to abandon my cozy, calm life for this chaos.*

But this wasn't my choice. This wasn't my *fricking* choice and I'm not the one who created the chaos here. Something is wrong in Neverton, and that something isn't me.

I straighten up in the driver's seat, overwhelmed with emotion but determined to hold myself together. My curiosity has finally done what everyone warned it would, and I've bitten off more than I can chew. The only thing left to do is see if I choke or swallow.

*   *   *

The drive home is spent alternating between blinding hope and certain doom. Every time I settle on one side, the other option pulls me back, until eventually I just can't take it anymore.

I pull over, idling on the side of the road while I pull out my phone.

The internal debate rages fiercely within me. Do I ignore this completely and hope for the best? Or do I call my parents and get a jump on whatever they might hear through the grapevine? There's gotta be a way to spin this, but after my recent troubles with the church, it won't be easy.

Some girls in the congregation are spreading rumors about me.

This angle works, I suppose, and it's better than nothing.

I call my dad, prompting a single ring before Luke picks up.

"Hey, honey," he starts, his tone jovial.

"Dad," I falter. "Hi."

A brief moment of awkward silence.

"What's up?" he finally questions. "You gonna be home soon? Dinner's on."

His familiar tone immediately puts me at ease as we slip into our well-worn father-daughter cadence. "Yeah. Sorry, I just . . . I wanted to get your advice on something. There's a few girls spreading rumors about me. I'm not sure how to handle it."

"Oh, honey," my father offers soothingly. "Come right home and we'll pray on it. Whatever it is, God's gonna sort this out for you."

"You're right," I offer, unconvinced of how effective that might be but happy to follow along. I'm suddenly wondering if I've overreacted.

My encounter with Ally could unravel this whole thing, but it could just as easily *not*.

"Lot of rumors going around these days, you can't trust 'em," Luke continues. "You hear what they're saying about butter?"

"No," I reply, a little confused.

"I could tell you but I don't wanna *spread it*." My father hits the punchline hard.

This is normally where I'd sigh loudly and get secondhand embarrassed, but his cheerful nature in this tense moment is enough to warrant a full cackle of unexpected laughter to erupt from my throat.

It feels so much better than a single fly spit take.

"Don't worry, Rose," my father insists. "I've got you. I've always got you."

He called me Rose, I realize. *It's honey or hon, sometimes even Honeysuckle, but never Rose. Not unless I'm in major trouble.*

"Seriously, Dad, thank you," I reply. "I'll see you soon."

I pull the phone away to hang up, but in this split second my ears catch something that sets me on edge. It's the beginning of a phrase, four words yelled to someone else as my father ends the call. I'm not sure what it means, but his tone is as different as night and day. He is shouting at someone, firm and sharp in his demeanor, just seconds after our gentle moment.

"Let me talk to—" he shouts, then silence.

I wait a beat, then finally pull back onto the road. I'm not sure what to make of this, but it's not enough to turn around. Even if it were, where would I go?

For now, I only have one option. Stay the course and hope for the best.

I've gotta be more careful. No more close calls like this.

Ten minutes later, however, I start wondering how much of a close call it really was.

I turn onto my street and find my mother posted on the corner, tears streaming down her face and a duffel bag gripped tight in her hand.

I slam on the brakes, clumsily coming to rest in the middle of the road as the two of us gaze at each other through the windshield of my borrowed car.

The last time I had a standoff like this I was staring down a literal demon, but this moment is equally terrifying.

I've got you. I've always got you.

Dad's words rip through me like a bullet, repeating over and over as the blood gushes from my heart and spills everywhere.

It's instantly clear someone has tipped my parents off. They know their daughter isn't satisfied with the answers she was given, isn't ready to go back to the way things were and pretend none of this ever happened.

The way I acted with Ally was desperate, or maybe I wanted to get caught, to close the curtain on this awkward farce I've been struggling to maintain.

My mother's expression is a lot of things, angry and frustrated and devastatingly sad. Her eyes are locked onto mine, somehow conveying an ocean of emotion without uttering a single word.

Finally, I creep forward, pulling up next to her and rolling down the window.

"What the *hell* are you doing?" Mom demands, fuming with rage as a shockingly rare curse word makes its appearance.

"Nothing," I insist. "Just coming home."

"You're asking people about Camp Damascus," Lisa continues, her expression faltering as devastating sadness overwhelms her. "*Why* are you asking about that camp, Rose?"

I consider denying this line of questioning outright, but I stop myself. I can't keep this up any longer.

"You sent me there," I retort.

"*Because we love you,*" she hisses, seething with rage. "Do you realize how much we spent to *save your soul*? Do you have any *idea*?"

"Half a million dollars," I flatly reply. "Then three hundred a month after that."

Lisa hesitates, struggling to maintain her composure as I reveal just how much I already know. I can see the quiet cadence of a desperate prayer dancing across her lips as she takes a moment to gather her thoughts.

Eventually, Mom points at a house to the right of my idling vehicle, a familiar blue rambler with a white picket fence circling the front yard. The Martinsons live here.

"Sexual deviance," Lisa announces, her jaw trembling as she speaks. "The daughter thinks she's in love with a *whore*."

I know what she's asking of me, but I refuse to play along.

"Sexual deviance," Lisa repeats, her gaze burning a hole through my head as she struggles to stay calm. "What would *you* do to help her, Rose? What's the right thing to do?"

I shake my head, lips sealed tight.

"Get out of here," my mom finally blurts. She pushes the duffel bag through my window, the heavy canvas tote landing on my lap with a thud.

"I'm—I'm sorry," I stammer.

"Was it worth it?" my mother demands.

Now directly confronted, I decide to finally answer. I'm no longer conflicted in my response, no longer overwhelmed by any judgment-based household thought experiment.

"Yes," I tell her bluntly, holding my mother's gaze. "It was worth it."

Mom stares back at me. She's trying so hard to stay angry, but there's simply not enough hate left to fill her veins.

She wants to see me as a heathen—a lost cause—but right now she sees her daughter.

"This was all for you," Lisa groans. "Your dad's waiting back at the house with some men from the congregation. They've got zip ties and duct tape. They're gonna take you back to Camp Damascus whether you like it or not, and I can't watch you go through that again. You might not remember it, but I will."

I've got you. I've always got you.

"So don't let them," I demand.

Somehow a smile manages to break out across my mother's face, Lisa briefly chuckling at this suggestion before sadness gradually creeps back in.

"It's so far past that now, Rose," she says, shaking her head. "You have no idea how hard it was to convince the congregation to step back after your crash, but you *still* couldn't stop looking for answers. Well, now they think you've found some, so it's not really our decision anymore."

I open my mouth to speak, but the words catch in my throat. I'm not sure what to say.

Suddenly, Mom's phone rings. She clears her throat and sniffles the congestion from her nose, stepping away from the car and picking up.

I hear the muffled sound of my father's voice on the other end of the line. I can't make out the words, but his tone is deep and frightening, the polar opposite of his casual tenor during our last discussion.

Our final discussion.

"No, I don't see her yet," Lisa offers, staring right at me. Her goodwill is barely hanging on by a thread. She listens for a moment, then loudly continues. "Sure, I'll let you know when I see the car. Okay. Yeah."

She hangs up.

"They're waiting to take you back," my mother reminds me. "You need to get out of here. Now."

I don't protest, rolling up my window and putting the car in reverse. I start backing away, but only get a few feet before a final thought surges through my mind.

I recall my mother's favorite house from our walks, the one tucked back in the woods where nobody can see it. There are no bake sales or women's worship groups there, just a quiet little cabin at the edge of the world.

I slam the brakes and drop my window once again, calling out to my mother.

"You should leave, too" is all I can think to say.

Lisa hesitates, her eyes burning through me. At first I think she's chosen silence as a final goodbye, but at the last moment she opens her lips to offer a parting phrase. "You are so, so spoiled," my mother says in disgust.

I continue my retreat to the main road. It feels as though my heart is connected to a string, this spiritual cable stretching like taffy as I back away. It battles to hold me in place, but the once-sturdy rope has frayed beyond repair.

The farther away I get, the more taut this string grows. It aches so badly, but finally, it snaps.

The strangest thing about all this is that I physically *feel* it happen, sense the very moment my heart breaks. It's a quick jolt to the chest, shocking me briefly then fading away.

I take one last look at my mother, offering a slight wave and receiving nothing in return.

As traumatic as all that was, my body somehow keeps me from accepting the full weight of what just happened. I'm strangely calm, despite my skin tingling and my head throbbing.

Everything else is operating on autopilot.

My hand mindlessly reaches up to pull the blinker as I turn onto a long, desolate backroad, and at the stoplight I have no problem pressing the brakes, then starting again when the light turns green. My body is a shell, the space within me hollow and empty, a blank void.

*   *   *

The only sound is the hum of my tires on the road, and this lonesome song stretches on forever as I cruise deeper into the woods. The trees fill in thicker and thicker on either side as Neverton disappears behind me.

I can sense fleeting emotions as they creep back into my brain, filtering through my mental safeguards one by one. Every time I accept a new portion of this awful reality, it stings and aches and hurts so bad that I want to scream, until eventually that's exactly what I do.

I open my mouth and let out an unbridled shriek, the fury spilling forth like I'm vomiting it from the depths of my soul. I pound the steering wheel with my fist, only stopping long enough to catch my breath and then erupting in another horrible, strangled bellow.

The car swerves a bit, not equipped for this kind of volcanic emotional display, and with the last bits of common sense I have I manage to pull off the drag in a plume of crunching gravel, rumbling down a side road and throwing my vehicle into park.

I scream again and hold it, my throat now burning from the abuse. I scream so hard I think I might throw up, and moments later that's exactly what I do, opening the driver's side door and ejecting my lunch and, somewhere in there, a single Americano sip across the ground.

When I finish, I wipe my mouth and fall back against my seat.

It's hard to remember the last time my body was this exhausted, but my mind keeps spinning away. While I'd love to take a break from any rational thought, I don't have that kind of time.

Technically speaking, this vehicle doesn't belong to me. It belongs to Luke Darling.

I've been driving his car since mine was totaled, but I'm guessing the police will soon be put on notice to get it back.

I take a deep breath, my eyes shut tight as I hold air within my aching lungs. I slowly let it out.

I realize now that I've been doing my finger patterns across the steering wheel. There's something deeply soothing about this orderly procession, every tap in its right place while the rest of my world falls apart.

A few verses about perseverance pop into my head—Matthew 24:13, Romans 2:7, and of course, Galatians 6:9—but I immediately push them away. Now is not the time for obtuse, two-thousand-year-old advice from dead men.

Instead, I look inward, crafting a proper verse of my own.

Rose 1:1–2. She raised a flaming sword, not to rend her heart, but to seal the wound where a heart had been. For those who cast her out did not know this steadfast flame, alight with righteous anger, would never cease until the heavenly kingdom fell.

As dire as this moment is, I can't help the smile that creeps its way across my weary face. That was pretty good.

I reach into my center console and pull out the list of campers, opening it up and taking a look. I've made notes along the margins for each potential target, ranking them by level of church involvement and marking the ones I'm comfortable approaching.

It's not much to go on, just small hunches based on whatever comes up when I run the names through an online search. A few have addresses scribbled beside them, and it's here I center my attention.

I select the address farthest out of town, making a mental note for tomorrow.

Rose 2:6. And when the morning came she pushed onward, because the wicked and the vile bore down from every side, and onward was the only direction she had left.

8

HOUSE
OF SAUL

There's a beauty to the long golden grass, an Old West cowboy ambiance to the way it stretches on and on around me, but as I roll through this sweeping landscape of farmland, I can't help feeling like I'm on the way to the gallows.

This is the place.

I stop my car, then pop the cap off my pen. I place my page against the steering wheel, drawing a line through the next name on my list: Saul Green. Attachment: *Mephasser.*

While previous investigations had brought me to pristine suburban locales, this address is a far cry from the rest. I'm parked in the middle of nowhere, arriving at the end of a long dirt road and flanked by unkempt fields. A few scattered trees frame this vast landscape—sporadic forests popping in and out while glorious Montana mountains rise far beyond—but for the most part the plains are nothing but yellow waves.

I climb out of my car and glance around, taking in this unfamiliar scene as the afternoon sun beats down from above. This particular acreage features a rare cluster of trees, tucking me away from the outside world.

Before me is a large farmhouse, the looming structure surrounded by vehicles in various states of disarray. Most of them are tireless and covered in rust, weeds grown up through their bodies over time and protruding from their engines in frozen eruptions of yellow and green. The farmhouse looks equally unused, the windows dark and a screen door barely hanging from its hinges. At one point, this home was likely a sight to behold, but the wear of age has really done a number on it.

Beyond the house is an enormous metal barn, this structure much fresher than the rest. It's large enough to evoke a full-sized airplane hangar, towering behind everything like a shimmering silver ghost.

Suddenly, a cacophonous sound erupts through the air at such a deafening volume it makes me jump in alarm. A flock of resting birds takes this as their cue to leave, leaping from their perch on a gnarled tree and escaping into the blue sky above.

My heart is pounding even harder as I struggle to understand the bizarre racket echoing across the landscape. It sounds like a sickening combination of sped-up secular rock and slaughterhouse animal squeals, a pig recorded midtorture and now someone's messing with the tape.

I glance back at my car and consider making an early exit, but the moment doesn't last. It's an instinctual reaction, not a thoughtful one.

I know what I have to do.

Focusing on the task at hand, I make my way out into the mess of mangled automobiles. The earsplitting noises are coming from the giant hangar, so I head directly for it.

The closer I get, the more my surroundings reveal themselves. While the aural cacophony is difficult to understand, it gradually dawns on me that this is music—barely—a screeching, grinding clutter of thrashing guitars and guttural vocal howls. It's just about the most unpleasant sound I could imagine, but I'm relieved to know I'm not privy to the actual death squeals of terrified swine.

I also understand the landscape much better, a clearer perspective as I approach the colossal hangar. There are even more cars parked directly in front of the building, but these vehicles are distinct from the rest. Here, sit beautiful automobiles in pristine condition, protected from the sun by a large sheet-metal overhang.

I'm not one to know much about makes or models, a blind spot in my trivia-hungry brain, but the vehicles appear quite luxurious. These are classic cars, either unused for decades or restored with breathtaking care.

A realization dawns on me. This dilapidated farmhouse isn't the sign of a resident who doesn't give a darn about *anything*, it's the sign of a worker so deep in their craft they can't find time for much else.

The massive hangar doors are cracked open, so I carefully limp around the edge and peer inside.

More cars are waiting to greet me, stuffed into every corner of this already crowded structure. It's an engineer's dream, chains dangling from the ceiling and vehicle parts stacked high on enormous cargo shelves.

A cascade of dancing orange sparks immediately catches my attention from across the garage, beckoning me onward.

I slink closer and closer, approaching a tall, mysterious figure in a metal welding mask. He's hunched over an engine block, diligently working away as sparks continue to spew from the vehicle's open hood and embers dance wildly across the ground.

Meanwhile, thunderous music churns from a nearby stereo, its volume cranked up so loud I can actually feel the vibration in my chest.

I stand watching for a moment, not entirely sure how to interrupt this engineer so deeply consumed by his work.

Eventually, however, I catch his line of sight, offering up a cautious wave.

The figure turns off his welder and stands upright, walking over to the audio system and killing the sound. He removes his enormous metal mask.

The face underneath is handsome, dark-skinned, and midtwenties, featuring a faint cascade of stubble along his broad jaw. His hair is messy and his eyes are strikingly light, but the most notable thing about this man's face is its expression.

He's overwhelmed with emotion, a nostalgic sadness welling behind his eyes while a smile of recognition creeps its way across his mouth. He knows me, and while this was a terrifying prospect in Ally's case, there's something deeply assuring about this man's demeanor.

"Rose Darling," the man sighs, my own name falling from his lips in a moment so unexpected it almost bowls me over.

Other than Ally, not a single person from the assignments list has recognized who I was, and *none* have reacted with this much genuine tenderness.

There's also a sliver of apprehension.

An image flashes through my mind, some tiny fragment of memory breaking loose from the greater blockage. I see this man with a sunburst acoustic guitar on his lap, his mouth open wide as he belts out a song to captivated campers. I'm watching from across the fire pit, equally swept away by his triumphant music.

The vision disappears just as swiftly as it arrives, but the feeling remains: Friendship.

"You remember camp?" the man asks.

"A little."

"How was it?" he continues, welling up a bit.

I've been plodding through this journey like a disembodied spirit: no family, friends or community left to remind me that I actually exist. I was starting to think I might've just disappeared completely, a phantom in some endless loop of unfinished business.

But I'm not a ghost, and someone who knows that has finally caught sight of me. Whether or not I fully recognize him in return is inconsequential.

"Not great," comes my understated reply, our conversation now a macabre inside joke.

Suddenly, my conscious mind takes the back seat as my emotions propel me forward, marching through the space between us and wrapping my arms around this unknown man in a powerful embrace. I can't help it as I begin to cry, letting it all out in a flood of blubbering tears. He holds me in return, pulling me close and enveloping me with his presence.

We stay like this for what seems like forever.

*   *   *

Saul places a glass on the large wooden table, then begins to unscrew the cap of a dark brown bottle. The sour scent of alcohol wafts across me when the top pops off, offering notes of the cleaning solutions I might find under a sink.

"What *is* that?" I ask, wrinkling my nose.

"Whiskey," he replies.

I have little experience with hard alcohol, but if it's all this pungent then I'm truly shocked by the worldwide popularity. The scent is only slightly less atrocious than that of coffee.

Saul turns to place the bottle back in his liquor cabinet, but stops abruptly. He swivels back to face me.

"You want some?" he asks. "Kingdom Kids are always two years older than their grade, right?"

"I'm twenty," I state, "and no thanks."

Saul nods and smiles as though touched by my response. He places the bottle back where it belongs, then stands for a moment. "So what *do* you drink these days?" he continues. "Still having root beer keggers?"

A flash of memories from my days in the congregation washes over me, recalling all the parties that felt wild and free despite existing tight under our parents' thumbs. It seemed very wholesome at the time, but remembering those people now makes me nauseated.

"Not anymore," I reply, shaking my head before stopping abruptly. "Actually, do you have root beer?"

Saul laughs. "Yeah," he admits.

"I'd like one, please," I say, prompting my host to head off into the kitchen.

As Saul clatters around in his fridge I take in my surroundings, my eyes working their way curiously across the dining room of the ancient farmhouse. This place was built to house a large family, but the windows have grown dusty with neglect and the peeling wallpaper is well past the point of salvaging. It's nothing but a skeleton now.

Saul returns with an ice-cold bottle of root beer, freshly uncapped and fizzing gently.

My host sets the beverage in front of me then returns to his seat across the table, flopping down casually. He still can't seem to wipe the smile off his face, basking in the presence of his old friend.

"How much do you remember about Camp Damascus?" I ask.

Saul considers this, leaning back in his chair and taking a long sip from his glass. I continue observing him during this quiet moment, making note of the little details I hadn't noticed from afar.

For one, Saul is absolutely covered in tattoos, the dark and intricate markings running down his arms and up his neck. His nose is pierced with a single ring on the right side, but his ears are chock-full of glinting silver and gold bars. The man's black T-shirt features a band's logo so distorted by violent spikes and spires it has become unreadable, and below this is a graphic depiction of vile, gore-soaked carnage.

I can't imagine seeking out the friendship of someone like this with my earlier mindset, yet here we are.

"I remember a lot," Saul finally replies, "but it's hard to tell what's missing, you know? Seems like every day I catch a glimpse of something new."

I nod, understanding precisely what he means. I'm on a quest to gather information and fill in the blanks of my memories, but it's frustrating to have no idea how large a hole I'm patching. It's like struggling to construct a puzzle without understanding the edge that borders it. The picture could be ten pieces wide, or ten thousand.

"I remember *you*," Saul continues, cracking a smile. "You've changed."

I laugh instinctively, then hesitate. "What do you mean?"

Saul considers his words carefully. "When's the last time you took a shower?" he finally asks.

In my previous world of youthful drama and high school politics, I might've been offended by this, or at least gone through the motions and pretended to be. Now, I just take his question at face value.

I take a lock of my own hair and hold it before my face, inspecting the ratty blond tangles. "I slept in my car last night," I admit. "We were friends?"

"Yeah, we were friends," Saul offers, then hesitates slightly. "I was your counselor."

This revelation hangs in the air between us, settling as we sip our drinks. I briefly consider anger, but the feeling passes quickly. Saul is tethered to a demon, just like I am.

"I didn't know," he assures me, an emotional weight in his gaze that's difficult to fake.

"Okay" is all I can think to say.

We're both giving this our best shot, but it appears brief mental flashes of some previous relationship aren't quite enough to cut through the awkwardness of strangers reuniting.

Suddenly, I tense up as a cold gust of air washes across my body, reacting to the stimulus in exactly the way I've been trained.

Pachid.

Something's not right, a break in the pattern. I erupt in a flurry of calculations, desperately wondering how this could happen while my mind remains free from impure thoughts.

"You good?" Saul asks, noting the concerned look on my face as my eyes dart across the room.

Eventually, my gaze finds its way to a gaping hole in one of the dining room windows, the glass corner broken just enough to let in a chilly gust of air.

"I'm okay," I reply.

Saul looks skeptical.

"What about you?" he continues. "What do *you* remember?"

"I remember the ceremony," I state. "That's about it."

Saul's eyes widen. "You remember the *tethering ceremony*?" he repeats, shaking his head. "I'm glad that's one of the few parts that hasn't come back to me yet. Hopefully it never will."

"Yeah" is all I can offer.

Saul nods, his expression changing slightly as a heartbreaking realization washes over him.

"Listen," he finally blurts, leaning forward. "I know why you're here, because I did the same thing for way too long. You've gotta drop it and move on."

I laugh. "There's nowhere left to *move on* to."

I can tell this simple response cuts my host deep, chilling him to the core. He seems viscerally unsettled by my words, thrown off course a moment before pulling himself together.

"I'm serious," he finally continues. "When I started remembering things I wanted nothing but justice. I read everything I could find on Kingdom of the Pine, just devoured the literature. I looked up old biblical texts. I even broke into three churches hunting for documents."

"You're way ahead of me." I laugh. "I've only done one."

Saul sighs loudly. "Well, keep it at that," he suggests. "There *are no answers*, Darling. Once they've got you tethered, there's no going back."

"But what *is* tethering?" I ask. "If you know there's no escape, then you must have a pretty good idea how it works."

Saul hesitates, staring off into space. "You're the one who actually remembers it," he finally counters. "Why drag me back into this? What else could I possibly offer?"

"I don't know," I reply, growing a little frustrated. "Listen, I understand this whole thing has become too much for you, but *I'm* not there yet. I'm still trying to sort it out, so if there's anything I should know, just tell me."

Saul straightens up a bit. He takes another drink of whiskey, but it's not the same casual sip as before. This time he downs the whole glass, as if to get that out of the way so he can focus on delivering his information. "Tethering means possession," he states bluntly. "It's demonic possession."

"But the *church* is doing it!"

Saul shakes his head, chuckling to himself. "Kingdom of the Pine runs Camp Damascus, the most successful ex-gay conversion therapy program on the planet," he expounds. "This whole city, whether it's the congregation or the tourism or just local traditions, it all revolves around the success of that program."

I'm listening closely, nodding along.

"Have you ever stopped to ask yourself *how* Camp Damascus is so successful?"

The official answer is that it "just is," and they can get away with this nonresponse because the numbers speak for themselves.

There are several rumors, however. One theory is the program relies on cutting-edge cognitive studies, developed with the help of Pastor Bend's Silicon Valley business connections who would rather remain anonymous. Using huge swaths of online data, they've determined exactly what steps one can take to remain pure.

Another theory is Prophet Cobel left behind additional sacred texts, a trove of hidden documents containing secrets of the universe from Jesus himself. These informational writings provide the congregation with a leg up against our competition.

Of course, the most common response is the classic one: it's just God's will.

I immediately recall these answers, tired regurgitations of congregation propaganda, then push them aside. "I have no idea," I finally admit.

"The church is invoking their own possessions," Saul explains. "They assign a demon to each member of their program—a watcher to keep every graduate in line. I'm sure you've noticed."

I nod, picturing Pachid's filthy, broken grin.

Saul climbs to his feet, heading to a study in the next room and calling out while he roots around. "The demons will keep you free from sin. They'll scare you away from impure thoughts and, typically, that's enough. In extreme cases, the demons will resort to violence. Sometimes they'll torture the one who's possessed, sometimes they'll eliminate the target of desire. Either way, Kingdom of the Pine has a thriving business with a spotless success rate."

"What about you?" I retort. "You're not a success. *I'm* not a success!"

Saul returns with a thick, leather-bound tome in hand. "We're not successful conversions? Really?" he retorts with a laugh. "I'm certainly not living the gay lifestyle I envisioned."

He's right. While our trips to Camp Damascus have left chaos in their wakes, any shred of my homosexuality has been pushed deeper into the closet than I could've ever imagined. Forget *acting on* my desires, it's dangerous for me to even *think* about them.

"But . . . you're still gay," I finally counter. "I mean, it doesn't actually work."

Saul is clearly intrigued by my choice of words.

"*I'm* still gay," I continue, using myself as the example.

Saul nods. "You're right," he admits.

"How did you learn all this stuff?" I continue, overwhelmed with curiosity. "I keep hitting dead ends."

Saul drops the weighty book on the table before me, the loud rattle making me jerk. "Spiritual study," he reveals, returning to his seat. "Prayer."

I stare at my host awkwardly. "Wait, after all this, you still believe in *prayer*? You believe in *God*?"

"You *don't*?" Saul counters with a laugh. "There's a demon attached to you, Darling! Are you really saying the devil is out there doing his wicked work, but now God is a bridge too far?"

I open my mouth to respond, but the words catch in my throat. He's got a fair point. I've been so wrapped up in my disillusionment with the church itself that I didn't even see what was sitting right in front of me, the mountains of evidence that *something else* is out there. Of course, it's difficult to tell what that something is, but throwing out the whole cosmic realm might not be the most logical course of action.

I haven't been pushing through this journey with as much balance as

I'd like, mostly because swinging hard to the opposite side of belief *feels* so good right now. I'm angry, after all.

Deep down, however, I'm analytical enough to know this isn't the best approach.

The results speak for themselves. I still haven't found the answers I'm looking for, and it appears the missing pieces were waiting in the last place I wanted to look: the realm of faith.

"You've got a point," I finally admit, "but I'm a little burned out on God."

Saul nods. "That's fair."

"I've seen demons, but the tethering ceremony is not *spiritual*," I continue. "They're not possessing people with ancient rituals and secret prayers, they're doing it with computers and coordinates. They have this machine . . ."

"A machine?" Saul repeats, his engineering brain now taking hold as he starts pacing back and forth. "What did it look like?" At this point a cartoon lightbulb may as well be flickering on above his head.

It suddenly occurs to me that Saul is having a similar revelation to the one I just had. He's been working to unravel this mystery through a lens of faith, and he's made great progress, but at the end of the day a complete solution has managed to elude him. His point of view is too narrow to encompass the whole mystery, just like mine was.

The key to both of our journeys lies somewhere in the middle.

"I couldn't really see it, I was strapped to a table," I admit. "I saw the tear, though. Some kind of hovering doorway ripped wide open."

Saul is nodding along. "That's how they climb through," he blurts, synthesizing the information out loud. "They're travelers arriving from *somewhere*. They phase through space."

"Exactly," I say, picking up the slack and offering a riff of my own. "If you stop thinking about them as spiritual entities and realize they're just *creatures*, it starts to make a little more sense. Animals have abilities we can't comprehend, like how sharks can sense magnetism. It's beyond our understanding, but that doesn't make them supernatural."

I can't help standing as the cogs in my mind begin churning at record speed. The information is coming too fast for me to sit still, joining Saul's movements as the two of us pace around the dining room like circling boxers. He's growing more animated by the second.

My fingers drum against my thigh.

"But they're coming from *hell*," Saul counters. "That's a spiritual place, not a logical one. There's no science behind hell."

"Why not?" I retort, dropping the reins completely and allowing my mind to run wild. "According to Hugh Everett III, there's infinite layers of reality stacked on top of one another. What we call *hell* might just be another layer."

Saul bristles at the suggestion, but I push onward, surprising even myself as words continue to spill from my mouth. I'm discovering my own sense of balance in real time, testing the edges of inspiration.

"That doesn't mean hell's not real, or that God's not real," I continue. "It's just a shift in our understanding of what that *means*. We're so used to looking at these things like they're outside the realm of science, but maybe they're just parts of the universe science hasn't gotten around to yet."

While the merits of these spiritual perspectives are clearly still up for debate, at least one of my burning questions has finally been answered. I now fully understand why this long-lost friend and I got along so well, despite seeming like polar opposites. We're both deeply inquisitive, different sides of a similar coin.

We complement each other.

This predisposition for deep analysis might also explain why we seem to be the only ones who've managed to remember our time at Camp Damascus, albeit faintly. We haven't been blessed by some incredible superpower from the great beyond, we're just curious.

Sometimes that's all it takes.

*　　　　　　　　　*　　　　　　　　　*

After years in a household built around stifling my excitement and curiosity, it's surreal to spend the afternoon here with Saul. Ideas spill out of me in a flood that ranges from diligently tested theories to half-baked flights of unbridled science fiction. We dive deep into everything we know about Kingdom of the Pine, laying it all out to understand where our knowledge overlaps, and where it doesn't.

Saul's right there to bounce these notions back at me, jumping in with thoughts of his own.

Like most everyone I meet, Saul's brain is quite different than mine, but he has the same drive for understanding and analysis. He can't help his deep craving for understanding the greater mechanics behind all things, which is likely how he's managed to make a living repairing cars and taking shop commissions.

We're on the farmhouse roof now, sitting just outside one of the upper bedroom windows where a gentle overhang provides space to watch the first blossoming colors of a glorious Montana sunset. Between us sits Saul's enormous tome of biblical mystery, a book I've been hesitant to crack open just yet.

Ancient religious texts and I aren't on great terms.

It's taken a moment to fully relax out here, and I was just barely convinced when Saul assured me the roof is stable and the few missing shingles are nothing to worry about.

Once I settle in, however, there's something picturesque about it, like a scene from one of the teen dramas I was never allowed to watch. The aching loss of my family remains, churning away at the pit of my stomach, but in this moment I detect the slightest bit of assurance through some other nurturing force.

What that force actually *is*, I have no idea.

Saul and I are posted quietly, our thoughts and theories finally simmering down in separate internal dialogues. His property stretches before us in the dying light, rows and rows of vehicles laid out in various states. Some cars are infected by long tufts of yellow grass, the weeds popping up through rusty hoods, while others are kept clean and fresh for pickup.

My eyes aren't on the cars, however.

A troop of prairie dogs has moved in, and Saul doesn't seem to mind as these little critters make their way through his metalworks. The animals pop out from various holes in the dirt, glancing around a moment and then diving back in on some unknown prairie dog mission I can't make heads or tails of.

Every once in a while, the creatures will approach one another and offer what can only be described as a kiss. It's not really a kiss, of course, and serves as another example of humans assigning some greater anthropomorphic meaning to instinctual behavior. In truth, prairie dogs locking their front teeth in greeting is a way of recognizing their family units, or potential rivals, and establishing complex social networks. It's pretty cute, though.

We project a lot of things onto other species. It's something I've always known, but the less I find myself relying on spiritual explanations, the more these biological realities stick out.

"They're just flesh and blood, like we are," I say, thinking out loud.

Saul glances over at me. "Prairie dogs?"

"Demons," I reply.

We sit a moment longer, letting this observation settle.

"They can drift through layers of reality," I finally continue. "There's a hidden biology there, and Kingdom of the Pine has learned to exploit it. They summon them here and put them to work. But *how?*"

"Maybe that's where the spiritual side comes in." He reaches over and opens the massive antique book that rests between us, its heavy binding hitting the loose shingles with a thud. I notice several pages in this section have been marked, and the one we've arrived on sports a glorious hand-drawn image.

"Take it," Saul offers, prompting me to begrudgingly lift this massive volume onto my lap.

The illustration features two priests holding down a ravenous demon and wrapping an iron collar around his neck. The creature has stringy hair and stark white eyes along with a set of lengthy, now-familiar digits. Behind them is a dazzling tear that hovers in the air, a portal to another world, just like the one from my flashback.

"Where did you get this?" I ask, running my fingers gently down the ancient page.

"Remember when I told you I'd broken into three churches?" Saul replies. "One of them was . . . pretty important."

I turn my attention back to the tome, unable to tear my eyes away as I continue onward. I gently flip from page to page, stopping at every marker. The next illustration is of a woman hunched over a clay bowl while a priest gently pats her on the back. A swarm of flies is erupting from her mouth and filling the basin.

"I tried to get as much information from this book as I could, but it takes forever to translate," he explains. "Most of it seems to be in Latin."

"*Bona res est scire,*" I reply, working over the text that accompanies the depiction of spewed-up flies.

I'm hoping for a concrete explanation, a step-by-step breakdown of every detail in the bizarre renderings.

Unfortunately, all I find are prayers.

"You understand Latin?" Saul gushes.

I flip deeper into the volume, my fascination and disappointment somehow growing in unison.

"*Prayer for the hungry, prayer for the broken, prayer for release,*" I announce. "I'll spend some time with this, but I've gotta be honest: the pictures are more helpful."

I pull out my phone and snap some photos of the massive walls of text, storing them for further study. The *prayer for release* shows a priest standing over a figure in shackles, confidently making some grand proclamation. The shackles around the bound man's wrists and ankles are cracking open, offering freedom.

"I think we're on the right track, though," I say.

I continue through the tome, but I notice Saul watching me with great concern.

"On the right track for what?" he questions.

"To stop them," I reply, looking up. "To expose Kingdom of the Pine and shut them down."

Saul shakes his head.

"Not gonna happen," he states. "It's a lost cause. They have so much more power than you think, Darling, and their influence goes *deep* in this town. It's not just an organization, or a church, or a camp; it's a culture."

"We'll see," I retort. "Maybe you're right. Maybe we can't shut the *whole thing* down, but I'm not gonna stop until I find her."

"Willow?" Saul replies.

I freeze, the very mention of this name flooding me with potent memories. I see the dark-haired girl standing outside a coffee shop as it pours down rain. I see her gently running her fingers along a row of book spines. I see her strolling ahead of me on a hike into the mountains, leading the way.

"Willow," I repeat, then swiftly push these thoughts from my conscious brain. "You knew her, too?"

Saul takes a deep breath and nods, slowing things down. He's hesitant.

"Do you know where I can find her?" I ask, my body tense.

Saul nods again.

"Tell me!" I demand, coming off much more aggressive than I'd hoped.

"I can't do that," he replies, solemn. "It's a death sentence. I know you miss her. God knows I miss someone, too, but as long as these demons are riding our backs, we have to stay away."

"Not if we exorcise the demons," I counter, a critical piece suddenly falling into place. "Actually . . . I'm pretty sure I already did that. I burned one alive."

Saul just stares at me, not sure if I'm serious or not. "You *what?*" he finally blurts.

I shake my head, just barely keeping up with all these new ideas as they come. "I locked Willow's demon inside a flaming car and killed it."

"How is that possible?" Saul protests. "They're so far beyond the limits of—"

"They're flesh and blood," I interrupt, reminding him of the tangible nature we've ascribed to these otherworldly beings.

Saul is still unconvinced. "Why would a demon *burn*?" he asks. "They're from a world of eternal flame. *So he called to him, 'Father Abraham, have pity on me and send Lazarus to dip the tip of his finger in water and cool my tongue, because I am in agony in this fire.'*"

I consider everything I know about these creatures and my encounters with them, walking through each of my harrowing experiences and allowing myself to catalog every moment. I think back to that time in my dark living room, and at the party, and my memories of the slab.

Suddenly, a chill tickles across my skin.

My heart skips a beat, fear pulsing through my veins and focusing my senses like a stiff shot of adrenaline. I shift awkwardly on the roof, glancing over each shoulder.

"It's just the breeze," Saul offers, noting my discomfort. "It gets chilly out here this time of night."

I'm reminded of my alarm over the draft downstairs, a simple cracked window all it took to put me on edge. It's sickening how much power a shift in temperature now holds over my mental state—Pavlov's perfectly trained dog.

The cool breeze comes again, washing over my body like a tear between worlds.

Suddenly, it all falls into place.

"Hell is frozen," I snap, sitting upright. "It's not a flaming wasteland, it's ice cold. Think about what it feels like when they're around, what happens when they open a tear to their world."

"Then why is every old Christian painting full of fire and brimstone?" Saul questions.

He already knows the answer, but he's unwilling to accept it.

"Because God didn't paint those," I reply. "The church did. *People* did. You know why Eve snacked on an apple in the garden of Eden? Because the Hebrew and Greek text said *fruit*, but the Latin translation for *apple* was a pun with the word *evil.* When St. Jerome translated it, he added the pun as a little joke, and now look at every Eden depiction. All of history altered by one guy's little translation gag."

"That's a tiny shift, not the exact opposite thing," Saul retorts. "If demons thrive in cold and fear the heat, why make a switch? Revelation 20:15, *and whosoever was not found written in the book of life was cast into the lake of fire.*"

"You ever hear that story about the Vikings discovering Iceland and Greenland, then switching the names to keep the lush beauty of Iceland for themselves?" I ask.

Saul nods.

"There's your answer. It's all about control," I continue. "It always has been."

This point seems to hit my friend the hardest. He's reeling from the implication, working it over in his mind as his expression evolves from doubt to dread.

"I'll see Willow again," I announce with confidence. "*Safely.* I know there's someone you want to see again, too."

"Yeah" is all that Saul can manage to reply, his voice trembling with emotion now.

I stand, minding the rickety roof under my feet, and place my hand on his shoulder. I can feel a profane eruption bubbling up within me and I push into it, refusing to silence myself. It might seem like a silly thing to care about, but it's not. This is *my* voice.

"Let's do something about it," I proclaim. "*Frick* Camp Damascus."

*　　　　　*　　　　　*

On the 14th of September, 1321, Dante Alighieri died in exile. He was called a lot of things—poet, artist, philosopher—but at the time his most prominent label was heretic. He was such a threat to the church that, eight years after his burial, Cardinal Bertrand du Pouget demanded the man's bones be dug up and burned at the stake.

Ask any historian how he died and they'll answer malaria, but history is written by the victors, and arsenic poisoning wasn't quite as easy to spot in the fourteenth century.

I've never read Dante's *Inferno*, which is strictly banned in the Darling household, but after spending the last two weeks researching all things hellish with Saul, I know the poem pretty well. .

In this early epic poem, the bottom layer of hell is described as freezing cold, an icy lake where Satan dwells.

This characterization didn't stick around, and look where it got Dante.

The last two weeks have been a blur of planning and scheming, Saul and I putting our heads together and manifesting something so much more than the sum of our parts. There's a madness to our focus, a parallel drive to prove ourselves in the face of a world that's cast us out.

I barely notice when the day of my high school graduation comes and goes without fanfare.

These days, my afternoons are spent helping Saul in his workshop.

Sometimes I'm a hands-on assistant, covered in oil and grease. We're both smart and curious, but Saul's engineering brain is unlike anything I've ever seen. I can certainly keep up, but there's a depth to his mechanical knowledge that I'll simply never possess.

Other times, I'll do nothing but sit nearby with my nose buried in Saul's pilfered spiritual texts, memorizing the prayers and keeping my host company. At this point in my self-extraction from the church, my religious curiosity is entirely clinical, but the information is important to understand as we determine what comes next.

Saying our enthusiasm is based on some kind of cathartic revenge would be disingenuous.

The true drive behind every twisting screw and buzzing saw, every turned page and highlighted text, is simple and breathtakingly obvious. It's the motivation behind nearly every epic journey since the beginning of time: love.

There are people tucked away in the back of our minds who mean everything to us, and while Camp Damascus made a promise to carve them out like a tumor, this guarantee was misguided. The church makes the same assurance to all parents who abandon their sons and daughters in this terrible place, claiming they'll fix something broken.

But they're wrong.

I'm living, breathing proof these "conversions" are all smoke and mirrors, the outward appearance of change over something that's internally immutable. Nobody who's graduated the Camp Damascus program is *ex-gay*, they're just even more tormented than before. They've been frightened and threatened into submission, a tactic that's been used against queer people for centuries.

The only difference is that now these threats have been outsourced.

In a darkly hilarious way it all makes perfect sense, the natural culmination of a philosophy that has colored my life for twenty years. Prophet Cobel taught us God wants his followers to thrive and *win*, that humility is important but it certainly doesn't supersede progress and growth.

Born of the Industrial Revolution, Kingdom of the Pine is very clear: when it comes to spreading God's love, you do what needs to be done.

According to the congregation, my sin outweighs any discomfort about demonic collaboration, and while this might seem like impossible mental gymnastics to outsiders, it makes perfect sense to me.

It's hardly the worst thing organized religion has come up with.

While I used to consume religious canon in a state of mystery and wonder, I now find myself utterly shocked that I ever believed a word of it.

Saul, on the other hand, claims he's closer to God than ever.

"You should come with me today," he says, setting down his tools and turning away from the workbench.

The wall behind Saul is covered in angular pipes and various machine parts, contraptions dangling from chains like some bizarre modern art experiment. This is its own kind of chapel.

"No thanks," I reply shortly.

"Today's the main event," Saul presses. "Gonna need all the support we can get."

I shake my head in utter shock, amazed the man can carry on like this despite everything Kingdom of the Pine has done to him. Saul is wonderful, and over the last few weeks of working together it has grown even clearer why we were friends in the first place. However, his continued dedication to the Lord is truly bizarre.

Between that and his taste in music, Saul is one of the most unusual Christians I've ever met.

"I'm fine," I state flatly, the same reply I give every Sunday afternoon before Saul makes his trek to a service at the tiny nondenominational church nearby.

We're far enough outside the county line that I'm not worried about anyone from Kingdom of the Pine showing up, but getting recognized isn't my biggest concern. My biggest concern is losing myself again.

"All good," Saul replies with a shrug. "I'll be back in an hour and a half, and then we can get started."

Saul hesitates, giving me one last chance to change my mind before finally removing his work gloves and tossing them onto a nearby bench. He strolls past, leaving me standing alone at the heart of his workshop.

I find myself suddenly awash in the heavy silence of this enormous metal structure. Moments later, the requisite eruption of sound from Saul's car stereo fills the void.

These sounds are just as abhorrent as when I first arrived, but for some reason I wish they weren't so far away.

I don't wanna wait around out here in the middle of nowhere.

Not alone. Not today.

Before big events, whether it was an intramural soccer game or the annual Christmas play, my dad and I had two important traditions. The first, of course, was a quiet session of prayer, a blessing to carry us forward and an offering of thanks to the Lord for carrying us this far.

The second was more specific to Luke.

My dad loved dumb jokes, and while these simple puns were also slightly groan-inducing, my exaggerated eye rolls were part of the fun. I spent my life building these rituals, and lately there's not much reason for family traditions without a family to carry them.

But I'm not on my own anymore.

Before Saul can leave, I spring into action, my body carrying me forward on instinct and propelling me from the shop into the late afternoon air. Saul has just started pulling down the driveway in what I've recently learned is a refurbished 1969 Mustang, but he stops when he notices me chasing after him.

My friend lowers his music and rolls down the passenger side window as I approach, gazing at me from behind the wheel.

"You finally gonna let God back into your heart, Darling?" he jokes.

I shake my head. "No," I reply. "Just wanted to ask if you remembered your bowl and spoon."

A confused look crosses Saul's face.

"Because it's gonna get a little *chili* today," I say.

My friend stares at me blankly.

"Alright," I sigh awkwardly, climbing into the passenger seat.

Saul smiles.

"Don't get too excited," I warn. "I'll come with you, but I'm waiting outside."

"Fair enough."

The second I shut the door he turns up his music and hits the gas, the two of us rocketing forward and throwing up a massive plume of dust.

The vehicle rumbles around me, its mighty engine literally shaking my body as hammering, caustic noise fills my ears. We fly down the dirt road then swerve out onto a long asphalt lane, taking off with such speed that my head slams back against the headrest and remains held tight.

Everything about this moment is the polar opposite of the quiet and well-manicured existence I used to care about, the family traditions I used to honor, but somehow a thread among these experiences remains the same.

I can't understand a word this vocalist is screaming at me, but according to Saul we are listening to full-on, dyed-in-the-wool Christian music. It goes without saying that we're literally *on our way to church right now,* so I'm hardly in a secular situation.

I can't help the smile that creeps its way across my face, nor the laughter that spills from my throat. For the first time in a long while, I'm actually having fun.

I reach over and turn up the squealing, shrieking, slamming noise even louder, allowing this aural swell to envelop my body. Grinning wide, I try my best to nod along, but I can't make any sense of the frantic, blast-beat rhythms, which only makes me laugh even harder.

Eventually, Saul and I pull into a small parking lot surrounded by thick forest, a tiny blue lodge tucked away in one corner. We find a spot and park near the handful of other cars, my friend shutting off his vehicle and plunging us into silence.

This is a humble place of worship, the antithesis of any massive, modern Kingdom of the Pine facility. It's a communal building, likely rented out to any number of rural folks, from Boy Scouts to swap meets to the occasional wedding reception.

On Sundays, it's a church.

"You sure you're not coming in?" Saul asks.

I nod confidently. "I'm never going in again."

My friend hesitates, not wanting to press the issue but finally asking a gentle follow-up. "Why'd you come on the drive then?" he questions. "Why not stay home if God's not calling to you?"

I could tell him a number of moving stories about praying with my dad before any big life event, but I spare him the details. This isn't about recreating what my father did in the past, it's about exploring what *I* do in the future.

"Tonight's important," I say. "I just wanted to be around other people. Isn't that the whole point?"

Saul doesn't confirm or deny my assertion, just listens.

"Obviously, there's more than one way to be religious, you're proof of that," I continue, "but then I can't help wondering, why bring God into this at all? Is your heavy metal really better with Jesus in the liner notes?"

"That was grindcore," Saul corrects me.

"Fine," I retort. I gaze out the window for a moment, watching believers filter in. They're greeted at the door by a smiling priest who shakes everyone's hands.

"There are things I miss about my old life, like community and family and just ... going to church on a day like today. You've shown me how someone could find love in that book on their own terms, but too many people around here have used it for hate."

Saul hesitates. "You wanna know what makes Kingdom of the Pine so scary?"

I don't attempt an answer.

"They may be ruthless and single-minded, but they're not doing this out of hate," Saul continues. "At least, they don't think they are. They're doing it out of a sick, ass-backward love."

"Either way, I don't wanna be a part of it," I proclaim.

Saul just nods, smiling to himself. "I'm just not okay with letting them define God's love. This is *my* little way of doing something about it."

We sit in silence for a moment, letting the words sink in. I'm beginning to realize my opinion about all this is much firmer than I thought, and Saul's is, too. This is something we'll never quite see eye to eye on, but despite all that, I'm so damn thankful to be sitting here with him.

The patrons finish trickling inside, the last of them finding their seats as the service begins. The priest takes one last look around before shutting the propped-open door.

"You should get in there," I suggest. "Don't worry about me. I'll be waiting."

Saul shakes his head. "Today, I'll sit out here with you," he replies, rolling down the windows.

"It's a big night," I protest. "If you wanna pray, go pray."

"*This* is my service," he retorts, dropping his seat back and relaxing as faint hymns begin to drift across this parking lot toward us. The choir within is sparse and modest, a vastly different tone compared to Kingdom of the Pine gatherings.

I gradually realize Saul's words could have two distinct meanings. Either he's fine with enjoying tonight's church service from a distance, or he understands I need company and his presence is a duty of friendship.

Either way, I'm thankful Saul's here with me.

We sit like this the entire time, listening to the wind in the trees and smelling the fresh Douglas fir as it wafts across our nostrils. The sermon inside is faint and muffled, unintelligible unless the whole congregation sings together, but that doesn't seem to matter much. I find myself shocked at how pleasant the whole experience is, the seething anger I've had toward Kingdom of the Pine briefly checking out.

Eventually, our service ends and Saul starts the car with a roar. We pull back onto the road, heading home through the shadowy forest as the sun makes its move from afternoon to evening.

I've courageously stared down Pachid before, but what we're about to do is a frightening leap beyond. I have no idea how this demon is going to react to the scenario we have in store, but I can only imagine she's not gonna be happy about it.

I reach over with one hand and hold my previously broken finger, remembering the last time I dared defy her. The fracture was a warning, and her next one will likely be less generous.

Fortunately, as we fly down the road I'm strangely energized. It's a familiar sensation, but one I didn't expect to revisit anytime soon. This is the way I used to feel right after church service, bounding out the door with a fire in my belly and feeling ready to take on the world.

It's an unmistakable mindset, but this time there was no real performance to accompany it, no submission to a higher power or prayer for forgiveness.

I just took a moment to rest and be thankful, and now I'm ready for anything with the power of a thousand suns behind me. The complicated, magical, deeply focused power of Rose Darling.

I'm ready to exorcise my demons.

9

HELL FREEZES OVER

"You look nervous," Saul says through a single wireless headphone in my right ear. "Don't worry. It's just a demon from the depths of hell here to keep you from being *too gay*."

I can't help laughing. "Well, when you put it like that, I suppose I could loosen up a bit."

I glance at the camera above me, peering down from one of the metal structures within Saul's enormous garage.

"I'm more worried about being posted in the middle of all these gasoline barrels," I continue. "Please don't pull the trigger early."

"I won't pull the trigger early," Saul assures me. "I also won't pull it too late, but just in case, you've got eyes on the RID?"

I glance over my shoulder at his homemade weapon, an ominous tank and nozzle that hangs quietly in the darkness. It's a little over-the-top, but Saul's engineering brain couldn't help itself upon learning the mortal weakness of our enemy.

Ranged Incendiary Device. Also known as a flamethrower.

"I can't believe you expect me to use that thing," I reply. "I admire your skills, but it looks like it'd just blow my hands off."

"Well, it's a last resort," my friend continues through my earbud, the faintest hint of defensiveness in his voice.

"How's everything looking up there?" I ask, hoping to catch a glimpse of Saul's crow's nest perched high atop one of these enormous metal shelves.

"Just wonderful," he confirms. "Cameras are rolling, the trigger is ready . . . now it's your call."

I take a deep breath and sit up in my chair, mentally preparing for what's about to unfold.

The newfound confidence I've gained has carried me far, but as Saul waits for my signal I find the wave of conviction finally breaking within me. Discovering my voice in the face of a toxic family life and an oppressive faith is one thing, but the worst they could've done was excommunicate me from a community I was already at odds with.

It's a painful, difficult journey, but the methods of Pachid are significantly more visceral.

A vision of Martina's broken body spilling from the closet fills my mind, her twisted head staring up at me with huge, bulging eyes.

My whole life I've heard stories about doing battle with demonic forces, but those dark energies were abstract and metaphorical, not a literal encounter with some undiscovered species.

"You sure you're up for this?" Saul asks, his voice filled with concern.

Correlation is not causation, and I know this. Just because flames trapped a demon within my vehicle, it doesn't mean this technique will work a second time. Our current data set is a single point in the middle of endless nothing.

Still, what other options do we have? We could test our theory and summon Pachid in a low-stakes situation, poking and prodding her with hot objects then cataloging her reaction, but would that really be any safer?

Or would that just give the creature time to adapt and plan?

I'd typically find confidence in prayer at a moment like this. Now, however, I find confidence in myself; mining strength from the simple fact that pushing onward is the only option we've got.

Rose 7:8. And upon the wicked she shall rain a mighty tempest of fire, smiting those who dared steal away her thoughts, but forgot to quell her vengeance.

"I'm ready," I finally announce.

"You're up, Darling," Saul affirms.

Huge metal shelving units loom on either side of me, big enough to hold car parts or even whole vehicles, but rigged with enormous, heat-conducting copper sheets. The rectangles are hanging high above each one of the four hallways that extend into various corners of the hangar.

It's a cartoonishly basic trap constructed at an extra-large scale, but as I gaze off into space these technicalities fall away. My eyes are wide open, but what I'm witnessing has nothing to do with the physical realm.

I'm gazing into the past.

Slowly, Willow's face appears through the haze. Typically, I'll get a flash of her smiling and laughing before I push these thoughts away, but this time her expression is something different. She's upset with me, disappointed after a misunderstanding.

It's not a big fight, just a little disagreement about some trivial thing, but the emotions it floods me with are breathtakingly potent.

As a potential reunion with Willow draws closer, my memories of our past life are starting to change. These dreams used to be marked with nothing but smiles and laughter, sunny days at the park or cozy nights indoors. It was perfect, but real relationships are never *perfect.*

In these visions, my bedroom still has a door. I hold my breath as I open it, slipping out with the care of a life-or-death prison break.

I can't believe I actually snuck out of the house.

I see a car parked down the street, Willow waiting for me to crawl out under the cracked garage door and sprint toward her through the darkness. We drive through the night and laugh and cry and buy terrible fast food, and Willow sings along because she knows all the words to these songs I've never heard. Sometimes she raps, and her lips are moving so fast I'm reminded of Baptists speaking in tongues. I tell her this, and she seems both confused and deeply moved by the compliment.

Other times, we sit at some late-night diner stuffed full of grizzled truckers and good ol' boys, but for some reason I'm not frightened by this scene. With Willow, it all feels like an adventure.

I see us sitting at a park in the light of day—the same place we accidently crossed paths in that chaotic reunion—and it suddenly dawns on me that this location was never quite erased from my mind. Willow and I were drawn here, unable to shake the habit of our meeting spot on the edge of town.

We lay out on a blanket and read, not saying a word to each other as we bask in the mere presence of someone we truly, unflinchingly trust. I remember deep conversations on this blanket about faith and love and the size of the universe.

"Are you with me?" she asks, calm and patient when I've started drifting away.

"No," I admit.

"Let me know when you are," she warmly offers.

Another time she's sobbing because a pet died—at least I think that's what happened—and when I try comforting her my words come out wrong and cold and strange.

She's upset at first, but we talk it through. I apologize, and she accepts.

Our relationship wasn't all sunshine and rainbows, but it was *real*. It was misunderstandings and growth and forgiveness and acceptance and, of course, the beauty that comes along with all that. We were so much more than a montage of upbeat music and endless smiles.

In those days, we weren't afraid to be ourselves, and that's something I'd never felt before.

A tear rolls down my cheek and I wipe it away.

"Yo!" Saul's voice suddenly erupts in my earbud. "There's a lot going on up here, Darling."

"Where is she?" I ask.

"I'm getting some weird signals on the monitors," Saul says. "The rip is forming down the hallway to your left."

I look to the aisle in question as the hangar lights begin to flicker sporadically. These intermittent flashes continue to build in severity as a wash of frigid air overwhelms me, chilling my body to the core.

"I see her!" Saul shouts. "Pachid's right in front of you!"

Gazing down the passage, I try my best to get a read on any shapes moving through the strobing corridor of scrap metal.

"I can't see anything," I report back. "How close?"

There's a loud clang as the lights shut off entirely, plunging us into darkness.

Every muscle of my body clenches tight.

"Sa-Saul?" I stammer into my earpiece. "You there?"

There's no response, just deafening silence as I sit here in the vast abyss. Outside the hangar there's still a bit of sun hanging in the evening air, but this large chamber leaves very few opportunities for light to creep inside. The only source is a few random slivers of illumination slipping through metal sheets.

The universe is almost entirely dark: made up of 95 percent dark energy and dark matter.

It suddenly occurs to me that I hold the keys to a simple, safe retreat, an easy way to make this whole ordeal come to a grinding halt and appease Pachid once again. All I have to do is stop thinking about Willow and let the past fade away, returning to my place as a "straight" Kingdom of the Pine congregant; at least for the moment.

It's an easy out, and clearly the safest choice, but what then?

I've been running long enough.

I stand and peer into the shadowy void, hoping to sense a change in the air, or catch the sound of approaching footsteps.

Instead, I'm met with utter silence.

An eruption of horrific screams suddenly fills my skull, and this time it's not Saul's music. A renegade signal has made its way into my earbud, prompting me to yank it out in shock.

These agonizing shrieks come and go in waves of static, oscillating in volume as I hold the device a few inches from my ear. It's a horrible noise, but through the chaos I begin to make out another signal, the familiar voice of Saul as he struggles to shout through the sonic wash. His shouting pierces the noise sporadically, a few desperate syllables at a time.

Even though I can't make out the words, the frantic emotions behind Saul's transmission are perfectly clear.

Without warning, the hangar lights flicker on in a handful of short bursts, flooding my vision like a camera flash. A figure is rushing toward me, the silhouette dark and strange against the brilliant illumination.

I cry out in shock, dropping the earbud as I stumble back and knock over my chair with a clatter. I turn and make a run for it, flooded with adrenaline as my mind snaps back into focus.

That was a rough start, but our plan is still active and the trap is ready to spring.

Fortunately, Saul designed the backup lever to be extra large and easy to find, even in complete darkness. I rush toward the switch and give it a hard yank, setting off a cascade of thunderous, split-second reactions.

Four bombastic slams erupt through the hangar, a square of copper panels falling into place. Heat washes across me as several torches ignite, blasting rolling flame across every wall of the superheated chamber that now rests over my former position. Above, a massive, flame-spewing device blasts down into the center of this area only slightly larger than a phone booth.

My eyes wide, I crawl backward through the dirt in an attempt to get away from the caustic heat and noise.

Then the screaming starts: the belligerent, unfiltered squeal of Pachid burning up.

I'm frozen in shock, staring at the billowing flames and glowing copper in awestruck wonder.

A frantic pounding begins to ring out through the hangar, starting fast and then slowly devolving into silence. The execution booth itself is loud as all heck, but this contraption can only run for so long.

Eventually, I pull the lever back into place, shutting off the gas and quelling the flames. The hangar lights flicker back on.

It feels as though Pachid's telltale chill has dissipated, but it's tough to be sure after getting so thoroughly roasted by the billowing flames. My skin is red and leathery from nothing more than a quick encounter with the chamber some ten feet away.

I take a moment to collect myself and get my bearings. "Saul?" I call out, raising my voice now that the earpiece is a mound of ash.

The single word echoes through the hangar with no response.

Too curious to wait for my friend's reply, I grab a dangling chain and start tugging. While copper is incredibly heavy (even heavier than steel, in fact), Saul and I devised a pully system that allows these four flat panels to be lifted with relative ease.

The metal sheet before me rises inch by inch, gradually revealing the charred body of a humanoid figure curled tightly in a wretched ball. The whole inner chamber is roasted to a crisp, even the dirt itself burnt and ashen.

I crank the panels higher until they lock into position, then step toward the carbonized remains.

"Hot damn," comes a voice to my left, prompting me to jump in surprise. I turn to find Saul standing in utter shock, his gaze transfixed by the warped figure.

The two of us creep forward until we're standing directly above Pachid's toasted corpse, the demon obliterated by flame. In this position her form appears eerily human, other than the bizarrely long digits that can be seen protruding from either hand. As far as her apparel, the only thing left is the iron collar around her neck and the metal name tag that was once pinned to the creature's red polo shirt. PACHID, it reads.

"You okay?" I ask my friend.

Saul doesn't answer for a long while.

I don't mind. While he's taking a moment to center himself, I appreciate something I haven't been able to enjoy in a very long time. I think about Willow, not in the usual fleeting moments or fragmented images that keep me safe and sound, but triumphantly diving into the deep end of my mind. I let the patchwork memories I've managed to gather overwhelm me, wrapping me in their warm embrace.

Before, this mental realm was prickly and frustrating. I wanted so badly to stay here, and I subconsciously yearned to bask in these thoughts while my consciousness screamed about danger lurking just around the corner. I was laying my mind on a glorious pillow while my body rested across a bed of nails.

But that fear no longer exists within me. I'm free.

"You ever wonder why they wear name tags?" Saul asks, interrupting my thoughts.

It's a simple query, but shocking in the fact that I hadn't considered it much until now. I'm aware of the demon's quirky attire, obviously, but the *implications* behind it had never really crossed my mind.

I don't know the answer, and I'm not sure Saul really expects one. He's grappling with the same thing I did after locking Willow's demon in my flaming car, coming to terms with the intrusion of something truly bizarre within our own concrete reality. It's one thing to believe in a collection of intangible supernatural forces floating through the ether, looming just behind the curtain of our world like ghosts, but these demons are *not* that.

These are mortal beings. While the things they wear and do may seem utterly bizarre, their oddities still weave together in a very real system of rules, regulations, and yes, name tags.

"I don't know," I finally reply. "Maybe they're at work."

After a long beat, Saul finally turns and begins to move back through the towering metal structures, making his way to the lookout while I follow behind. We move in silence, eventually arriving at a ladder that leads up to the platform above.

The two of us climb quietly and slowly, processing these events at our own pace.

Reaching the top, we find Saul's extra-large computer monitor and a humming processor tower next to it. He was perched up here for a clear sightline of the hangar down below, but in the sudden darkness this extra effort was nullified. Even his vast assortment of wireless cameras were less useful than we'd hoped.

"Everything crashed when the power surged," Saul informs me, unusually deadpan as he goes about his business.

He sits down in his chair and gets to work, sorting through a cascade of potentially corrupted files.

Video clips pop onto Saul's screen, half-finished recordings from various cameras placed around the hangar. I see one from the main entrance of the large metal building, and another directly trained on the trap. Yet another view is angled down a hallway between towering metal shelves.

Saul plays this clip and we watch closely, the lights flickering as a tear in reality begins to appear before our very eyes. Onscreen, the camera is trained directly upon the shimmering line of blue light that quivers in the air with strange, erratic motions.

This is the second time I've witnessed this phenomenon. The first was back at Camp Damascus, albeit through a haze of vague memories that wash in and out of my conscious mind.

The tear grows wider and wider until I can see right through it, a stone chamber lurking behind. Somehow, the extremely low temperature of this otherworldly location can be visually observed, a clear shift in the air before the mysterious opening. When Pachid steps through the slit, a faint icy mist billows from her nostrils and mouth.

Pachid exits the wormhole and stops abruptly, smiling as she gazes off into the empty space before her.

The video feed goes dead as the file corrupts.

"That's where we lost power," Saul explains.

He opens another recording and presses play. This view is positioned at a random corner of the hangar, far from the action.

"Some of the cameras were picking up intermittent signals," Saul continues. "You know how horror movies love to have TVs with random creepy imagery? That trope could've evolved from a very real phenomenon."

"I've never seen a terror film," I retort.

Saul frowns. "I guess you'll just have to trust me. I think demons innately amplify transmissions from . . . hell, I guess. These aren't just *random* images, they're intercepted audio and video feeds."

I watch as static begins to overtake Saul's recording, two sources transposed over each other amid the visual snow. Eventually, the feed finds clarity in a location that's distinctly familiar.

My breath catches in my throat as I'm transported back to Isaiah's birthday party, instantly recalling the grotesque imagery that appeared on television while we were playing truth or dare. The recording I now watch is nearly identical, featuring the same shaky handheld camera and blunt lighting.

This video feed offers no sound as it creeps through the darkness of another world, slowly making its way over frigid stone walls in a seemingly endless labyrinth of chambers.

Saul and I are entranced by the transmission, our eyes glued to the recording as our hearts pound away within our chests.

The camera view tightens in on one of the walls, very slowly rolling across the topography of the rough surface. Up close, frost is clearly visible in the space between faded stones.

Eventually, tiny pink roots come into view, hanging across the cold surface and covered with a glistening wet sheen that reflects the light of the camera. As the view moves from root to root, the network rapidly becomes more complex, a cascading pattern of tendrils laid out next to one another and growing in thickness as they drift upward to a central point.

I start drumming my fingers against my leg in a familiar repeating pattern, instinctively struggling to release some of the pressure within as the camera continues onward. Something horrible is coming. My reptilian brain knows this, but I'm too curious to look away.

Movement sweeps across the roots, the quick, repetitive motion of some strictly timed machine. It moves past the camera once, twice, three times, every stroke scheduled to perfection. Meanwhile, the transmission reveals these tangled pink tendrils are pinned to the wall in certain places, a handful connected to plastic tubes of some unknown liquid.

Higher the recording drifts, until finally something familiar and human emerges into view at the top of the screen. It's blurry and over-lit, but I immediately recognize this pale form as a severed human neck, the bloody carnage exposed while various black tubes push deep within. The roots extending downward are not roots at all, only the stripped-bare web of a fully revealed nervous system with no flesh or bones to protect it.

A startled gasp escapes my throat as the camera pulls back to reveal a writhing, squealing head. The eyes have been removed from their sockets and the mouth is sewn shut, but the subject is very much alive as a macabre contraption pulses back and forth across their exposed nerves. Who knows how long they've been hanging here.

The file suddenly glitches and freezes up, our recording interrupted by the power surge.

I stagger back, feeling the powerful urge to vomit as a wave of disgust and nausea washes over me.

"What the . . . *heck* are they doing to these people?" I sputter.

"It's hell," Saul offers flatly, staring at the frozen screen. He doesn't need to elaborate any more than that.

*   *   *

I emerge from the hangar to find myself surrounded by the glorious Montana evening. A breathtaking sunset is already well into its nightly bloom, oranges giving way to deep indigos as the gloaming arrives. The vastness of this world is overwhelming, especially now that I have the freedom to explore it.

It's a picturesque sight, almost enough to scrub the horrific visions of a literal hell from my mind.

Not quite, though.

I don't look back as I make my way past abandoned vehicles and pristine, refurbished luxury cars, eventually arriving at the front door of Saul's old farmhouse. He stayed in the garage to continue fine-tuning our gear.

The farmhouse door is freshly painted in a light, cheerful yellow, the first of many upgrades I've started making around here. Fixing the broken dining room window was another.

I know what it's like to get lost in your own focus, so I don't blame Saul for the way he's let this place fall apart. Fortunately, there are two of us living here now.

The second the cozy indoor air hits me I feel a potent surge of relief.

I make my way over to the living room couch and collapse into it, immediately erupting in a fit of tears as I hold the pillow against my face and allow myself a moment to *feel.*

Once more, I bask in the memories of Willow in all her glory. We're dancing in an apartment—her apartment—headphones on as she giggles at my awkward moves. She puts an arm around me to show me how it's done, and in this gesture our eyes lock. We stare at each other, our loving gazes somehow permeating time and space as I watch from my cage of the present.

I've been here before, but it's never been safe enough to let the mental tape play this far.

Our bodies have stopped swaying to the music as our lips curl up in slight, knowing smiles. A bizarre, beautiful standoff is humming with youthful energy between us, every micro-expression tempting the next.

I remember wanting to lean in so badly, but that craving was flanked by a sickening dread of what might happen if I did. Maybe I'd been reading this escalation all wrong, taking a close friendship and blowing it out of proportion in a deeply inappropriate way.

But even then I knew this wasn't true. I was just making excuses at the edge of a high dive, terrified to jump.

She's worth the leap, though.

I lean in and kiss Willow, sparks momentarily erupting across the cosmic space between now and then. Somehow I can *feel* her, the ghost of these memories still hiding within the cells of my body.

I hold this moment for as long as I possibly can, basking in an overwhelming sense of grand *belonging* that permeates everything. I can't remember the last time I felt this safe, accepted by Willow without a shred of pretense.

Eventually, however, my recollection starts to fade. Our lips part as Willow drifts away, dissolving into the abyss from which she came.

The tears stop flowing and my body's natural oxytocin gets to work, endorphins spilling across me from the magical depths of my brain. My heart slows to a reasonable pace and my breathing calms.

I'm just about to fall asleep right there on the couch when, suddenly, a blast of thundering sound prompts me to sit up in alarm.

I'm used to Saul playing his music in the hangar, and by now I've memorized most of these wild deathcore thrashers by heart. This, however, is something completely different.

I narrow my eyes and stand up, listening to the thumping beat that rattles through the entire farmhouse. It's shockingly rhythmic and danceable, an upbeat, major-scale bassline weaving its way through the pattern.

This is pop music.

I approach the living room window, gazing out across the fleet of vehicles in the yard. Beyond them lies a small patch where the grass is slightly more maintained than the surrounding wilds. It's just outside the hangar entrance.

By now the sky has darkened enough that I can barely make out the silhouette of Saul as he stands in the middle of this natural stage, completely motionless and staring off into space. He's got something strapped to his back and holds what appears to be a small tool in his hand.

The music continues at full volume, rumbling across the dark forest around us with bubblegum tones. I was never allowed to listen to secular music at home, but I recognize this song as something I heard friends listen to on rare occasions.

It's one of those tunes that seeped its way into the popular consciousness, unavoidable to even the congregation's most overprotected children.

A boy band sings this one.

Johnny or Donnie or Joey or Justin or Nick or AJ or Howie, their names rolling through my mind like secular apostles.

Saul remains motionless for a while, listening to the thunderous pop jam as the darkness blooms around him. The stars are making their grand entrance, just barely twinkling across a glorious cosmic cascade.

But he's not alone.

A second figure appears in the tall grass, stepping out and revealing their awkward, gangly shape. This is the tallest demon I've seen, a rail-thin humanoid with pale skin and long black hair. They're sporting the same red polo as the others, and based on the proportions of their lanky frame I can only imagine how difficult sizing must've been.

My first instinct is to run out and help Saul, to make sure he has all the support he needs while literally facing down his demons, but I don't move an inch. As crazy as it sounds, giving Saul this space is the most supportive thing I can do, consequences be damned.

If it were up to me, every one of these creatures would be dealt with in a safe, organized system, coaxed into our new machine one by one and dispatched with precision and efficiency. Saul and I are not the same person, however, and his personal journey is not for me to insert myself.

Instead, I watch with rapt attention as these two figures face off, Saul coming to terms with his past as slamming pop music paints the scene with unexpected vibrancy.

Saul is yelling something at the demon now, his face overflowing with emotion as he says his piece.

The particularly tall creature tilts its head to the side, taking Saul in for a moment, then abruptly springs into action. The demon makes its move, striding toward my friend with a sudden conviction that causes my breath to catch.

Saul, however, is ready.

My friend lifts the tool in his hands to reveal its true nature in spectacular fashion, a brilliant orange burst of superheated flame erupting from his grip and engulfing the monster. My eyes go wide as I instinctively pull back from the window, washed in the reflection of this fiery display. The makeshift device, cobbled together from a fuel tank, a large spray nozzle, and an igniter, was a last resort if things went sideways with the trap.

To be honest, I hadn't really expected the flamethrower to work at all.

The wave of tremendous heat strikes the demon and it crumples to its knees, succumbing to the unrelenting roil that spills across its roasting form. It lets out a frantic shriek, struggling to flee but unable to find its bearings as Saul pushes forward. I can tell the warmth is difficult for Saul to take, even from his side of the device, but his conviction doesn't waver.

He continues screaming at the demon, his exact words lost in a haze of slamming pop music and rumbling flames, but his intent is coming across just fine.

The demon is crawling away now, dragging itself hand over hand before collapsing, a charred crisp in a metal collar.

Finally, the flames relent.

Saul pulls out his phone and turns off the music. He stands quietly for a moment, then turns to the window, locking eyes with me.

Saul hoists up the homemade flamethrower confidently.

"It works!" my friend calls out.

10

LADY OF
THE FLIES

I stare at the rectangular notecard in my hand, this blank space just as vacant as my expression. I've been sitting out here on the hood of what I now know is a 1966 Ford Falcon, my legs crossed as I perch quietly upon its rusted metal skeleton.

It's been long enough—and I've been quiet enough—that the prairie dogs have returned from their initial scare, no longer afraid of my presence. One of the creatures pops up from a hole no more than ten feet away, staring right at me in a way that becomes impossibly distracting.

"Hey!" I finally shout, dropping my pen and the empty notecard. "I'm working!"

The prairie dog is unfazed, frozen in place.

This standoff goes on for quite a while, until my opponent abruptly retreats. It's not my dominance that triggers this move, however, but the arrival of Saul, who's now strolling down the driveway toward us.

Saul's tiny earbuds are so loud I can hear him coming. The chaotic sound of tinny blast beats echoes across his property, disrupting the still of the morning as he returns from his routine dawn walk. My friend shuts off his music and pulls out the buds, tucking them away in the pocket of his hoodie.

A few of the prairie dogs still remain, but Saul makes quick work of that. "Yo!" he shouts, immediately causing the stragglers to scatter. He lets out a frustrated sigh, shaking his head. "The animals are taking over. I knocked down some cocoon in the back of the garage, and it was like *this* big." Saul holds up his hands, positioning them approximately one foot apart.

I'm trying to be a good friend and react accordingly, but my thoughts are elsewhere.

"You alright?" he asks. "You were in the same spot when I left."

I glance down at the blank notecard in my hand, then back up at Saul.

His expression is one of deep recognition. "Tonight's a big night," my friend acknowledges.

I nod, crinkling up my nose a bit. "I usually write out talking points for social events, but I don't know where to start," I explain.

Saul's initial reaction of shock is quick and instinctual, but he catches himself, immediately shifting into bemused acceptance. "Okay, sure," he offers. "No luck?"

I shake my head.

I shouldn't be too hard on myself, really. After a brief email to Willow in which I assured her it was now safe to meet, she agreed on a time and a place—this evening, at a bookstore one town over. Looks like I've set into motion what could be the most important conversation of my life.

No pressure.

"I usually come up with three talking points, maybe five. Just facts I can discuss or questions I can ask," I explain. "This meeting is pretty specific, though. First, I'll probably tell her about the demon's weakness against fire, which I can then connect to a greater historical conspiracy from the Christian church. Did you know there's a painting from 1495 called *The Holy Family with the Mayfly?* Albrecht Dürur is the painter, and it—"

"Wait, wait, wait," Saul interjects, raising his hand to cut me off. "I can see why you're having a hard time. Can I give you some advice?"

I nod.

"You're coming at this from the wrong angle, Darling."

I take a beat. He's right, but I'm not sure what to do about it. "Help me," I implore.

Saul laughs. "When's the last time you saw Willow?"

"A few months ago. The night of my wreck," I reply. "It wasn't great."

He nods. "Let's treat this more like a date and less like you're teaching a history class."

"So ... nix the questions?" I translate, preparing to lose the notecard.

Saul immediately shakes his head. "The card is your thing, Darling. Never be ashamed of the card. Let's just brainstorm some *date* topics."

My friend takes a seat on the hood next to me and starts mulling over options.

*　　　　　　　*　　　　　　　*

I'd imagined what this moment would feel like, predicted all the ways it would change me, but now that I'm actually here I'm mostly shocked by the emotional dullness.

I yearn to be fully open, but deep down I'm too frightened to expose my heart like that—terrified I've come all this way to learn it was a fool's errand.

Maybe memories are all I'll ever have.

I'm standing outside a bookstore, checking in with myself before making the leap and heading through the door, but now that I'm here the nervous tension I'd expected is nowhere to be found.

I'm numb.

Standing out here by some shop I don't remember patronizing, in a small town I don't remember visiting, I might as well be one of the demons. Phasing through the world. Barely here.

But everything changes when I push through the door.

I'm immediately greeted by a wave of emotional warmth and the scent of old books, an innate sense of relief wrapping its arms around me. The emotions come on so swiftly that it's arresting, stopping me in my tracks as I stand in the doorway and take in my surroundings.

The shop is large for Lebka Rock, this neighboring hamlet just outside the county line, and I'm impressed by the stacks and stacks of books that stretch deeper into the belly of the building. We're on the bottom floor of some historical structure, likely the tallest establishment in this whole town with a whopping two stories.

An older man behind the counter looks up and smiles.

"Oh, hey" is all he says.

"Hi," I reply. "Where's your science and nature section?"

The man behind the counter gives me a confused look, then shrugs and cocks his head to the left.

I follow his gesture, creeping deeper into the stacks. Though it's nothing short of a paperback labyrinth, it's amazing how cozy this place feels. I could easily get lost in here, but I'm not entirely sure I'd mind. The only pang of unease I feel is when I creep past the religious studies section, a floor-to-ceiling bookshelf with various offerings from Pete Bend. Several fresh copies of *Craftsman Soul* are stacked high and ready for the taking, while new and used selections from his back catalog cover the rest. I note the title of a particularly thick tome, a two-word reminder of the Camp Damascus catchphrase: *Love Right.*

Eventually, my journey into this glorious maze comes to an end.

I stumble upon a small corner nook, the kind of place where you might pull down a novel to check out the first few pages, then look up to realize an hour's gone by. There are two chairs tucked away back here, and in one of them a familiar vision is waiting.

Willow Crogall is sitting quietly, a beguiling young woman with chin-length raven hair and dark eyes. She's wearing a black jean jacket, tightly fitted over a charcoal tee.

Our gazes meet and, unlike last time, neither one of us turns away. We don't feel conflicted about our paths crossing, or sense nauseated fear at the pit of our stomachs over what might happen next. Willow, to her credit, is a big part of this greatly altered reaction. She could've easily ignored my email.

This meeting is not a decision to be taken lightly, more than just a rekindled romance. For Willow and me this situation was life or death, right up until the very moment my tethered creature collapsed to the dirt in a scorched heap. For all Willow knows, I'm just pretending our problems have been solved, meeting up with a long-lost love despite the demon that still clings to my back.

But that's not the case, and I'm thankful Willow has given me a chance to prove it.

Still, she's apprehensive. I want to erupt in a moment of catharsis, wrapping my arms around her in a warm hug, but despite this strangely familiar location and her willingness to meet up, the tension remains.

"You really killed him?" Willow immediately asks. "My demon?"

"He's gone," I reply.

"You're *sure*?" Willow's lip trembles slightly.

"He's . . . pretty dead," I say, recalling the billowing flames and the creature in the back of my car, thrashing about as he cooked alive.

"And yours?"

I nod. "Also dead."

She hesitates, just as nervous as I was when I realized our shackles might finally be broken. Willow looks away for a moment.

"You haven't seen him for a while, have you?" I continue, already knowing the answer.

Willow shakes her head, finally turning her gaze back to mine. Tears are welling up in her eyes, the emotions within struggling to rip forth as she valiantly holds them at bay.

"Do you know where we are?" she asks.

The question is surprising, taking me slightly off guard.

"I . . . don't know," I reply. "Lebka Books?"

Her eyes stay fixed on mine.

"Do you know where we are?" Willow repeats, only this time there's a strange desperation in her tone. She's *begging* me to answer, pleading for me to get this right.

I give it a moment, allow the space to permeate me. I take note of the worn wooden shelves, the soft acoustic guitar ballad ringing out from a radio at the front counter. I close my eyes, wondering what it is about this place that resonates so deep, then suddenly pop them open.

"This is where we met," I reply with startling confidence.

Willow finally breaks, launching from her chair and marching toward me. She wraps her arms around my body, pulling me close and embracing me in a way that is strangely heartbreaking—a bittersweet juxtaposition of how good it feels and how long it's been. We stay like this for an exceptionally long time, rocking from side to side in the hidden bookstore nook as we simply exist in each other's presence.

In all my memories and all my dreams, it was never this good.

Eventually, the two of us pull away from each other, staring eye to eye as we consider what happens next. I feel a deep and powerful compulsion to kiss her, and I can tell she feels the same, but for some reason we hesitate.

We've got some catching up to do, and although we have quite a history together, there are still plenty of things to relearn before diving back in.

Instead of kissing, we untangle and drop into the chairs.

Willow's camera is sitting between us on a small table, held tight in a sharp leather case. She extracts it, lifts it up and snaps a picture of me, then puts the device away.

"I've been taking a lot of photos," she explains. "When you lose your memory for long enough, you start to think about capturing the little moments more often. It makes me feel better knowing the things I shoot won't disappear."

"Not this time," I confirm.

It takes a moment, but eventually the incredible weight of the statement washes over me. We sit in silence a moment longer, taking it all in.

"Did you write notes for this?" Willow suddenly asks, a knowing grin creeping its way across her face.

"You know about that?" I blurt, fighting back a deep surge of embarrassment.

"I know all kinds of things about you," Willow replies, laughing, then suddenly realizing how uneasy this moment has made me. "It's okay. We've brainstormed topics together."

This does, in fact, make me feel better.

"Can I see?" Willow implores.

"The notecard?"

Willow nods.

I pull a folded-up card from my pocket and hand it over, watching as she opens it and reads quietly to herself. I watch her expression shift from amusement to adoration to deep introspection.

"It's dumb," I say.

Willow shakes her head, then hands the notecard back.

"My name's Willow Crogall," she starts. "Legally speaking, it's Magdalene Crogall, but let's keep that between us. The first time I told you this, you never mentioned it again, so I trust you. I'm twenty-one years old. I'm a Gemini, which doesn't matter because I don't believe in astrology. My favorite dessert is cinnamon rolls, and my favorite movie is *The Thing*. You've never seen it, but one time you sat through it with your headphones on and an open book in your lap, because you knew it meant a lot to me. You looked up once during the dog transformation scene and never looked up again. One time, on a mission trip to Las Vegas, I snuck into the Great Britannica Casino and a drunk guy gave me a $100 chip, but I was too scared to collect the cash so now I keep it in my bedside table. I've been living on my own since a fight with my parents three years ago."

I'm listening intently, legitimately thankful for this rapid-fire format.

"My folks were still supporting me while I did online courses, until they found out about us and cut me off," Willow continues. "They wouldn't help with rent unless I spent some time at Camp Damascus. That was the deal." She hesitates a moment, wrestling with some deep internal wound.

Willow's lip trembles slightly as emotions well up, then subside.

"I didn't take it seriously," she reveals, her monologue drifting to a stop.

I fold up the notecard and slip it back into my pocket. "I . . . don't remember any of that," I admit. "I remember other things, though."

Willow smiles. "Maybe we can fill in the blanks together."

She reaches out and places her hand over mine.

"Let's leave," Willow blurts. "If we're together, what the hell does it matter? We won. You killed two fucking *demons*. How badass is that? The story is over and there's a happy ending!"

I take a deep breath, mulling over her suggestion in my mind. It's a wonderful thought, a dream scenario ripe for the taking. I want so badly to just reach out and grab it, to accept Willow's offer and hit the road, never looking back and forgetting these horrible people ever existed. By now I'm no stranger to temptation, and this is my most potent temptation yet.

But I just can't do it.

"That sounds really nice," I gush, "but there's something I've gotta do."

Willow's expression drops. "Oh god," she sighs. "After all this time, you're so different but you're so . . . *you*."

"There are people at that camp who need our help," I reply. "This season, and the next season, and the next season. We can't just let it keep happening."

"We literally can," Willow retorts.

"It's dangerous, and it's stupid. You don't have to help me, and I wouldn't expect it. All I'm asking is that you wait for me to finish what I started."

"I've been waiting a pretty long fucking time," Willow replies, getting emotional again.

"I know," I admit. "I can't believe I'm saying this, because I've been waiting, too, but we have to help those kids."

Willow is silent, listening.

"I spent a lot of time doing work for Kingdom of the Pine," I explain. "I ran donation projects and brought in money for the church. I thought I was helping people, and in some ways I probably was, but I was also funding some pretty horrific stuff. Namely *demonic conversion therapy.*"

"You had no way of knowing," Willow replies sympathetically.

"Actually, I *did* have a way of knowing," I continue. "I should've been paying more attention, but that's not the point. The point is, I was doing all these things because God said it was right. My whole life, that was *always* the motivation, but is that *real* genuine good? Is something righteous if you're doing it because you're worried about getting punished if you decline?"

Willow is nodding along. She knows where I'm going with this, and it's clearly something she's thought about, too.

"I wanna do something *good*," I continue. "Not out of fear of punishment, or because someone else told me it was the right thing. I wanna do something good for goodness' sake. I *know* I don't have to help those kids; I've got no obligation and it would be a hell of a lot easier to just skip town with you. The fact that I don't *have* to do any of this is exactly why I'm going back to that camp."

Based on the way she shut down our previous meeting, I get the feeling Willow knows exactly what I'm talking about. She's been running from her *own* truth for a long time, and while that's easy enough with a demon on your heels, the moment you get to slow down is a double-edged sword.

It's also the moment you've gotta confront what you've left behind.

"I'll help," she finally replies.

"Wait, what?"

Willow nods, then says it again with a little more confidence, as though she's still convincing herself. "I'll help," she affirms, nodding along. "What's the plan?"

I hesitate, slightly embarrassed by the brutal simplicity of it all. "We're gonna break in and smash that machine," I finally declare. "They can't tether any demons if there's no way to summon them in the first place."

"Where's the machine?" she asks.

"I'm not entirely sure," I reply, "but I know how to find out."

✳   ✳   ✳

Willow's choice to leave her apartment and join Saul and me at the farmhouse is an easy one. She's aimless out here, and while this little studio brings back a surge of wonderful memories for me, I can tell it has gradually evolved into a place of great pain for her, a wound she's yet to let heal.

Her place is located directly above Lebka Books, a store she claims brings people from miles around, thanks to their unique finds and impressive selection of used paperbacks.

Willow opens the door of her apartment and pushes inside, immediately getting to work as she stuffs things into a large duffel bag. I follow behind to discover another familiar location in need of filling in, the abstract world of my memories suddenly faced with the intricate detail of reality.

I've laughed and cried here, even tried to dance, but as I stroll to the middle of this small rectangular room I finally get to *exist*.

As Willow maneuvers around me, gathering various all-black pieces of clothing and cramming them into her bag, I allow my eyes to drift across every square inch of this space.

Her bed is stuffed into one corner, well-made but so overwhelmed with massive, cozy blankets that it will always appear slightly disheveled. The wall next to it is absolutely covered in photographs, the images ranging in size from tiny, white-rimmed Polaroids to a few enormous posters. The subjects vary, featuring glorious Big Sky landscapes or discarded cigarette butts, but the grainy style remains consistent.

"You took all of these," I announce, framing the question as an awkward statement.

"Yep," Willow replies from across the room, still going about her business. "That's a little different from the last time you were here."

My gaze drifts to the other side of the room, a wall that immediately causes an innate pang of discomfort to wash through my frame. A large, extra-wide bookshelf runs from floor to ceiling, taking up most of the space save for a small portion of the wall that remains exposed. This exposed wall is where a framed poster is hung, featuring an eerie yellow symbol that I've never seen before.

The shelves are covered in strange paraphernalia. A skeletal rat sits under glass next to an assortment of pinned beetles. Jars and bottles are lined up next to this, organized and filled with crafty ingredients, and a collection of black books line the shelf under that. A turtle shell and a taxidermied bat call the next row home.

Everything about this display screams *occult*, a subject I certainly don't care much about these days, but it still rings some malignant Christian alarm deep within me.

Be cool.

"Pagan stuff," I offer, mustering up the most casual and convincing nod I can. "Awesome."

Willow stops packing, glancing over at me in confusion. "What?"

I nod at the shelf. "You're into witchcraft."

Willow cocks her head to the side.

"You don't remember dating a witch?" she asks.

She holds this expression as long as she possibly can, until she finally can't hold back any longer and erupts in a fit of laughter.

"I'm just fucking with you. I like nature," she replies, "but I don't *believe* in . . . well, anything."

"Oh," I falter. "Okay."

"Plus, that stuff looks pretty cool," she continues.

My eyes drift over to the poster. "What about that symbol?"

Willow raises her eyebrows.

"That?" she asks, grabbing a remote off the counter and pointing it at her nearby stereo. "That's Wu-Tang Clan."

Willow presses play and a beat drops, the rhythmic sound vibrating through her apartment. I'm immediately transported to that night with the headphones, recalling the way we danced together despite the fact that I had no idea what I was doing.

The song cascades across my ears, heavy and raw and beautiful. A rapper confidently brags over this staccato piano line, making his case with intoxicating bravado.

"Are your neighbors gonna get upset?" I ask.

She smiles. "I'm moving out. I don't give a fuck!"

I begin to nod along with the music, well aware of how awkward I look but not really caring.

"If I can dance to it, then I like it," Willow continues, getting back to work as she pulls a few books from the shelf and tosses them into her duffel.

"Then you will *not* like Saul's music," I reply.

I watch as Willow finishes up her packing, the past and present meeting at a beautiful crossroads in my mind. The last time I remember being in this room we were quiet and scared, hidden away with two sets of headphones in the dead of night.

But Willow's not afraid to announce her presence anymore, and neither am I.

✳   ✳   ✳

Short of another break-in, finding more information about the inner workings of Camp Damascus is nearly impossible. We briefly consider another journey into the depths of a church outreach center, hoping to stumble upon some records or blueprints, but eventually decide the element of surprise should remain in our favor. They don't know we're planning something, and at the moment that's a massive asset.

It's all or nothing. If we're going in, then we better be taking care of that machine. Multiple trips just aren't worth the risk.

Even sniffing around Neverton City Hall for old construction documents proves a bridge too far, Kingdom of the Pine's tendrils creeping into every corner of this small town. We've been excommunicated, three young heathens who've swiftly gone from vital community members to a rot at the core of the apple.

Time also appears to be a finite resource, and I can feel the grip of the congregation closing in. Someone from the church stopped by Saul's property yesterday, handing out home-printed Missing Person fliers with the face of yours truly plastered across the front.

Saul was deeply bothered by this, and when the canvasser left he spent a good three hours making sure my old car was not just tucked away, but fully dismantled. For the first time, he seemed viscerally upset about giving me a place to stay, liked he'd bitten off more than he could chew.

We all knew how terrifying Kingdom of the Pine could be, but Saul was especially worried. When I tried consoling him, his answers were short and sharp, and he declined to discuss because "you wouldn't get it."

I've been told that a lot, so it cut deep, but for whatever reason I felt like he might be right this time.

This morning Saul built a gate at the bottom of the drive.

Fortunately, despite all the roadblocks between us and a technical, physical layout of Camp Damascus, their penchant for advertising has become their undoing. Everyone living in the greater Neverton area has seen the commercials, years and years of video documentation that shows off the grounds in stunning detail. I've seen plenty of them myself, but I've never actually studied the footage long enough to link the visual fragments in my mind.

As our memories gradually return, the information within these ads might just manifest a coherent map of the place.

The problem is, Camp Damascus isn't exactly advertising their dungeon. No matter how well we recollect the campground layout, it's what's likely *under* the dirt that matters.

With this in mind, I've extracted myself from the video analysis completely. While Saul and Willow download old commercials and gradually sketch a scale map, I'm trying my best to keep my brain fresh from any outside influence.

The possession room's location lurks somewhere deep within me, and the best way to dig it out is likely the same method that revealed its existence in the first place. As demonstrated in the back of a speeding ambulance, epinephrine seems to unearth significant caches of my buried thoughts.

Of course, that was a very specific circumstance. Injecting a pen full of adrenaline into my heart right here on the floor of Saul's living room is probably not going to yield the results I want. Still, there are other drugs that have shown promise in pulling back the hazy veil of long-term memory loss.

"This is my parents' worst nightmare," I announce, gazing at the living room ceiling with a pillow behind my head. "Their gay daughter and her lesbian girlfriend in a spooky old farmhouse doing drugs with a metalhead."

The analytical part of me worries these trips into my subconscious mind could be more imagination than recollection, and that's a legitimate risk. Our options, however, are limited, and we're taking the precaution of keeping me far, far away from any Camp Damascus commercials. If I return from my trip down memory lane with a description that matches Saul and Willow's research, we're likely on to something.

This plan is not foolproof, of course, but it's what we've got.

Saul approaches, kneeling down next to me and handing me a cup of hot tea. I don't ask him what's in it, just sit up and take a long sip from the warm beverage. I can't help the grimace that works its way across my face.

"That's terrible."

"Sorry!" Willow calls from the kitchen. "You want more honey?"

"I just wanna get it over with," I reply. I take another long pull from the cup, swallowing as much of the bitter, putrid liquid as I can.

"I feel like we should be playing some groovy tunes for you," Willow suggests, strolling into the room.

"This needs to be as objective as possible," I counter, closing my eyes and leaning my head back against the single pillow. "No tunes, no talking, no people."

I expect a response as Willow and Saul excuse themselves, but no words come in return. For a brief moment I consider opening my eyes to check if they're still around, but I hold myself back.

Instead, I do everything I can to melt into the ground below me, disappearing within myself as I slip deeper and deeper into the empty canvas of my own mind.

Very, very slowly, the weight of the air on my skin begins to change, shifting away from my familiar location and placing me somewhere mysteriously abstract. I've cleared my mind, crafting a blank space for any memories to reveal themselves in a vibrant display.

Unfortunately, the more I struggle to eliminate any conscious thought, the more random musings on *thought itself* slip past my defenses.

Becoming a blank canvas is hard.

As soon as I realize these sneaking ideas have overwhelmed my brain I push them away, but other intrusive thoughts quickly pile in to take their place. I find myself wondering if Willow still thinks I'm attractive.

We still haven't kissed outside of a memory.

I need to stop chasing these mental threads, to allow myself a moment of true relaxation.

What if you just fall asleep? What if these aren't memories, they're dreams?

The vast darkness of my own mind offers no response: an endless, silent observer. Eventually, another question wanders aimlessly through my conscious brain, taking up space.

What if you're already asleep?

Frustrated, I decide to open my eyes and check this hypothesis, but I quickly discover the option is no longer available. My body has disappeared completely, a lonesome consciousness drifting aimlessly in the vacuum of space.

I struggle to lift my eyelids again, to wrangle control over a physical form that's no longer there and immediately find myself in a state of full-blown existential panic. If I had a heart, it would be beating much, much faster now, but there's no heart to speak of and no frame to hold it.

I can't even tap my fingers.

Unless, of course, I can somehow create them.

I make one last attempt to open my eyes, only this time I accept the endless landscape for what it is: a prison of my own design. This frightening place is not truly an infinite abyss, just the illusion of one.

The truth is, *I'm* in charge here, and while the physical form I'm accustomed to has been stripped away, there's nothing to keep me from making a new one.

Rose 11:4. Let there be Rose.

With that in mind, I focus deeply on creating a new body. I push with all my might until, eventually, I can feel the weight of my arms and legs, the gentle beating of my heart within my chest. I sense my lungs expanding and contracting in a deep, steady rhythm.

I open my eyes.

The dilapidated ceiling of Saul's farmhouse living room has disappeared, replaced instead by a stark vision of pristine clarity. Morning light stretches across a bright white ceiling in a warm rectangle, welcoming me home as I return from a state of deep slumber.

I sit up, glancing around to find myself in a small cabin, well-maintained and quite chic despite the four twin beds crammed into the limited space. A huge framed poster hangs on the far wall, featuring the silhouette of a crucifix and a short message from First Corinthians.

God is faithful; He will not let you be tempted beyond what you can bear. But when you are tempted, He will also provide a way out so that you can endure it.

At one time, this passage would've filled me with warmth and encouragement. Now, it does nothing but put a bad taste in my mouth.

I climb out of bed, glancing down to find I'm clad in a green-and-white T-shirt with the words CAMP DAMASCUS printed across the front, along with a cartoonish image of several pine trees and yet another crucifix.

The light cascading across my ceiling is streaming through a set of barely opened blinds.

I approach the window and open them with a single swift movement, revealing a large field of well-maintained grass and an American flag waving valiantly from a pole in the middle. On the other side of the field is a row of stark white cabins, which I can only assume run parallel to my own and several others. Beyond that is a thick evergreen forest, but I can make out a second flag pole in the distance, likely marking another clearing.

Strangely, there are no other campers to be found.

I turn back and face the room, preparing to head outside and take a look around, when something bizarre stops me in my tracks. I freeze, gazing at the far wall to discover my shadow has disconnected from my body.

While I've moved to the left, the proud silhouette remains firmly planted, hands on its hips in a confident pose.

I hold my hand up in a cautious wave, watching as the shadow remains steadfast in its defiance.

"Come on," I finally call out, growing frustrated. "We gotta go!"

My shadow shakes its head.

"Yes," I demand. "*I'm* the one in charge here."

I watch as my shadow pantomimes a state of exaggerated laughter, buckling over as it heaves and quakes. Moments later, the silhouette stands back up and shakes its head.

Growing frustrated, I march toward the wall in an attempt to reconnect this trick of light with my physical form. The shadow is too quick, however, leaping out of the way and jumping up onto one of the twin beds.

"Hey!" I yell, irritation bubbling up within me.

I rush to the shadow's new location and it springs away for a second time.

"Get the *heck* back here!" I cry, flailing wildly as I attempt to grab the abstract form.

To my shock, it actually works, my grasp somehow causing the shadow to trip through my hands and go toppling into one of the other beds. The silhouette clambers to its feet as I charge toward it, making another dive. I grab again, only this time I manage to get a good hold of my shadow's leg, yanking it to the ground and dragging it toward me as the outline struggles to pull away.

"You belong to *me!*" I shout, lost in the moment. "Not anyone else! You understand? You're *my* shadow!"

Despite the silhouette's best escape attempts, I eventually manage to reconnect the figure's feet with my own. After a good bit of wrangling, my shadow calms down and falls in line, duplicating the movements of my body. It slips back into place like a fitted shoe.

Before I have a chance to enjoy this morsel of success, however, the cabin door flies open with a loud bang.

I glance over to find Saul standing in the doorway, light beaming through and illuminating him with its radiant presence. He's immediately familiar, but the man who stands before me is quite different from the Saul I know today.

While his arms are still covered in tattoos, the piercings are nowhere to be found. His demeanor is more enthusiastic and bright-eyed than I'm used to, and he sports a tight yellow shirt with the words JESUS ROCKS emblazoned across the front. Depicted under this text is a large boulder that's been rolled away from a cartoon cavern entrance.

An acoustic guitar is slung over Saul's shoulder, and he gives it a powerful strum.

"Rise and shine!" Saul calls out. "Another beautiful day!"

"Oh . . . yeah," I blurt, taking a minute to collect my bearings and fall in line. I stand up and try my best to act natural.

"You about ready to rejoin the group for today's *temptation talk*?" Saul asks, flashing his brilliant smile.

I nod instinctively, playing along.

Saul is unconvinced, gazing at me with doting skepticism. It's utterly bizarre seeing him like this, the same kind heart wrapped in a strangely alien package. I understand this reality isn't a *pure* recollection, that I'm gazing through the funhouse mirror of my subconscious mind, but there's still truth hidden deep within my brain.

I may not *really* be talking to an earlier manifestation of Saul, but this approximation certainly arrived from somewhere.

Saul takes off his guitar and gently rests it against the wall, then strolls over and sits directly across from me on one of the beds.

"You'll probably have a lot to talk about then, huh?" Saul posits.

"Yeah," I reply, not exactly sure what I'm agreeing with.

"You know why we don't mix campers from the west cabins and the east cabins," Saul continues. "You're a smart girl, I don't need to tell you this."

I nod along.

"That's the thing about temptation," Saul continues. "It doesn't care how smart you are. Sometimes being a deep thinker makes it *worse.*"

I take in his words, listening intently and offering up my best expression of humility. "You're right. I'm sorry," I gush.

"You've gotta understand, Willow's trying to get through this process, *too,*" Saul continues. "If you make contact, you're not just setting yourself back, you're setting *her* back."

"Understood," I reply with a nod.

Saul hesitates a moment, his expression shifting into a bemused chuckle. "But that's not why you're here, is it?" my friend asks.

The distinct change in his demeanor helps me relax a bit, and instead of following my previous strategy of lying low, I find myself pulled in the opposite direction.

I shake my head. "You're right, that's not why I'm here."

"You're looking for a way down below," Saul continues.

I nod.

My friend laughs again. "How do you even know it's underground? Because there's stonework? You can find stonework anywhere."

"So it's *not* underground?" I press.

Saul shrugs. "I have no idea, I'm just the charming bad boy metal shop counselor who leads worship songs."

"There's *shop class* here?" I ask.

"Gotta teach the guys to be guys," Saul replies, a twinge of sadness in his voice.

I sharpen my focus on the task at hand, driving home my direct line of questioning. "You *really* never noticed a suspicious room?" I ask. "A basement?"

"Nope, but you did," he retorts.

My heart skips a beat as I realize I'm closing in on something important, the abstract nature of this strange world coalescing into coherent truth.

"What did I notice?" I implore.

"Everyone's split into two groups, the west cabins and the east cabins," Saul continues. "There's a central gathering place between the two, with a mess hall, a rec center, and a church for worship."

"I remember."

"There are no south cabins," Saul continues. "The lake is to the south. Which leaves one option."

An image of an overgrown trail flashes into my mind, a path away from the mess hall that hasn't been walked in years. A sign is posted at the base of this unused route.

"The *north* cabins are under renovation," Saul and I announce at exactly the same time.

A vision of these humble, white-painted structures abruptly manifests. I see myself creeping through the ferns, bathed in darkness on my way to visit Willow as I catch sight of these cabins from the corner of my eye. They look perfectly functional to me, well-maintained and manicured but with no campers to be found.

"Are they *always* under renovation?" I ask.

"I don't know," Saul retorts. "I'm just a manifestation of your own memory."

"I'm gonna check them out," I announce, standing abruptly. "You coming with me?"

Saul also stands, strolling over to his guitar and picking it up. He hoists the instrument with a broad smile and plays another triumphant chord. "I've gotta go lead some morning worship tunes," he informs me. "Have fun, though."

With that, my friend exits the cabin, a joyful swagger in his step. He begins to strum loudly, playing a powerful, uplifting song that rings out across the empty field.

"Hey!" I rush to the door and call out, stopping Saul in his tracks. "How will I know which cabin it is?"

He turns back to face me, briefly pausing his strumming. "Follow the rot," he gurgles, his voice dropping several octaves. "Flies love rot."

My expression sours with confusion, but as Saul continues on his way it becomes apparent that this is the only hint I'll get. As my friend leaves he begins to sing, his voice carrying beautifully through the morning air.

"*Lord! You're all that I need! Lord! You're all that I live for!*" he belts, wandering away.

I watch Saul continue into the distance before turning my attention to the left, my gaze falling upon a row of thick trees at the edge of the clearing. There are no cabins on this side, just the darkness of the woods, and it's this darkness I'm drawn toward.

I stroll down the porch and make my way across the wide open field, marching toward the tree line as a single metal link raps softly against the flagpole.

A distinct chill begins to creep its way across my skin, growing more and more pronounced with every step until I reach the edge of the woods and realize my teeth are chattering.

I stop here, gazing into the forest in an attempt to catch sight of some hidden collection of cabins. Unfortunately, there are none to be found, yet an uncanny psychic pull tempts me onward.

This clearing is to the west of camp center, so the north cabins must lie diagonally through the woods.

I make my way into the thick overgrowth, pushing ferns away as fallen branches and dead leaves crunch underfoot. My eyes are peeled, but I'm following my instincts now, allowing the inertia of my subconscious mind to take hold.

It's not long before a third clearing comes into view: the north cabins.

Unlike the other sections of Camp Damascus, this one doesn't feature a flagpole to mark its location. However, every other aspect of the clearing remains eerily similar. The grass is just as neatly trimmed, buildings freshly painted with the same stark white pigment from across the site.

There are ten cabins in all, two rows of five on either side of the clearing.

My heart pounding, I approach the closest structure and make my way onto the porch. I take a moment to peer through the front window, discovering nothing but a dimly lit room identical to the one I woke up in. When I open the door, I find more of the same.

Aside from the breathtakingly low temperatures, there's not much to see here.

Instead of gradually making my way down each row, I decide to focus my efforts and listen to the voice within, the whispering part of my subconscious brain that has made all this possible.

Returning to the middle of the field, I close my eyes, allowing the swift current of memory to take hold. *None of this is real*, I remind myself, *but deep below these veils of symbolism lies a hidden truth.*

It's not long before a faint, darting buzz draws my attention to the right. I open my eyes and glance over to locate a single mayfly dancing through the air, fluttering this way and that before swooping off toward one of the cabins.

The insect sways with a strange meandering tumble as I follow along, and despite its gradual movement, the general direction is clear. I walk slowly behind the fly's wandering trail, following across the field until I'm standing directly before the middle cabin on the left side of the clearing.

It's here my six-legged companion lands on the first wooden step, gazing up at me with its bulging, crystalline eyes as it furiously rubs its dirty little hands together.

I meet the tiny creature's gaze.

Suddenly, an eruption of caustic, sonic drilling prods me to stumble back in alarm, losing my footing and slamming against the grass as I stare up in disgust at a churning black mass. The cabin is absolutely covered in flies, the creatures swarming so thick they look like a heaving, undulating paste that's been spread across the entire structure. The sound in my ears is a deafening, overwhelming drone, a horrible sound that fills the clearing as the creatures swirl and pulse, a living tornado of filth. They roll off the cabin like dancing fire, drawn to the rot.

My eyes snap open and I sit up with a gasp, prompting Willow and Saul to pull back in shock. I've returned to the warmth of the farmhouse, slamming back into my body with a powerful thud that jerks the air from my lungs.

"You okay?" Willow asks, placing her hand on my back.

"Ye-Yeah," I stammer, the word tumbling forth awkwardly as I struggle to find my voice. I'm still reeling from what I've seen, the rolling boil of mayflies charred across my mind.

Willow gives me a moment to catch my breath.

"Did you remember?" she finally asks.

"I don't know," I admit. "Things were pretty ... abstract."

I turn my attention to Saul. "Was there a third set of buildings in the woods?" I ask. "A clearing for the north cabins?"

Saul leans back a bit, his eyes staring off as he struggles to remember. "I think so," he confirms, "but I never saw them. They were under renovation when I worked at Damascus."

"I think they were *always* under renovation," I say.

Saul locks eyes with me. "Do you know which cabin we need to search?"

I've seen the cabin, and while the mass of flies was likely just a symbolic manifestation from the depths of my subconscious, the location itself is clearly marked.

However, the logical, scientifically minded part of my brain pauses. This segment of my personality has been growing stronger every day, and now the sword it wields into psychic battle is dominant. There's nothing concrete about my findings, and the assertation that *any* information gleaned from an abstract drug trip holds water is highly suspect.

Sure, there's plenty of evidence to suggest repressed memories lie dormant in the subconscious, but reading these images like tea leaves is just as silly as the religion I've turned my back on.

Is this just a new Trojan horse for faith to use as it creeps back into my life?

Maybe a little faith isn't so bad, a voice abruptly offers from deep within me, bubbling up from the darkness and making a profoundly simple case.

Find balance.

To be fair, this all-or-nothing approach has been getting exhausting. The further away I get from my time with Kingdom of the Pine, the more I'm realizing it's not so much the *faith* I'm upset about, it's the hate and fear disguised as concern and charity. Faith is just a vessel, and while it can certainly be used to justify truly horrible things, maybe I'm letting the aggressors off the hook by blaming faith itself.

"I have a pretty good idea which cabin to search," I finally reply, imagining the deluge of swarming flies.

"Good enough to make a run at this?" Saul asks.

The opposing sides of my mind finally collapse into each other, swirling together like buckets of red and yellow paint as they synthesize into a brilliant orange. This new tone floods across everything, igniting a powerful force within me.

"Yeah," I declare with a nod. "Let's go back to camp."

11

STRAIGHT STREET

As Willow's car winds its way up the hillside, we each begin to prepare in our own way.

In the back seat, Saul reveals a set of wireless headphones and dives into his private concerto of thundering guitars and grinding deathcore rhythms, nodding along to the music.

Willow drives, but her cameras are locked and loaded. There's even a tiny video recorder strapped to her forehead, endlessly cataloging from Willow's point of view.

Meanwhile, I've pulled out my phone for a last-minute cramming session with all the information at our disposal. I'm going through my old notes, flipping back and forth between personal findings and scans of Saul's mysterious tome. I've gone over this stuff so many times I can recite it by heart, yet I push onward.

Continuing our approach to Camp Damascus, I'm particularly focused on the Prayer for Release, trying my best to memorize the strange pattern of words. These incantations are mostly in Latin, but they also feature lines of a bizarre language I've never encountered before. What's more, these passages don't read like a traditional prayer. They're not speaking directly to God for assistance but, instead, coming off like how-to instructions.

It's utterly bizarre for a religious text, and deeply fascinating.

My fingers tap out various fractal-like patterns as I read, keeping me focused. I don't even notice I'm doing it until I glance over to catch Willow gazing at me from her place in the driver's seat.

I stop abruptly, my fingers seizing up as I recall every time my parents scolded me over this habit.

Willow, on the other hand, just smiles.

"It's okay," she assures me, reaching out and placing her palm on my leg.

I melt, not just from her physical touch, but from her unquestioning acceptance of the things that make me unique. Willow is incredible, and I can only imagine falling for her a second time has been just as easy as the first.

Still, coming together under such strange and traumatic circum-stances is difficult. We've held each other, but we still haven't kissed.

All in due time.

After much debate, the three of us decided to break into Camp Da-mascus as a unit instead of any one person going alone. Of course, sneaking *anywhere* is easier when there's a single individual hoping to remain hidden, but at this point the journey belongs to all of us.

Besides, now we can split the work between three distinct positions.

As the only person with a recollection of the tethering chamber (drug-induced or otherwise), I'm leading the charge and focused solely on getting us to the correct cabin.

Saul, on the other hand, is tasked with keeping us safe.

I glance at the large backpack sitting next to my brilliant friend, the enormous tank of his homemade flamethrower barely fitting inside the canvas. We've made a pact not to harm any fellow humans tonight, but demons are another story. Just because we've taken care of our own dark passengers, that doesn't mean there aren't plenty more of them out there.

Meanwhile, Willow is recording every step of the process.

This evidence may or may not come in handy, depending on what we find tonight. Back at Saul's place we've still got the charred body of a literal demon stashed away, but who knows where we can entrust this incredible supernatural evidence.

It wasn't just Kingdom of the Pine who taught us that demons thrive in fire when it's actually their greatest weakness, it was the entire Christian establishment over several centuries.

The corruption runs deep.

This fire versus ice discrepancy could've started as a little secret between two people several thousand years ago, the liars dying off before they ever had a chance to come clean about their clever switch. Likewise, it could be a clandestine truth that every religious leader, across all denominations, is well aware of.

Is turning Pachid's body over to the Neverton Police Department going to do much of anything? Or will the corpse just disappear a few hours later as some fixer from Kingdom of the Pine slips out the back door of the morgue?

How about the FBI? How high does the reach of our congregation, or *any* congregation, go?

I guess we'll find out.

Suffice to say, we've decided to collect as much evidence as possible, then worry about what to do with it later.

I turn and gaze out the car window, watching the lights of Neverton twinkle below in the humble little valley of deep, dark forest. Perched on the mountainside above, Camp Damascus watches over everything.

I find a single tiny light below and focus on it, allowing the distant yellow glow to burn into my gaze.

"Sexual deviance," I whisper under my breath, repeating the words of my mother on the day I left. "The daughter thinks she's in love with a beautiful, sweet girl who accepts her exactly the way she is. How do you help her?"

The words are so soft that nobody can hear me, but I give it a moment of consideration all the same.

I didn't have an answer at the time, but by now an understanding has grown within me. It's not about the solution, because the question is flawed. There's nothing deviant about me.

If I had to reply, though, I'd consider the new family I've suddenly found myself with, the ones who accept me exactly as I am. I'd consider the way I feel right now in the passenger seat of this car, simmering with joy despite the horrific and dangerous mission I'm about to embark upon.

The answer is simple.

I'd love her.

We pull off the main road, rumbling up onto a sightseeing turnout as gravel crunches softly underneath the car tires. Willow parks, shutting off her headlights and plunging the scene into vast, endless darkness. Up here, the only illumination is the light of a massive full moon that hangs silently above.

We've arrived.

"Everybody ready?" I ask.

Willow nods.

Saul stops his music, pulling one of the wireless headphones away from his ear. "Hell yeah."

"You really think you should be listening to loud songs while we're trying to stay alert?" I question.

"What's the point of busting into a conversion camp to slay demons with a flamethrower and smash up their possession machine if you're not gonna listen to black metal while doing it?" he retorts.

It's a fair point.

"Fine," he finally continues, offering a compromise. "I'll turn it down."

As we climb from the car I'm immediately bathed in a palpable sense of unease. The air shift is sudden, washing me in the damp coolness of the night, but it's not just the natural feeling of the forest that's getting under my skin.

Something is just *different* about this place, whether it's a mental trick I'm playing on myself or some strange unknowable phenomenon. We've barely touched the edge of the congregation's property and I can already sense its psychic weight.

There's no such thing as psychic weight, I remind myself.

"Everyone good?" I ask, pulling out a plastic angel mask and placing it over my face.

My friends nod, following my lead and donning masks of their own.

"Want me to say a prayer?" I joke.

This prompts a chuckle from Willow, but Saul is not impressed.

"Lord, guide us with your hand," Saul murmurs, more to himself than anyone else. "You are my war club, my weapon for battle—with you I shatter nations, with you I destroy kingdoms."

While the power of prayer no longer moves me, Saul's inclusion of Jeremiah 51:20 is admirably fitting.

Willow is less impressed. "Let's fuck this duck. Amen."

As the three of us begin our trek into the darkness of the lush woods, I can hear Saul behind me, still mumbling a plea for spiritual protection under his breath.

We creep silently through the forest, eyes darting from side to side as we hike into the wilds. It's disorienting at first, but eventually we begin to notice the soft lights of Camp Damascus slipping through trees in the distance.

At this late hour, the radiance is much less pronounced than it might usually be. It's nothing more than a dim glow, small lights around important walkways and structures offering just enough illumination to satisfy the Montana fire and safety code.

These lights also serve as great directional markers.

Soon enough, the trees begin to thin out for a view of the first flag-pole from my vision. There's no safety lighting on the large metal needle protruding from the canopy, but the moon casts everything with just enough silver glow to make out a faint shape as our eyes continue adjusting.

I'm still struggling to gather my bearings, but the longer we travel, the more I find myself tapping into something more powerful than the map Saul and Willow so diligently prepared. There's a compass hidden deep within me, a transcendent path buried under the ever-present mental fog.

Being here in person, however, is causing the fog to lift.

We pass the first clearing, sneaking along the outer edge and avoiding the main camp facilities. From here I can just barely make out the ominous croaking of frogs as it drifts from the nearby lake, their nightly drone filling the air.

The woods fall away in an abrupt change of scenery, revealing a small clearing lit by nothing more than the celestial bodies above. There's a path leading to and from this rectangular opening in the forest.

At one end of the clearing an assortment of haybales are stacked, creating square, segmented walls about five feet tall. A large paper target is affixed to each bale in circular red-and-black displays. A bullseye lies at the center of each, and this section of the paper is ripped and torn from multiple arrow piercings.

We've stumbled upon the range.

The three of us waste no time crossing this open area, uninterested in the technicalities of the Camp Damascus archery program. Unfortunately, reaching the halfway point triggers an unexpected sound from the forest before us.

I halt in my tracks, the noise so loud that even Saul can hear it through his blaring headphones. The three of us freeze in place, not entirely sure how to react to the unexpected commotion.

Saul's music stops.

My eyes quickly scan the dark cluster of trees, the hammer of my heart thrusting raw adrenaline through clenched muscles and veins.

Another rustle from the darkness.

Staff members just *seeing* us would immediately put this mission in jeopardy, not only tonight, but for every night that follows. We've gone straight to the source, maintaining the advantage of surprise, but the moment our presence is noticed that edge comes crumbling down.

Of course, this is also predicated on the idea that we can outrun—or outfight—whoever finds us, and this staff is likely well-versed in hunting down runaways.

Another rustle causes my body to clench even tighter, a coil seconds away from popping off and launching me back the way we came.

Suddenly, an enormous stag emerges from the ferns, its antlers regal and sharp. The majestic animal pauses before us, motionless under the light of the moon.

We gaze quietly at each other, each species appreciating the moment, but when the creature continues trotting on its way I can't help noticing something strange hanging from its hind leg. The shape is unexpected, looking like a deflated balloon, but with nothing more than a brief glimpse through the shadows it's impossible to tell what it is.

The deer disappears, but not before stumbling slightly, its antlers knocking awkwardly against a tree.

"Did anyone else see that?" I whisper, swatting away a single fly that buzzes around my head. I glance at the others, who offer silent nods, but by then my only focus is on the figure standing behind them.

"Oh *frick*," I blurt, staggering back in a moment of shock. My voice is much too loud, but the utterance happens with such instinctual force that I can't possibly regulate my volume.

Saul and Willow turn abruptly, equally startled as we maneuver away from what I can now see is a camper with a compound bow in one hand and an arrow in the other. He can't be older than sixteen, sporting shaggy brown hair and a vacant, slack-jawed expression.

"Hey," the boy mutters, his voice matching the despondence on his face. "Is archery starting?"

We're backed against the hay bales now, not quite ready to run but feeling deeply uneasy about the spacey demeanor of this armed teen.

It's the middle of the night, certainly not time for archery.

"Probably not" is all I can think to say.

The boy's eyes dart to me and he raises the bow slightly, an expression of startled fright taking over. "Oh!" he blurts, pulled from a trance into some bizarre waking nightmare.

I immediately reach up and pull off my angel mask, hoping this might quell the camper's apprehension. It seems to work, but his arrow remains notched.

"What's your name?" I ask, keeping my tone as soft and even as possible.

He scrunches his face up, thinking hard. At first the lack of an immediate answer seems mildly amusing to him, but his good-natured expression quickly melts into worry and confusion.

"Did you bring me here?" he asks, his voice wavering as panic sets in. He grips the bow even tighter now, prompting me to raise my hand in a gesture of peace.

"No," I say. "Not at all."

Willow pulls off her mask and steps up next to me, offering her silent support.

"Do you wanna get out of here?" I ask the camper.

For a moment the haze of confusion breaks and he seems perfectly cogent. The simplicity of this question has struck something deep within him, momentarily flipping a switch.

His eyes well up with tears that glisten in the moonlight. The camper's parade of emotions has finally settled on a horrible frown of agony and regret. He nods along in confirmation, apparently so consumed with these blooming feelings he can barely find the words.

"Yeah," he finally sobs. "I wanna go home."

Willow and I exchange glances, not sure how to react, while Saul hangs back in silence. The mask is still covering his face.

"We can help you," I continue. "Do you—"

"Is archery starting?" the boy suddenly interjects.

"Uh, no," Willow replies.

Panic creeps back into the camper's tone, his emotional loop starting anew.

"It's not time for archery yet," I assure him.

I step back a bit, moving closer to my friends and lowering my voice. "How do we do this?" I whisper. "We've gotta help him."

Now *both* my companions are silent.

"So we're just gonna leave him out here?" I blurt, frustrated.

Willow hesitates.

"Rose," she finally starts. "How many people are we saving tonight? One of them, or all of them?"

I glance back at the camper, whose grip on the bow is tightening. His emotions shift so rapidly it's hard to keep up.

"What are you talking about over there?" the kid abruptly calls out, his voice jarringly loud in contrast to our pristine surroundings.

"Shh!" I hush him, swiftly breaking away from my friends and marching toward the boy.

My sudden movement is too much for the camper, who raises his bow and notches an arrow. "Hey!" he shouts.

I throw my hands in the air, immediately heeding his warning and backing away.

"I know you're confused, but you've gotta be quiet," I plead.

The boy narrows his eyes. "Did Pops send you?" His arrow is still pulled back and pointed directly at my chest.

As I back away, Willow steps in front of me, a maneuver that's slightly frustrating until I realize how sweet it is.

Saul finally breaks his silence, ripping off his angel mask and stepping forward.

"Your dad didn't send us," Saul assures the panicking camper, his voice calm and collected. "I know this is all very confusing, but check this out—the moment's gonna pass. I know you feel so fucking *terrified* right now—trust me, I get it—but the more time goes by, the more things are gonna fall back into place. It's all gonna make sense."

This isn't true, and I know it. Saul, Willow, and I are incredibly lucky to have our memories back, but based on my interactions with other Camp Damascus alumni, this is rare and likely random.

This kid might be out here forever wondering if it's time for archery.

Fortunately, I'm not the one doing the talking here, Saul is.

"Everything's gonna be fine," Saul continues with deep conviction. "You're good."

Even in this breathtakingly tense moment, my friend's charm shines through with nothing more than a few simple words. I can see why they hired Saul, because connecting with these young campers is second nature to him.

The frightened boy slowly lowers his bow, but just as this occurs yet another kink in our plan arrives. Two flashlights are bouncing through the darkness toward us, yellow beams slicing through the space between trees.

"Oh shit," Willow blurts, a universal consensus.

They must've heard our new friend's panicked yelps, drawn to the commotion.

I spin abruptly, frantically searching for a place to hide. The edge of the forest is pretty far away, and crashing through branches and ferns would likely be a dead giveaway. Instead, I opt for the only other choice, swiftly ducking behind one of the square haybale targets. Saul and Willow follow suit, the three of us pressed tight as we make ourselves as small and quiet as possible.

Heck. Heck. Heck. Heck.

I know I should keep my head against the hay, but as usual my curiosity gets the best of me. I cautiously peek around the edge, watching the scene unfold.

A man and woman have emerged from the forest, Camp Damascus counselors dressed in their usual green-and-white uniforms. Their sweeping flashlights make it hard to see any faces, but their eerily cheery demeanor is more than apparent from the vocal tone.

"Hey, buddy," the woman coos. "What's going on out here? We've been looking all over for you."

"I—I don't know," the camper stammers, deeply distraught.

I retract my head as the counselors lift their flashlights and sweep the area, not entirely satisfied with the camper's answer. One of their lights pauses on the haybales we're tucked behind, lingering for a moment.

All it would take is one slip of the tongue for our whole plan to fall apart, and in the short time we've known this anxious camper, I can't imagine we've accumulated much goodwill.

"Sounded like you were arguing with someone out here," the counselor notes.

There's a long pause, long enough that my lungs start inexplicably hurting and I suddenly realize I've been holding my breath the whole time.

"Is archery starting?" the camper finally asks.

"I asked you a question," the counselor presses.

"You did?"

There's a long pause.

The light on our target finally moves along, a deep sense of relief washing over me as I slowly relax.

"No archery tonight," the other counselor chimes in. "Bright and early tomorrow. Let's get you back to your bunk, huh?"

"Okay, yeah," the camper replies.

Soon enough, the group can be heard making their way back up the trail from which they came.

The last thing I hear is one of the counselors quietly speaking into a communication device. "We found him. Tell security we're fine over here. Yeah."

Eventually, the night is plunged back into its previous state of overwhelming stillness.

"Let's go," I announce.

We don't have time to dwell on the strange encounter, quickly returning to our mission as we push onward to the forbidden side of camp.

It's not long before we arrive at another clearing, this set of bungalows just as immaculately groomed as the first. I've been here before, and as my eyes bear witness to these familiar buildings in two distinct rows, a faint gasp escapes my lips.

We've made it to the north cabins.

✳   ✳   ✳

For a place that's supposedly never available to use, it's shockingly well-kept, the lawn tight and the stark white cabins freshly painted without a blemish to be found. Of course, there's plenty of metaphorical rot lurking just below the surface, but you'd never know it.

The second *rot* crosses my mind I receive a visual flash, a reminder directing me to a very specific cabin. I recall the flies billowing off it like rolling flames, their caustic buzz so concentrated and loud that it sounds like a power drill boring into the back of my head.

"That one," I announce, pointing toward a small, inconspicuous building.

We hurry along the edge of the clearing, not daring to cut through the exposed middle ground. All the while, Willow is quietly snapping photos, her shutter falling into a steady rhythm like the tick of an old clock. Digital files tend to corrupt around these creatures, but analog film should fare better.

Soon enough, we've arrived at the cabin's front steps. I gaze up at the humble white structure, my eyes transfixed on the door.

"You ready?" Saul asks from behind me.

I *am* ready, but for some reason I can't muster the willpower to move. My body is quaking, trembling with anxiety and fear.

5, 4, 3, 2, 1.

4, 3, 2, 1.

3, 2, 1.

2, 1.

1.

My hands hang at my sides, frantically tapping out patterns in a subconscious effort to calm myself down.

Unfortunately, it appears this situation is a little too potent for my usual coping method to earn results.

Fingernails grow faster during the summertime, and they tend to grow even faster on a person's dominant hand.

Julius Caesar ordered the amputation of captured warriors' thumbs, so even after they were freed, they could never bear weapons.

"Five, four, three, two, one. Four, three, two, one. Three, two, one. Two, one. One," I whisper under my breath.

I force myself to stop, focusing my internal strength in an effort to halt these dancing fingers and keep the pithy facts from spilling through my brain in an avalanche of distraction. I take a deep breath and let it out, mustering up another mental push that will, hopefully, propel me onward.

Unfortunately, all the heart in the world can't seem to compel my body.

Vena amoris *is said to be the only exclusive vein in the human body, traveling straight from your ring finger to your heart. It's a myth.*

Willow steps up beside me and places her hand over mine, not palm to palm but facing the same direction. It's an unusual position, prompting me to glace down at our digits in confusion.

Willow's fingers begin to move, dancing in unison to my very specific pattern. A strange wave of relief washes over me as our fingers tango like this in utter silence.

My taps are not magic, and while I often walk them across any surface I can find in moments of stress, performing these steps will not completely alter my reality. This is not a miracle cure.

What *does* move the needle, however, is the sudden reminder of just how close Willow and I were. I have no recollection of showing these patterns to anyone, yet the girl beside me can repeat every step in perfect unison.

She's got my back. So does Saul, for that matter.

My birth family never understood these subtle movements, either ignoring them completely or reacting with downright contempt. However, my chosen family doesn't seem to mind. In fact, they're quite happy to dance along.

I step forward, finally releasing Willow's grip and continuing up the porch.

I cautiously peer through the front window. This cabin is exactly how I saw the one in my vision, although it appears one bunk has been moved to the room's opposite corner.

Last time I climbed through a window in the dead of night I triggered a silent alarm, and I'm not looking to make the same mistake twice.

With that in mind, Saul steps up next to me, following my lead. He gazes through the glass to assess the scene, pointing down at a small metal square attached to the window's inner edge. It's a security system, set to activate the moment the seal has broken. One can only assume there's another unit affixed to the cabin door.

Fortunately, we've planned ahead.

Saul pulls off his backpack and sets it down with extreme care, prompting me to recall the highly explosive, flammable equipment held within. Apparently, Saul also saved enough room for a simple flathead screwdriver.

"All these premade cabins have cheap windows," my friend whispers, his voice slightly too loud thanks to the grinding heavy metal in his earbuds. "They're all the same."

Saul gets to work, slipping his screwdriver between the pane and its wooden frame. He does this very, very slowly, working his way along the edge. Once the surrounding material is broken, Saul begins his process of carefully extracting the glass as a single, complete rectangle. He moves achingly slow, carefully pulling away the glass.

"Oh!" Saul abruptly jerks, the pane dipping sharply in a moment that causes my heart to skip a beat.

Saul reels slightly, somehow managing to regain control of the delicate rectangle. I can see now that a large, wispy cocoon is tucked away in the darkness, hidden on the inside edge of the frame. It's stringy and delicate, like torn cotton candy, sticking to Saul's knuckles as he pulls away.

"*Ugh,*" Willow blurts in revulsion.

Saul carefully sets the pane down, stepping back and wiping the white threads away on the fabric of his shirt. A scowl of disgust overwhelms his face. "I saw one of these in the garage," he recalls, making sure every last strand is cleaned off his hand.

Peering in through the opening, I take note of three wispy white pods affixed to the inner wall. The largest of these cocoons—the one Saul touched—is about a foot long and cracked down the middle to reveal a hollow interior. The others are smaller, two- and four-inch ovals of webbing that are still busy gestating whatever's inside.

I also note the security trigger. It remains affixed to its window frame, undisturbed.

Saul picks up his backpack and throws it over his shoulder. "Be careful. That stuff's nasty."

Saul, Willow, and I climb through our freshly crafted entrance, glancing around the shadowy cabin where moonlight barely seeps. I'm tempted to pull out a flashlight, but the chance of this faint illumination alerting someone is just not worth the risk.

Fortunately, I know where to begin my search.

I motion for my friends to help, pulling the relocated bunk away from its wall to reveal a wooden door below.

"Oh *my,*" I gasp, realizing my visions were correct.

There could just as easily be a security device hidden behind this door as the last one, but with no way of telling and no possibility of turning back, there's only one thing to do. I step to the side, then reach down to grab a large metal handle affixed to the oak frame. With one firm tug, I pull the door open to reveal a set of industrial metal stairs leading down into some unknown chamber below.

My companions and I exchange glances—uneasy, but ready to do what needs to be done.

The ground flattens out at the bottom of this staircase, transitioning into a long hallway constructed with clean gray sheets of metal. The floor of this area is lined with ultramodern strips of glowing blue lights, illuminating the scene from below.

Taking the lead, I make my way down the steps.

As Willow closes the trap door behind us, the atmosphere shifts yet again. While the campground had a rustic, natural flow, this basement feels downright futuristic. We might as well be roaming the laboratories of some billion-dollar computing firm.

"What the fuck?" Willow whispers, unable to hold back her amazement any longer as we continue down the otherworldly hallway, bathed in blue.

We cautiously round a corner.

I stop in my tracks, confronted by a long row of chambers lining either side of the space before me. Each cell is protected by an enormous pane of translucent glass, but it's not their high-tech construction that catches my attention. Instead, my focus is drawn to the bodies huddled in the corners of each chamber: young adults, teenagers, and children stirred from their slumber by our unexpected visit. There are more than thirty people down here, with one to three captives in each bare metal cell.

The majority of these captives remain sleeping on the floor, but the ones who notice us quickly rise to their feet with expressions of utter panic.

Their terrified faces are gut-wrenching.

Immediately, I pull off my angel mask, struggling to calm them down.

As the captives rush toward us, they're greeted by walls of thick glass. The barriers appear to slide upward when unlocked, but without a method of triggering the doors, there's absolutely no way for us to aid an escape. Not yet, at least.

Next to me, a preteen boy is pounding against the barrier, crying out as tears stream down his face. I can't hear a thing despite standing no more than a foot away from this terrified child. His mouth hangs wide, but not so much as a muffled scream can be heard.

Willow and I immediately get to work searching for a lever that could trigger the release of these captives, but it quickly becomes apparent that whatever we're looking for must lie in the chamber beyond. Meanwhile, Saul pulls a metal hammer from his bag, raising it to shatter one of the panes before I reach out to stop him. "Too loud!" I warn.

Saul hesitates, then insists. "We've gotta get them out of here."

"It's not gonna work," I explain, shaking my head. "Look at them banging away from the inside. These are polycarbonate panels, and they're thick."

Saul's anger and frustration begrudgingly dissolves into crushing defeat. By the time we're ready to search the next room our friend is standing in utter silence, eyes blurry and lips curling back in an expression of searing emotional pain.

"I can't believe I was part of this," he moans, the words barely understandable as they emerge from his mouth in a quivering mess.

"You didn't know," I reply, hoping to reassure him.

"Didn't I?" he blurts, then shakes his head as he redirects the question inward. "I can't remember. For all I know, *I* was the one who brought them down here."

Technically, he's right, but right now the last thing he needs is to parse *technicalities.* My friend needs support.

I step toward Saul, placing a hand on his shoulder. "And now you're trying to get them out."

Willow chimes in supportively. "You were in a *cult.*"

Saul clenches his jaw, still deeply troubled. Around him, terrified children hammer against their glass prisons in utter silence, crying for help.

"That's the thing about Kingdom of the Pine," he finally admits. "The stuff they believed, the messages they pounded into our heads . . . none of it was that weird. They're just the thousandth little twist on the exact same book."

Saul's right. While the congregation is clearly up to something deeply troubling, the basic foundation of their beliefs is not much different than that of any sect to come before. They may be a little more hard-nosed and a little more open about their utilitarian approach, but their principles are, well, pretty average.

That's the scariest thing about them: they're not that special.

"Let's just fix what we can," I suggest. *"Rose 15:30. For the righteous sword of truth is so sharp that even half swings will graze a bone of incredible depths."*

Saul just stares back at me, and in the moment of silence I realize how unusual that was. "Are you making up your own Bible verses?" he asks.

"Uh, yeah," I admit. "Up until this point I hadn't said any out loud, though."

Saul considers this a moment, then nods, wiping away his welling tears. "Sick. That was super metal."

It's going to be a while before he can work through his guilt as a piece in this macabre puzzle, but right now he's found enough strength to stay sharp and focused on the mission at hand.

As we continue onward the prisoners call out in mute terror, their mouths agape and their eyes flooded with tears as they no doubt beg us not to abandon them.

"We'll be right back," I mouth, struggling to communicate this relatively simple message that has been rendered nearly impossible to transmit.

I'm so torn up about leaving that I briefly lose focus on where we're headed. As we push through the large metal door at the end of the hallway my perception is a scattered mess, but it's yanked back into a state of high alert when the horrifying contents of the new chamber reveal themselves.

The room is perfectly square, with a door positioned on both the left and the right walls. The strips of blue illumination have fallen away, replaced instead by a sterile overhead fluorescence. The centerpiece of this chamber is an enormous glass tank that sits along the entirety of the back wall, each section partitioned into several internal compartments. Some of the chambers are empty, while others teem with little black flies that swirl like a dark, undulating hurricane. Others host masses of webbing—wispy cocoons in various sizes affixed to the glass.

The remaining tanks, however, are the most alarming.

I step forward, the familiar, curious part of my brain overloading as it struggles through a sludge of disgust that might otherwise keep my thoughts at bay.

Held within this partitioned tank are collections of large, foot-long invertebrates, the groups spaced out and paired off in a way that seems deliberate.

I've grown up near enough farms to recognize a selective breeding arrangement.

The creatures themselves are plump and round, like gray, football-shaped worms. They're moist and glistening, and although the tanks are just as soundproof as the ones in the hallway, I can only imagine the awkward squish their moist bodies make as they crawl around in these barren habitats.

"What *are* they?" Willow groans, too revolted to draw any closer to the strange creatures.

I continue approaching the back wall, overwhelmed with both terror and wonder.

This species is unlike anything I've witnessed in the animal kingdom, yet there's something strangely recognizable about them. While there's little about their features that relates to our natural world, they *do* sport qualities of the demons from *somewhere else.* Their skin is the same wretched pale grey, sagging and sick, and a small line of dark, stringy hair runs along the ridges of the apparent invertebrates. It's matted against their wet bodies in an awkward, broken line.

"Demon larvae?" Saul questions from behind.

"Could be," I reply, taking a moment to consider. "Or maybe just another species from the same place. There's plenty more than *Homo sapiens* in our world; I don't see why there would only be demons in theirs."

I draw closer still, leaning down to the glass for a better look. I'm no more than a foot away from one of the bizarre creatures when the pudgy worm turns toward me, noticing my presence.

We stay like this for a moment, frozen in a curious standoff.

Slowly, the tip of the strange organism begins to expand, opening to reveal a dark, four-fanged mouth that stretches into a distinctly square orifice. The maw is dripping with thick, glistening mucus.

"Oh wow" is all I can think to say, the inquisitive part of my mind fully overriding any good sense I might otherwise harness to pull away.

Before my friends have a chance to call out and remind me, a purple tube erupts from the creature's mouth in a quick snap, slamming against the side of the tank and prompting me to stumble back in shock.

The hollow proboscis, which features a frighteningly sharp point, rubs against the glass for a moment as it struggles to catch hold. When this doesn't work, a cascade of tiny white eggs begins pumping forth, spilling across the bottom of the tank. I can only assume those were intended for placement somewhere deep beneath my skin.

I take a moment to catch my breath, then collect myself and stand up straight.

"I don't think those are larvae," I state, nodding to the unhatched eggs at the bottom of the tank. Several dead flies lie scattered about next to them. "I think it's the final product."

My mind is churning through new information as I struggle to make sense of it all. This is fascinating, but the implications are nauseating to process.

For the first time, I'm a little thankful for the memory loss.

"Some creatures that bite need to go unnoticed. Leeches and mosquitos evolved to secrete an anesthetic once they've attached to their host, which allows them to feed," I explain, thinking out loud. "A species could *easily* evolve to produce something even more powerful than a simple numbing agent. Something to make you forget you were ever a host to begin with."

I glance back at my friends. "We've probably got some eggs in us."

"You do," announces an unexpected voice from the doorway on our right.

12

THE CONQUEROR

The worms were such a horrific detour that we've completely let our guard down. Now, turning to face our unforeseen visitor, I find myself staring into spectacled eyes I know all too well.

My "therapist," Dr. Smith, stands before us with a disappointed look on his soft, bearded face. His demeanor is far from threatening, but glancing down I notice there's a gun gripped tightly in one hand.

I step back a bit, staring down the barrel of his weapon. I'm not around guns often, and the mere presence of one puts me on edge, let alone a pistol trained directly on my chest.

The average nine-millimeter bullet travels up to 1,500 feet per second.

"Don't worry," Dr. Smith continues. "The flies won't ever grow up, that's been bred out of them. Some Ligeian gestate longer than others, although it depends on their exposure to certain radio waves."

Dr. Smith hesitates, then corrects himself.

"Well, not *radio* waves," he explains.

I instantly recall the strange, unknowable aura that radiates from every demon. The way it wreaks havoc on electrical currents and audiovisual transmissions. The idea that this emanation has an additional *biological* effect doesn't surprise me, especially on a potentially symbiotic species like these worms.

Dr. Smith points at the tanks. "Regardless, none of them should stick around long enough to become . . . that. Most of them never gestate at all, but there's always a few seeded oranges mixed in with the seedless. Lucky you."

One of the worms rises upright in its tank, tracking my movements like a stout, slimy cobra.

"The eggs eventually dissolve," he continues, "but as you can see, Ligeian produce quite a few of them with a single puncture. Unfortunate side effect; we really just need them for the memory loss. *Great indeed, we confess, is the mystery of godliness.* He works in mysterious ways."

"You think *God* made those things?" Saul scoffs.

Dr. Smith shakes his head. "No, but he brought them to us for a reason. Hi, Saul. Do you remember me?"

Saul just glares, but his eyes reveal the answer. He doesn't remember at all.

"It's nice I happened to be on shift tonight," Dr. Smith continues. "Catching the three of you like this is very poetic. Magdalene was never *my* patient, but she certainly made things interesting for me."

"Willow," she snaps.

Dr. Smith shrugs, ignoring this. "I'm only here on Thursdays, so the chance of you running into a doctor who might just shoot you in the back was fairly high."

"Eighty-five and some percent chance it was someone else on duty tonight," I announce. "Fourteen and change it was you."

"And that's not enough for you to regain a little faith?" Dr. Smith asks.

"No," I reply flatly.

Saul steps forward, prompting Dr. Smith's fingers to dance across his weapon in a strange, subconscious reply.

"Bullshit," Saul snaps. "You made a deal with the devil, and now you're gonna lecture us about who has the most faith?"

"*And after you have suffered a little while, the God of all grace, who has called you to His eternal glory in Christ, will Himself restore, confirm, strengthen, and establish you,*" Dr. Smith retorts. "This is a small price to pay to change the world! Look at you! You've all been delivered from your sins of the flesh!"

Saul shakes his head. "*And on this rock I will build my church, and the gates of hell shall not prevail against it,*" he counters.

"*And there are varieties of ministries, and the same Lord,*" Dr. Smith snaps back, then laughs a bit. He's pleased with himself. "I could do this all day."

I can't take this anymore. "It's almost as if the Bible can be twisted into supporting whatever point of view you want," I blurt.

Dr. Smith breathes in slowly and lets it out, assessing the situation. I can see now that an office lies behind him, featuring a simple desk and some filing cabinets stacked high against the far wall.

It's nothing like the ritual chamber from my previous vision, no flat wooden table or humming, whirring machine.

He notices me glancing over his shoulder and smiles.

"You're here for the machine," he observes. "Hoping to shut off the holy radiance of our Lord and Savior like it's a light switch? You've read enough of the good book to know God's will doesn't bend because you're upset over His tough love."

Willow angrily interjects, unable to hold herself back any longer. "You dumb fuck, you're attaching demons to innocent kids. You're not speaking for God."

"We are *saving* them!" Dr. Smith cries out. "Saving *you*! Do you know what those things do once they drag someone to hell? The horrible things they carry out on those who let sin overtake their lives? Kingdom of the Pine may be ruthless, but we are *not* cruel."

"I saw one of them twist a girl's head around backward," I retort.

"With *righteous purpose!*" Dr. Smith angrily counters, growing frustrated by this audience that dares question him. "*We* instill the mercy of God in them, quick and painless. Have you seen what happens when they're left to their own devices? The transmissions from beyond?"

A flash of horrific imagery fills my mind, visions of human bodies flayed alive and left to suffer. Nauseating displays of exposed nerves plucked like guitar strings. He's absolutely right; these creatures are brutal when left to their natural habits.

"You've seen what happens to those who spit in the face of God," Dr. Smith continues, his expression softening, "and that's not something I want for *any* of you."

He hesitates, his rage fading.

"Let's get you tethered again," he finally offers.

"No fucking way," Saul interjects.

"I'm afraid you don't really have a say in the matter," Dr. Smith replies. "You must understand, I can't just let you walk out of here. You're a threat to the decent work we're doing."

"Don't do this," I blurt. "You can pull out any shred of Scripture to convince yourself the ends justify the means, but if God is this brutal, what's the point of worshipping him in the first place? If the big guy is really signing off on this *torture*, then I'm not on His team whether He's real or not. I don't think you wanna be on that team, either."

Dr. Smith listens intently. If I didn't know any better, I'd think I spotted the faintest flicker of empathy lurking behind his cold expression.

Saul steps forward to interject. "We're not asking you to question God's existence. We're not even asking you to question His motives. We're saying your *interpretation* might be off. God is infallible; man is not."

Dr. Smith falters again, his face cracking even more. At this point, the fury has disappeared completely.

He's deep in thought now, genuinely touched by our words. "I'm in awe," Dr. Smith finally observes, chuckling to himself. "The devil has a very clever tongue. In my younger years, I might've gotten swept up in that. Unfortunately, you're too late."

"It's never too late," I plead.

Dr. Smith laughs. "No, I'm afraid it's literally too late. I pushed the security alarm the second you came down those stairs."

My blood runs cold. "What?"

"They'll be here any time now," the doctor continues. "You didn't really think I'd have some *come-to-Jesus moment*, did you? Jesus is already guiding my hand."

A wave of crushing defeat overwhelms me as I recognize the awful truth. We're trapped.

I have no doubt Willow will be gone forever this time, diligently scrubbed from the depths of my mind. She'll be cast into an endless nothingness, some faint yearning I'll never quite put my finger on.

Dr. Smith glances at Saul, eyes fixating on his backpack with sudden curiosity.

"Open it up," my therapist demands, lifting his gun just enough to remind us it's there.

Saul lowers his bag, bringing it around front and unzipping the pouch. "It's nothing," my friend assures.

"Careful now," Dr. Smith continues, noticing the tank of Saul's flamethrower. "Bug killer? How'd you know?"

Saul nods, shooting me a quick glance.

Dr. Smith laughs, lowering his guard for a moment. "Trust me, you're not going to kill those things with a chemical you'd find at the hardware store. They're tough little critters."

Without warning, Saul pulls the trigger of his makeshift flame-thrower. The weapon is pointed sideways, angled away from any particular target, but the plume of fire and heat is so powerful it causes Dr. Smith to stumble back in shock.

There's an earsplitting bang as he reflexively fires his weapon, a bullet rocketing into the glass habitat nearby with a hearty crack. A deafening crash of glass follows shortly behind, but I'm too focused on rushing Dr. Smith to give it a second thought.

I leap through the air and tackle him with all my weight, somehow managing to knock the gun from his hand and shove him against the wall.

At this point, I have two distinct paths. I could go for Dr. Smith's weapon, or I could dash into his office and slam the door behind me.

The answer seems obvious, as I'm not interested in leaving Willow and Saul to fend for themselves, but I quickly discover another factor is at play.

A cascade of sloppy, gurgling squeals fills my ears.

The tank may have featured several partitions, but the front was constructed from a single pane of glass that now rests shattered on the floor. The bulbous worms within are now crawling forth, rolling over the ledge and plopping to the ground with alarming speed.

I glance at Willow and Saul across the room, watching as they back toward the opposite door. We're separated by a scene of utter chaos, but at this point there's not much we can do about it.

"Go!" I cry.

Dr. Smith rushes for his weapon as I retreat into the office, throwing the metal door shut just in time to see my companions do the same on their side of the chamber.

I back away from the door as frantic yelps begin erupting from the opposite side. As the squealing creatures grow louder, so does Dr. Smith, and soon enough his voice transforms into a muffled jumble of desperate prayer.

Another gunshot rings out, then another, each bang prompting me to jump in alarm. I stumble a bit as I back into the desk behind me.

Dr. Smith's voice quickly grows more frantic, transitioning from anxious speech to shrieks of utter terror. Whatever's happening on the other side of that door sounds horrifically painful, a chaotic blend of stabbing proboscis, crawling wet invertebrates, and the frenzied stomps and kicks of Dr. Smith as he struggles to keep them at bay.

Eventually there's a loud thump as what must be the doctor's body collapses to the floor. His screams have devolved into guttural, heaving groans, animalistic and sloppy in a way that's difficult to imagine for this straitlaced blowhard. He retches loudly as the crawling, squishing noises slowly fade away.

Then, silence.

I think about calling out, making sure Saul and Willow are safe and sound in their opposing chamber, but there's too much space between us. I'd need to head back through the middle room.

Instead, I get to work searching this office for another exit. It doesn't take me long to find a row of switches built into the side of the desk, each one labeled with the name of a specific chamber in this underground lab.

Some of the switches are illuminated, glowing yellow. I can only assume this means the deadbolts they control are active.

I get to work turning off the hallway locks, hopefully allowing the prisoners to make their escape. I notice one of the levers is marked with the label LIGEIAN TANKS. This must be connected to the chamber I just escaped from.

"Rose?" a weary voice suddenly calls out from behind the door, causing my breath to catch in my throat.

I freeze, every muscle in my body clenching tight.

"You left me in here with those things." Dr. Smith screams, then repeats himself at an even more manic pitch. He's furious with anger and struggling to comprehend the audacity of his former patient. "You left me in here *with those fucking things!*"

The light below the metal door shifts as I hear Dr. Smith climb to his feet. I can hear him shuffling toward me, prompting an immediate flip of the LIGEIAN TANKS switch as I throw the deadbolt tight.

The door handle jerks once, then again with even more force.

"For he is the minister of God to thee for good. But if thou do that which is evil, be afraid!" Dr. Smith screams from the other side.

There's a loud bang and a blinding flash. I jump in alarm as a well-placed bullet tears through the lock and shatters it completely. Seconds later, Dr. Smith throws his weight against the door, slamming it open as he stumbles into the room with an awkward stagger.

The man's clothes are covered in a haphazard assortment of small tears, the holes soaked with glistening spots of fresh blood. There's a circular wound on the side of his face, as well as on his right hand just above the tightly gripped pistol. His glasses are shattered, but they still rest precariously upon his nose.

A single, straggling worm hangs lazily from the doctor's side, its proboscis still not ready to let go.

Behind Dr. Smith, the floor is littered with tired invertebrates, the pale creatures much less aggressive than they were just moments earlier. Their football shape has altered slightly, flattened out like a well-squeezed tube of toothpaste. They chortle happily, satisfied and sluggish.

"*For he beareth not the staff in vain!*" the doctor continues, a fire in his eyes as he lifts his weapon and points it directly at me.

I cower against the back wall, throwing my hands up to cover my face as though these thin stalks of flesh could do anything to stop a bullet.

Dr. Smith stands no more than five feet away, a point-blank shot should he choose to take it.

Gradually, however, a look of confusion slowly creeps its way across Dr. Smith's face, an awkward furrow of his brow as something particularly distracting flutters through his mind.

"*For he bears not the . . . rod in vain?*" the doctor continues, shaking his head. "Do you remember?"

I do remember. It's *beareth not the sword in vain* from Romans 13:4, but I don't respond.

"Do you remember, Annie?" he continues.

Who the heck is Annie?

Dr. Smith shakes his head, struggling to rattle something loose within the depths of his mind. He's growing more disoriented by the second.

"Was I supposed to pick up the eggs?" he asks, then catches sight of the gun in his hand.

Dr. Smith lowers the weapon. "Annie?" he asks, tears filling his eyes. "What's this?"

The doctor awkwardly opens and shuts his mouth, curiously working the muscles as though he's never felt them before. He looks worried.

"I can't—I can't grow," he stammers. "Grow good soon. That's true."

Dr. Smith takes another step toward me, but his gaze continues to drift. Words keep tumbling from the man's mouth, but every passing phrase makes less and less sense until they're gurgling out in awkward grunts.

My mind darts chaotically, but I can't help returning to Dr. Smith's revelation about the worms and their selective breeding program. The creatures have been propagated for varying degrees of memory loss, gestation rate, fertility, and lifespan.

Now, the man has inadvertently volunteered himself as the ultimate human trial, a host to every variable.

Dr. Smith begins to shake, convulsing wildly. He fires his gun into the floor several times, rolling through a series of deafening blasts that quickly transitions into the hollow clicks of an empty chamber. He won't stop pulling the trigger, however, fitfully jerking his appendages like a ragdoll.

Dr. Smith coughs loudly, a spurt of flies erupting forth in a wild black plume.

The man's gaze meets mine, as though I might provide some guidance in his state of utter confusion, but all this does is repel me even more. Flies are crawling across Dr. Smith's eyes, spilling from his tear ducts as he struggles to wipe them away. It's not long before the insects are pouring from his ears and emerging from unknown places under his clothing. He continues to cough as the mass of humming mayflies overwhelm him, but no matter how desperately he struggles to clear his throat, he finds himself even more obstructed. He is choking, gasping for air but inadvertently swallowing more and more of the black insects.

Soon enough, there's just too many flies for air to pass through. Dr. Smith slams to the floor, convulsing wildly as flies continue to pour from every orifice of his body. Their drone is overpowering, the sheer mass of the swarm elevating from a buzz to a terrifying roar.

I'm still frozen in shock, and the only thing that pulls me from my trance is fear of what might've happened to Willow and Saul in the opposite chamber.

Keeping my distance from the roil of insects, I edge just close enough to flip the desk's LIGEIAN TANK switch, unlocking the central room. I stagger to my feet and carefully exit the office.

Here, the worms don't seem very concerned about my presence, barely acknowledging me with their squeaks and gurgles as I tiptoe around their deflated bodies. After expelling every egg they had, the creatures are spent.

Reaching the other side, I push through the door to find Saul and Willow resting against a familiar stone wall, struggling to catch their breath. An assortment of mechanical parts are scattered haphazardly around them, a broken machine stripped down to the cogs and gears.

Willow jumps up, rushing forward and throwing her arms around me. We hug for a moment, my eyes drifting across the chamber behind her in stoic recognition. I see the huge metal slab and the straps that wrapped around my wrists and ankles. I see the rolling pedestal that once held a diabolical machine and now sits empty.

"We did what we could," Saul offers as Willow and I release our grip on each other. "Bent and warped as many pieces as possible. I'm taking the important stuff with me."

My friend motions to his backpack, which is now stuffed with mechanical parts.

"I opened the cells," I blurt. "We gotta go. Security's coming."

"They're probably already here," Saul counters, his expression faltering slightly.

He's right, and I know it.

Saul puts down his bag and pulls out the flamethrower. "At least this time we'll remember what happened," he announces, preparing his weapon and eyeing the exhausted worms that litter the central chamber.

13

JUDGMENT

Because we're no longer bound by the need for silence, the way out is much faster than the way in. The futuristic cellblock is wide open, captives freed and nowhere to be found. Hopefully, they've escaped deep into the woods by now.

Our feet slam against the metal floor of this long underground passage, shadows cast upward from the cold blue glow below. They look enormous as they whip across the walls.

Saul, Willow, and I are well behind the fleeing prisoners, and with little time to spare our focus is on the quickest getaway possible.

So long as it's not too late.

The answer comes as we emerge from our underground bunker, screeching to a panicked halt at the top of the staircase.

We're surrounded, a cascade of floodlights aiming down at the building from every angle. Brilliant illumination pours in from the windows, and the front door sits wide open before me.

I shield my eyes, barely noticing the two figures who stand on either side of us.

"Oh good, we were just about to come down and get you," a woman says gruffly. "Now we don't have to. Hands up."

We follow their orders, returning to the world above in a complicated mixture of victory and defeat.

We've been caught red-handed, and Kingdom of the Pine clearly has no problem enacting brutal judgment as they see fit.

That said, we've managed to exterminate the worms, trash their demon-summoning machine, and set a whole dungeon of prisoners free. We did what we came here to do, despite fumbling the escape.

Our captors pat us down, removing Willow's cameras and stripping away Saul's tools, including the flamethrower. They're likely searching for Dr. Smith's weapon, but find nothing.

This must be the security force, a well-armed tactical squad that's suspiciously absent from any starry-eyed Camp Damascus infomercials.

"Come on out," calls a strangely familiar voice through a booming megaphone. "Let's get a good look at these little rascals."

We step onto the front porch, shielding our eyes as they adjust to the brilliant lights that strike down from every angle. The captors behind us push roughly onward, keeping pace as we stumble toward the open field of the north cabins. There's a crowd of figures surrounding us, but I'm too disoriented to comprehend much more than an abstract parade of silhouettes.

As I approach, a cold wave washes over me.

"Alright, shut 'em down," calls the familiar voice. The megaphone crackles slightly, a strange, oppressive drone humming through it.

The glowing beams disappear, plunging us back into a state of reasonable illumination. It appears the enormous spotlights were mounted on trucks, three of which are positioned around us. I can only assume the congregation uses these vehicles for tracking down runaways.

This, however, is far from the most shocking thing about our welcome party. Yes, a handful of uniformed security guards have arrived, but they're relegated to the trucks in back. Instead, we find ourselves surrounded by four distinct types.

The first group I recognize are escapees, kids previously locked away down below that we set free during our invasion. They're shaking and scared, cowering in fear after a brief moment of freedom that was offered unexpectedly, then ripped away just as fast. They've been put through the wringer tonight.

The second group are counselors, clean-cut and watching with a faint, almost undetectable smugness. There are about a dozen of them, which gives slight credence to the notion that not everyone who works at Camp Damascus knows the true extent of what happens here.

Then again, does it really matter if you're just *evil*, as opposed to *over-the-top cartoonishly evil*?

Third is the security force—twenty or so well-armed soldiers, clad in all black and mixed in with the others.

However, the last group of figures are the ones who draw my focus the most, the ones that cause my breath to catch in my throat and my veins to flood with frigid ice.

Looming behind the humans is a flank of white-eyed demons, pale and wretched as they smile with those bizarre grins. They're a variety of sizes and shapes, but feature similar renditions of stringy black hair that hangs around their heads in awkward patches. Their red polo shirts all match, name tags perfectly affixed to their chests. A single iron shackle stays tightly wrapped around each of their necks.

The counselors and security team are unfazed by this demonic presence, but the campers are petrified. Some do everything they can to look straight ahead and pretend nothing's there, while others can't help glancing back in a state of awestruck dread.

"Oh *no*" is all I can think to say, these simple words falling from my mouth in an expression of preemptive defeat.

A man steps forward, lowering his megaphone and calling out to us with a booming voice that's no stranger to addressing a room. I recognize him immediately. Our host is Pastor Pete Bend, the head of Camp Damascus, himself.

Pete's near-supernatural charisma is immediately apparent, the blood of a salesman coursing through the body of a spiritual leader. His hair is buzzed tight on the sides and longer on top, juxtaposing salt-and-pepper temples with a distinctly modern cut. Even at this late hour he's immaculately dressed in a fashion-forward jacket and an extra-long tee. A set of trendy sneakers rest upon his feet.

The only religious paraphernalia to be found on Pastor Bend are the cross that hangs around his neck and the traditional red band around his wrist. This denotes all congregation leaders, a reminder of Prophet Cobel's sacrifice: his left hand for an audience with God.

Pastor Bend clears his throat. "The megaphone was picking up a little feedback from my infernal coworkers," he explains, then raises an eyebrow in an exaggerated performance. "Notice I didn't say *friends*, I didn't say *family*, I said *coworkers*. We all have people we don't enjoy working with, right?"

Pastor Bend pauses for us to respond, but nobody's willing to play along. Instead, we just stare at the man in awkward silence, forcing him to continue his impromptu sermon without audience participation.

"You go in for a heart transplant and you discover your doctor is using an assistant who is absolutely *terrible*," Pastor Bend continues. "This guy's killed the last five patients he worked on. He's constantly leaving scalpels inside the chest and sewing people up, just terrible. Guess what, though? This assistant gets along with your doctor *really* well. They're best buddies."

Pastor Bend pauses for dramatic effect, all eyes trained on him. He's relishing this moment in the spotlight, unable to keep himself from putting on a show.

"Now your doctor says, 'Listen, I know my assistant is terrible at his job, but he's a real sweetheart. I've got this other assistant who could help us out, but I can't stand the guy. He's one of the world's greatest surgeons, never made a mistake, but he's also a real jerk,'" Pastor Bend continues.

"Get to the point," I call out, sick of this achingly transparent presentation. Everything about Pastor Bend's delivery is fake, a friendly cadence that all great preachers can channel at the drop of a hat. I used to feel perfectly at home when someone delivered a message in this bright-eyed manner, but now it just makes me nauseated.

"The point is: Who would you want to operate on you?" Pastor Bend continues. "Even better question: Who would the *hospital* want to operate on you? It would be downright criminal to let the unskilled assistant work just because they were pals with your doctor. You deserve the best treatment you can get."

I'm trembling now, struggling to shake the cold that exudes from the nearby demons.

"Doctors have an ethical imperative to use all the tools at their disposal when looking after your body," Pastor Bend continues. "*We* have an ethical imperative to use all the tools at our disposal when looking after your *soul*."

"Good luck with that," Willow retorts. "Your machine is fucked and those little worms are all dead. You're not converting anyone."

A look of disappointment crosses Pastor Bend's face as he glances at the security guards behind us. One of them nods in confirmation.

"Kingdom of the Pine paid millions for the blueprints to that machine. It took years to build," Pastor Bend explains, "but wrath is just as much a sin as lust. You'll find nothing but forgiveness from Kingdom of the Pine. The Ligeian worms, however . . . that's a problem."

Pastor Bend turns on his megaphone and holds it up to his mouth, clearly frustrated. "A really big problem," he announces, his voice cutting through a haze of distant screams and dancing static before shutting off the megaphone and returning it to his side.

Pete's clearly got more to say, but my mind is already jumping ahead. I chart the most logical course of this standoff, and I'm not thrilled with the place where I end up. Those worms served a very specific purpose, and with this tool eliminated, the congregation might just have to make us forget the old-fashioned way.

They're going to kill us.

"You and the campers you've released are now a huge liability—not to me, but to the future sinners yet to be saved by our world-class conversion program," Pastor Bend explains. "It's our moral obligation to save as many people as we possibly can. We're here to help you . . ." The pastor trails off, waiting for a response that doesn't come.

Pastor Bend tries again, opening his arms and speaking a little louder this time.

"We're here to help you . . ." he calls out, finally prompting a response from the counselors.

"Love right!" they shout back.

Willow reaches out and takes my hand in hers, squeezing hard. She's also beginning to realize where things are headed. Even more devastating, she's confronting the fact that there's no way out.

I squeeze back, but the gesture is instinctual. Right now, my mind is elsewhere, rushing down every possible path and struggling to find an outcome that doesn't end in utter disaster. We're trapped, and I know it, but I can't give up that easily. I keep allowing my curiosity to push even deeper into the recesses of my mind, following every option to its logical conclusion and then starting over again once there's no reasonable options left.

I glance over at Saul, noticing that he's fervently praying under his breath. He's desperate for answers, throwing any sense of rationality to the wind and following a path that feels right.

Over the last few weeks I've accepted what a foolish exercise this is, but there's also something about it that makes me extremely jealous. Saul and I have reached the same dead end, but my friend has hope while I recognize there's none to be found.

Willow squeezes my hand again, a tiny gesture that strikes deep.

Of course there's still hope.

"Please appreciate how difficult this is going to be for our staff," Pastor Bend continues. "Camp Damascus is about healing, not pain, and I hope you can find peace knowing the end will be quick and easy. In their natural state, demons are driven to torture those who sin, but so long as they're working for us they'll be nothing but efficient."

Three demons step forward, one for each of us. Around the circle, the other creatures place their powerful hands on the frightened campers before them.

This is it, I realize. This is where I receive the answer I was *really* looking for, the biggest question of all. Am I about to go out like a light, or is there something more?

Tenet number four: I will persevere when my body does not.

As these final moments loom, a strange thought crosses my mind.

I've spent my whole life in a deeply destructive collective, pinned to the hard end of a philosophical extreme. When my pendulum swung back the other way I had plenty of momentum, but I never really got the chance to experience life in the middle.

I never had much balance.

Truth be told, I probably would've ended up on the blunt and logical side of things, but a little vacation along the median sounds fun. My faith was all or nothing, and I suppose that's fine, but I'm curious what it might've been like to responsibly dabble.

The demons who stepped forward begin marching across the grass toward us, closing in for a simultaneous execution.

More regrets begin to wash over me: mysteries that will never be revealed, puzzles that will never be solved.

Is the entirety of their world just freezing underground torture chambers? Why are they wearing those polo shirts? What's with the shackles around their necks?

An idea washes over me, a connection that I never could've made within a completely logical state. Now that I'm seconds away from death, however, I'm willing to experiment with the mysterious and unknown.

Just the tiniest bit.

Words begin tumbling out of my mouth, not the traditional prayers I was raised with, but a bizarre Latin passage from Saul's occult demonology tome. I've got a specific text in mind, the one that felt less like a prayer and more like instructions for some holy artifact.

The Prayer for Release.

The image from that page is still burned into my mind, a priest standing over his disheveled captive and spontaneously releasing their bonds through some power beyond our understanding.

I quickly rattle off the words, fully expecting that this incantation will do nothing and I've reached the end of my mortal coil. Fortunately, I'd been studying these passages so diligently that even now, in this moment of tension and fear, I recite them with perfect accuracy.

Just a few more steps before the demons arrive, the pale, smiling creatures reaching out with their long-fingered hands.

Crack!

The demons hesitate.

Crack! Crack!

The unexpected clang of three popping shackles resounds through the clearing.

The creatures halt, broken iron hoops falling from their necks.

Metallic snaps continue ringing out as the remaining demons are freed, their collars tumbling off and landing in the grass with a cascade of dull thumps.

"What the hell just happened?" Saul exclaims, backing away.

"I don't know," I admit, utterly shocked.

Pastor Bend's eyes are wide with disbelief. "What did you do?" he cries, shaking his head from side to side and sporting an oddly sympathetic expression. "I offered you a painless death, and now they'll drag you to *hell!* It's in their nature to punish the sinful and depraved. We commanded them with mercy in our hearts, but now they're free."

The pastor wells up with tears and begins mumbling through a prayer, not for himself, but for us.

Standing before me is a pale, saggy-skinned demon with long, sunken features and huge white eyes. Her name tag reads EISHETH.

Up until now, I've only witnessed these creatures sporting a frightening, wide-mouthed smile, but with a flickering, trembling grimace her expression begins to shift.

The stance of these demons is swiftly adjusting, the monsters no longer carrying themselves with perfect posture. The sharp twitches that once coursed through their fingers at random intervals have disappeared, finally releasing them from their rigid, locked-in stature.

"No. Please," I beg, backing away from Eisheth in a state of sickening panic.

The rest of the captives are crying and whimpering now, cowering in the face of spiritual judgment.

Suddenly, a deafening squeal of feedback rips through the air, erupting not only from Pastor Bend's megaphone, but over the entire camp's PA system. I flinch in alarm, momentarily reaching up to cover my ears as the sounds transform into a swirling collage of random audio sources and radio waves from beyond. I can hear the frantic screams of hell through this wash, accompanied by the rolling drone of some foreign-language news report. A baseball game pops in and out for a moment, and soon enough this random flood of sound lands on an unexpected broadcast of blasting, grinding deathcore, amplified directly from the headphones still playing inside Saul's pocket.

I cower under Eisheth's gaze, face-to-face with the judgment I've been promised since I was a child. All of my decisions, every personality flaw, every white lie or venial sin hoisted upon the scale and settled accordingly.

For God will bring every deed into judgment, with every secret thing, whether good or evil.

I drop to my knees and close my eyes, but in these final moments I don't ask for forgiveness. I don't accept Jesus as my savior, and I don't suddenly repent the love I feel for Willow. She's still holding my hand, and as the scales of good and evil weigh this gesture through the stern glare of some higher power, I only squeeze tighter.

If they've got a problem with this, then *frick* 'em. They may be powerful, but they're wrong.

Eyes closed, I hear the screaming begin, not just transmissions from beyond over Saul's caustic, crushing music, but cries of agony and fear from all around me. I brace for impact, dreading the first horrible stab of pain, but the pain never comes.

Instead, I sense Eisheth rushing past me with a babbling squeal. A gun blast erupts from behind us, joining the chorus of wild bangs that ring out through the clearing as my eyes pop open.

It's complete chaos. Demons gallop through the darkness, propelling themselves forward on their hands and feet like wild animals, then launching through the air to tackle their fleeing prey. Campers scatter, some tripping and tumbling while others scramble to aid their helpless friends. Truck lights flicker erratically while more gunshots crackle and pop, counselors and security guards firing desperately at their targets to watch as the bullets phase right through them. Meanwhile, a vicious assault of pummeling Christian deathcore washes over the scene in a hellish soundtrack that, honestly, couldn't be more fitting.

Willow tugs my arm, yanking me from my trance.

"Run!" she screams.

The three of us take off across the clearing, weaving through this unbridled landscape of violent pandemonium. My eyes dart from one brutal scene to the next, struggling to chart the safest course of escape.

A dropped handgun catches my eye. I rush to grab it, scooping up the weapon before realizing I have no idea what I'm doing. These bullets will do nothing but pass through our demonic adversaries, causing as much physical harm as my speeding car did.

But the web of potential outcomes isn't finished just yet.

I suddenly remember Saul's flamethrower, the backpack that housed this contraption now lying several yards behind us.

"Wait!" I cry out, slowing Willow and Saul.

I raise the gun, gazing down the barrel and noting that the pressurized tank of Saul's device rests halfway exposed from its bag. I also note that, unlike in the movies, a bullet striking any pressurized tank and causing an explosion is almost impossible.

I take my chances, shooting once, twice, three times; then finally unloading on my target in frustration. The bullets either ping off the tank or disappear into the dirt around it. As the chaos blooms and my clip empties, I readjust for one final shot. It would take a genuine miracle to accomplish the feat I have in mind, but I suppose stranger things have happened this evening.

Steady. Hold your arm straight. Don't breathe when you fire.

I pull the trigger one last time.

Nothing. My bullet thumps awkwardly into the grass, a dull ending to my very bad idea.

I lower my gun and drop it to the ground in defeat, but as I do this a figure steps up next to me. It's Willow. She grips a rifle in her hands, her eyes trained diligently on the tank. She presses the gun's butt tight against her shoulder, perfectly fixed as her one open eye peers steadfastly down the rifle's sight.

She pulls the trigger.

A billowing plume of flame erupts before us, so sudden and brilliant that I can't help gasping aloud and shielding my eyes. The wave of fire reaches some three stories high, swiftly igniting two of the nearby cabins and scattering globs of liquid flame across the field.

Willow offers little more than a smirking shrug, but the moment of victory is short-lived as a shrieking demonic man rears up behind her. Willow swivels and fires another shot, but her bullet passes right through the creature's body with a turquoise crackle.

The demon grabs the rifle with his long pale fingers and tears it from Willow's hands, tossing it over his shoulder and letting loose another wild screech.

I pull Willow back, not wasting another second in this pandemonium.

"This way!" I shout, taking the lead and altering course.

We take off sprinting in another direction, bobbing and weaving as a strange new sound fills the air, a flourish of hollow snaps and cracks.

It takes a moment, but when I finally chart the source of these noises I'm appalled to the core. The demons are neglecting to kill their prey outright, as their motivations are much more thorough than some instinctual creature hunting for food. Instead, it appears they're methodically breaking the bones of their victims, sometimes snapping the neck and other times destroying all four limbs in a complete set.

Meanwhile, those caught by the demons continue screaming in pain, confused why their body no longer obeys any desperate commands.

The demons roughly drag their victims across the ground or hoist them over their shoulders, then manifest a blue, glowing tear in the air before stepping through to the other side.

They're keeping them alive on purpose.

"Out Satan!" screams a belligerent and wide-eyed Pastor Bend, rushing up to us with a crucifix thrust forward. "Saint Michael the Archangel, defend us in battle, be our protection against the wickedness and snares of the devil. May God rebuke him we humbly pray!"

He's doing his best to exorcise our demons, but the demons were never ours to begin with. We didn't summon them. We didn't nourish them. We didn't throw collars around their necks and train them.

The victims of Camp Damascus were minding our own business when these forces of darkness were *thrust upon us* and given a name, an act perpetrated by the congregation itself.

Yet, despite all this, I'm still compelled to help him.

I wave my hands in Pastor Bend's face, struggling to interrupt his religious diatribe. "Run for the woods or stay by the fires!" I shout. "They hate the fire!"

It's only now that I realize how little Kingdom of the Pine understands about the very power they've harnessed.

Pastor Bend continues bellowing his prayer, a metaphorical fire in his eyes while a literal blaze looms orange and magnificent behind him. "And do thou, O Prince of the Heavenly Host, by the power of God, thrust into hell Satan and all evil spirits who prowl about the world seeking the ruin of souls!"

I suddenly notice a gun gripped tight in Pastor Bend's left hand, a crucifix on one side and the threat of violence on the other. He's not just hoping to remove demonic influence from our bodies, he plans to remove the bodies as well.

It's too late for us.

"Wait," I blurt, throwing my hands up.

The pastor lifts his hand in a sudden jerk, ready to fire a bullet right between my eyes.

Before he gets the chance, however, a long-fingered appendage whips through the darkness and grabs Pastor Bend by the skull. He cries out in shock, struggling to fire his weapon at the creature behind him, but a swift snap of the wrist renders Pastor Bend utterly helpless. He drops the gun.

The demon behind Pete Bend slams something into his upper back with a quick and powerful movement, immediately prompting the pastor's eyes to go wide and a spurt of deep crimson to eject from his lips. There's a hollow thump to accompany this movement, then a strange tearing sound as the demon pulls swiftly upward.

The whole thing happens so fast it's difficult to fully grasp, my mind reeling at the creature's brutal efficiency. It's using a tool of some kind, a metal scooping device attached to a handle and an oblong glass tube.

In a matter of seconds, Pastor Bend's eyes pull back into his head, the wet spheres yanked through the rear of his skull along with the man's brain and spinal column. He doesn't even have time to cry out in shock, emitting nothing more than a faint gurgle as his body collapses to the ground.

Meanwhile, the demon shuts the bizarre, tubelike device with an audible click, sealing it tight. Light blue liquid blasts into the glass cylinder with a powerful, hissing injection, filling the container and completely submerging this precise selection of Pastor Bend's nervous system. His eyes bob and slide against the side of the glass, staring back at me as the demon abruptly turns and hauls them away.

There are no eyelids left to narrow or widen, but I get the distinct impression Pastor Bend is keenly aware of what's happening, still sensing the blue liquid as it sloshes around his brand-new form.

A jagged, glowing rip in time and space appears before the demon, opening wide as the creature slips through, then swiftly closing behind.

Aside from the mangled shell of a body that lies before us, there's no trace they were ever here at all.

Keep moving.

Once again, we turn and dash away from the raucous bedlam, weaving through plumes of flame that rise higher and higher as they spread into the forest. I lead our trio along the edge of the towering blazes, slinking close to the heat in an effort to keep the demons at bay, but the farther we travel, the more I realize these efforts are meaningless.

As my analytical mind continues to churn, the truth gradually becomes apparent. The creatures aren't after us.

As we finally reach the edge of the clearing, I slow my retreat and turn back to the chaos.

"What are you doing?" Saul cries out, anxious to push onward. "We gotta go!"

My eyes dart from one macabre scene to the next, the pattern I've been sensing now fully revealed in all its diabolical glory.

Across the clearing my gaze locks with a crowd of other campers, tired and scared but completely unharmed as they watch the chaos unfold. I recognize each and every one of them as captives from below, along with the boy from the archery range.

We're all here, and not a scratch on us.

Meanwhile, screams of horror continue ringing out through the night, camp counselors receiving judgment from the very creatures they hired to do the judging.

Religious lore of all stripes teaches of entities who act as enforcers, and if you believe in these creatures then the truth of their verdicts often comes as a package deal. If angels and demons exist, their motivations might as well fit the profile we've laid out for them.

Now, however, I know the truth.

Whatever these beings are, whether spiritually manifested or defined by the same science that governs the rest of us, it's clear their moral scale is not perfectly calibrated with the church's.

Certainly not as much as the congregation would have me believe.

I have no doubt the culture of these monsters revolves around pain, punishment, and judgment, but once the church's shackles fall away, they answer to an even *higher* cosmic assessment of right and wrong.

What that is, I'm not sure, but it certainly doesn't have a problem with gay people.

Forcing bigoted views on others and ramming them through a destructive system of conversion therapy, however, appears to be a massive ethical transgression.

I watch as the boy from the range starts gathering his fellow campers, calling out to them in a fervent, triumphant tone. The others are nodding along, raising their voices to join him, and although the cacophony of grinding thrash metal and breaking bones is too much to hear exactly what they're saying, I think I get the point.

Soon enough, the former prisoners are gathering large sticks from the woods, wrapping fabric around the ends, and then igniting these makeshift torches with the nearby fires.

The camper from the archery range pumps his fist in the air one last time—delivering the most ferocious battle cry an angsty teen has ever mustered—then starts trudging his way through the woods, back toward the camp's faculty center. The rest of the campers follow close behind.

✳   ✳   ✳

As Camp Damascus continues to burn, echoes of snapping wood and bone filling the air, our trio turns and disappears into the forest. We're headed the opposite direction, taking our time without the threat of demons or the people who haphazardly wield them.

We move in silence.

It's not long before we arrive back at Willow's vehicle, standing on the edge of the mountain and gazing across Neverton below. It's an absolutely glorious vista, and while I've witnessed it plenty of times, there's something special about tonight's.

A weight has been lifted, not just from us, but from every victim of that terrible place.

I glance over to catch Saul enjoying a similar moment of reflection. He's not wearing any headphones, his meditation holding its own without the help of any particular soundtrack.

Willow steps next to me, and as she does I turn to meet her gaze. Our eyes lock, and suddenly a powerful urge overtakes my body.

"Hey" is all she says, a million little things communicated within the breathless tone of this singular word.

I can't help the smile that works its way across my lips, an uncontrollable display of the lurking joy that bubbles its way to the surface and fully consumes me.

We don't hesitate, refusing to wait a second longer before our lips meet in a passionate eruption. We melt into each other, all the stress and strain and fear that kept us at arm's length finally crumbling away.

This is so much better than the memory of our last kiss, not only thanks to the visceral warmth of her body against mine, but for the future that lies stretched out before us. This isn't just some hazy recollection that could dissipate at any moment, it's the real thing.

Memories come and go, but the present is ours.

Within the softness of her lips and the tickle of her hair as it frames my cheeks, I discover a safety unlike anything I've ever known, a sense of true acceptance.

Meanwhile, the flames continue billowing into the sky behind us, a raging inferno where Camp Damascus once stood. The blaze is so large that its orange, mountainside glow illuminates the entire Neverton valley.

My shadow stretches on for miles, fully engulfing the city below.